ONE OF US

JEANNIE WAUDBY

RP|TEENS
PHILADELPHIA • LONDON

First published in Great Britain in 2015 by The Chicken House, 2 Palmer Street, Frome, Somerset, BA11 1DS, United Kingdom, www.doublecluck.com.

First printed in the United States by Running Press Book Publishers, 2015.

Printed in the United States

Books published by Running Press are available at special discounts for bulk purchases in the United States by corporations, institutions, and other organizations. For more information, please contact the Special Markets Department at the Perseus Books Group, 2300 Chestnut Street, Suite 200, Philadelphia, PA 19103, or call (800) 810-4145, ext. 5000, or e-mail special.markets@perseusbooks.com.

ISBN 978-0-7624-5799-1

Library of Congress Control Number: 2015930722

E-book ISBN 978-0-7624-5820-2

9 8 7 6 5 4 3 2 1
Digit on the right indicates the number of this printing

Cover images:
Seamless Plaid 0018 © AvanteGardeArt
Group of People © Thinkstock/Rawpixel Ltd.
Cover and interior design by T.L. Bonaddio
Edited by Rachel Leyshon and Imogen Cooper
Typography: Trade Gothic, Heavyweight, and Fairfield

Published by Running Press Teens
An Imprint of Running Press Book Publishers
A Member of the Perseus Books Group
2300 Chestnut Street, Philadelphia, PA
19103–4371

Visit us on the web!
www.runningpress.com/rpkids

For
PETE
RORY
KIRSTEN
AND
CARA

CHAPTER 1

I'M NOT AFRAID of spiders or snakes.

I'm not afraid of graveyards at night.

I'm not afraid of deep, dark water.

I'm not afraid of ghost stories or horror movies.

And stations? I make myself get on a train every day.

But I am afraid of the Brotherhood.

Normally you can see them—you know who they are, with their scarlet-checked clothes. They stand out. But today, as people hurry through the sleet to Central Station under umbrellas and raincoats and scarves, I can't tell the difference between us and them.

I keep watch through the slanting snow, because how can you face a danger you can't see? A person who looks like any other person, but who secretly wants to kill you and everyone like you? I don't know why I'm thinking like this now, when I have to make this journey to school every day. What would the odds be, for me to be caught up in another bomb at Central Station?

Slowly the crowd funnels into the station. I look up at the sign looming over the door: *One City, Two Ways*. That's not how it is, though. Everyone knows this is a divided city. Under the cover of the doorway, umbrellas swish down and people pull rain hoods off and unzip coats. Now I can see everyone for who they are. Ordinary citizens, dressed in the usual dark clothes we all wear these days. And the Brotherhood. Dotted through the crowd in their signature check.

I edge into the station just as three Brotherhood boys are pushing their way out. One boy crashes into me, his hands fending me off. For a second his dark eyes stare into my face. Then he says something sideways to his friend. They all laugh. What did Grandma used to say? *Never make eye contact with a Hood, K. It's like dealing with an angry dog—if you turn away, it won't attack you.* So I turn away.

"Do not abandon your luggage at any time. If you see unattended baggage, move aside and alert staff . . ." *I hate these announcements.* I shuffle into the station along with everyone else. *They make me jittery.* Steeling myself, I head toward the elevators that take us down to the tunnels.

Deep underground, the platform's already crowded, and a man elbows in front of me as he struggles to get two huge suitcases closer to the edge so he can be first on the train. Someone jumps on my foot, and I wince. It's a little boy pulling on his dad's hand. He's looped the strap of his backpack over his forehead like a headband. That makes me smile.

It's then that I see the bag on the bench, brown paper with string handles. As soon as I notice it, I look around for the owner. It's habit. But I can't see who it belongs to. That means it's alone—"unattended." And the more I look at it, the less it seems like just a bag. Who left it there? The Brotherhood boys upstairs flash into my mind. Should I pick up the phone on the wall and report it?

As I move toward the phone, the little boy points

at the bench. "Daddy!" he calls. "The cupcakes!"

His dad turns, still holding his son's hand, and darts across to the bench. He grabs the bag, and as his eyes meet mine for a second he half-smiles sheepishly. I hear someone tut.

Warm wind heralds the train, which rushes out of the tunnel and comes to a screeching halt: "Watch the gap. Move right down inside the train cars . . ." The doors swoosh open, and the man with the suitcases starts heaving them on. I wait behind the boy and his father. The train's packed, like it always is at morning rush hour.

I could wait for the next one, but then I'll be late for school.

I put one foot on board.

A bone-shattering, chest-crushing *bang* lifts me into the air.

And everything slips away.

—

WHEN I OPEN my eyes I can't see or hear a thing. There's just a heavy, ringing silence and a terrible smell, a *fearful* smell, that hits the back of my nose. Smoke and something else underneath. I start coughing and my hand flies up to cover my face but hits a rough surface right in front of me. A wall? Where am I? I feel the panic rising, then stop myself. *Stay still. Take little breaths.* Something trickles down my face. Blood?

What happened . . . ? There was a noise, a blast, and I fell . . . Don't know where I am, but I have to get out . . . Get out, K!

I struggle to my feet, but there's no room to stand. Something solid's above me, forcing me to crouch. I try to move back, but there's no space there either. I reach up and touch a sort of metal ceiling, bulging in toward the rough wall in front of me, or is it not a wall . . . is it . . . is it the platform? I reach above me, and there's a gap. *Watch the gap* . . . That's when I realize: *I'm under the train.* At any moment it could tip over and crush me. Metal slides against the back of my hand. It's moving!

Now I'm panicking and screaming, screaming for help—I know I am, except I still can't hear or see in the darkness. My hands scrabble at the wall, at the platform edge, reaching up from underneath the train. There's smoke in my eyes, in my throat . . . The smell's in my mouth . . . *Please* . . . I can't move, I can't breathe. Every mouthful of air is a choking cough, bringing poison, not oxygen, into my body, and all at once I see it clearly:

I'm going to die.

Then a hand clasps mine. A warm, soft, human hand. Strong and safe.

I feel my own hand close around it. I am never letting go.

Another hand reaches down and clamps itself around my other wrist, and little by little I am lifted up, up, squeezing through the gap and onto the platform.

I fall forward, my face smacking against the concrete. My mouth fills with blood and ash, dust mingling with iron, choking me. My eyes are streaming in the gray smoke.

Whoever lifted me out is still holding me, hoisting me to my feet. A man. I still can't hear anything, just the blood thumping in my ears. I clutch at his clothes but can't hold on: he's wearing something hard and slippery. Dim light now, and I can see the train is right in front of me, the doors buckled over the gap where I was thrown. That's what was moving above me. And there's the man with the two suitcases. But he's lying half in and half out of the carriage. His eyes are closed and his mouth is moving. There's a figure kneeling next to him. They're holding hands.

My head starts to spin and my legs go, and suddenly I'm being picked up and carried away. The smoke's fading, the smell too. The train never even left. It's still waiting at the platform but with blasted doors and twisted metal. We're climbing stairs, I think. *Yes, you can't use an elevator in a fire. I should try to walk,* I think, and struggle to get my feet down, but that makes us both fall, hard, onto the steps.

Sound slams into my head: "Evacuate the station. Move calmly to the nearest exit. Evacuate the station. Move calmly . . ." The ringing isn't in my head. It's the station alarm.

I start to cough again, choking coughs that I can't control, and my rescuer leans in to me, patting my back. He looks young, but he's got a scarf tied around his mouth and nose, so only his eyes are visible. His chest is rising and falling because he's struggling to breathe too. I want to ask him about the suitcase man, but I still can't talk, can't think.

His arm tightens around me and we begin climbing again. One, two. I cling to the pocket of his jacket.

Leather: that's why it's so hard to hold on to. Five, six. It takes a long time. Ten, eleven . . . I lose count. And all the while, the alarm's ringing and the disembodied voice is shouting: "Evacuate the station. Move calmly to the nearest exit . . ."

That's what we're doing, *moving calmly*, his arm around me, my arm around him, two strangers clambering to safety. I almost faint again, but I hear his voice near my ear: "Not far now. Stay with me."

And then there's daylight ahead, the gray light of winter gleaming through the glass roof of the station. I make my legs walk up the last few steps, and fall on to my knees, racked by a coughing fit that tears through my rib cage. Other noises rush into my ears: sirens from outside the station, shouting and screaming and running feet . . .

When I stop coughing he gets me to my feet, puts his arm around my waist and walks me across to a bench under the display board. He helps me sit and crouches in front of me, taking the scarf from his mouth. Under his sandy hair his face is streaked with sweat and ash. His gray eyes are level with mine and I can't look away. No one has ever looked at me so kindly. Not since Grandma.

"Thank you . . ." I cough out.

"You OK?" He takes a bottle of water from a woman who has come up to us, and unscrews the lid, passing it to me.

I nod, even though we can both see I'm not. "What about the man with the suitcases?" It's all I can think about—his moving lips, the figure kneeling next to him holding his hand.

The gray-eyed man gets up and sits heavily beside me. Then he shakes his head. "I think you're the last one to walk out. I was going to leave, but then I saw your hand come up from under the train."

I take a sip of water, but it doesn't wash away the taste of smoke and blood. Now I start to notice what's around me: police and paramedics and rows of stretchers. People are huddled in groups—some in dark clothes and some in Brotherhood red. From their grimy faces and hair they must have been on the platform too. Smoke drifts up the staircase from the tunnels below. There's an ache in my chest.

"What happened?" I ask. "Was it a bomb?"

"An explosion," he says carefully. "It's too early to say what caused it. Listen . . . if you're OK you should go to the cafe across the square. They're setting up a first-aid post there so the paramedics can use the station for the badly injured and the fatalities."

Fatalities. He's matter-of-fact. What about the suitcase man—is he no longer a person, just a fatality? I can't make sense of it so I just stand up. The gray-eyed man takes hold of my elbow.

"I'm fine," I say too quickly. "Really. Thanks." But what I'm thinking, illogically, is: *All I want to do is stay with you.* He makes me feel safe.

"Well, in that case, I'd better go." He looks across to the police cordon.

Of course. He's obviously with the emergency services. "You're a policeman?"

He looks back at me. "What?" Then he nods. "Oh yes, a policeman. That's right."

He touches my shoulder and his gray eyes seem to smile at me, as if we've always known each other. "Take care."

"Thank you," I say. It's not enough for someone who's just saved your life, not nearly enough, but he just nods again and turns away as if he's used to it.

I should've said a better thank-you. I stumble to the exit. I didn't even ask his name. Without him, I would still be wedged in the gap between the train and the platform, surrounded by crushing metal and stone, breathing the terrible smoke, the smell I can still taste in my mouth. Or maybe not breathing at all. I turn to look for him, but he's gone.

The little boy from the platform is there, though. He's standing very still, his arms hanging stiffly at his sides. He hasn't got his backpack around his forehead anymore. I look for his dad, but a policewoman comes and crouches in front of him. She says something close to his ear, because it's even noisier out here with the sirens shrilling, then she takes his hand and leads him away. I see his face, running with ash and tears, and even from here I can make out the word he's crying, over and over: "Daddy."

I have to get out.

—

OUTSIDE, THE FREEZING wind feels good against my face. For a moment I lift my head and look up at the dark Old City towers with the Brotherhood Meeting Hall spire looming up the hill behind the square. I close my eyes and open my mouth, letting the sleet run in. The main road outside the station is closed except for police cars and ambulances, but in front of me the square is full of people running toward the station or just standing, staring.

I walk slowly across the square, head down against the driving sleet, forcing myself toward Fred's Cafe. After a few steps I look back at the station. There's a tendril of smoke twisting from the entrance—how does it form such a graceful curve? If I was painting it, I'd let the smoke and cloud merge together, make those tiny dots of movement opaque. Pastels? Or maybe charcoal, black and dense. Like the smoke from a crematorium. I give myself a shake. How can I even think of my drawing now?

It's steamy and warm in Fred's Cafe, *my* cafe, where I go every morning before getting on the train. It's packed but someone immediately comes over with a blanket. I don't know why, but I'm still shaking. I sit down in a corner so no one notices me. There's a television above the counter. Scrolling across the bottom of the screen are the words, *BREAKING NEWS . . . SUSPECTED BOMB AT CENTRAL STATION . . .*

I feel the shock, like a fist, deep under my ribs. I knew it. *That* was what I felt as I walked toward the station. I was afraid and I didn't know why. The group of Brotherhood boys in the entrance flicker into my mind. Is the Strife starting up all over again? What about the Reconciliation process?

Fred brings me a mug of tea. "Sugar, for the shock," he says. "You're hurt, K. Were you there?"

I wipe my face and my fingers come away red. "I'm fine," I say, but I know he's not convinced.

"Someone will clean that up for you in a minute," he says.

I pick up the mug, but my hand is trembling so much that I have to hide it under the table. And the TV subtitles keep on rolling . . . *BROTHERHOOD BOMB* . . . My teeth are chattering . . . *CASUALTIES AT CENTRAL STATION* . . . I clutch my mug and stare at the screen.

I think of the Brotherhood boy who collided with me in the station doorway. I want to run back and catch hold of him, make him tell me he was the one who did this, make him look at the people on stretchers in the station. Make him look that little boy in the eye.

How can you face a danger you can't see? A person who looks like any other person, but who secretly wants to kill you and everyone like you?

I turn my face toward the wall. I can't cry here, in the crowded cafe.

Fred strides back to the counter. "Hoods," he says, knocking the TV off at the switch. "They'd kill us all if they could."

CHAPTER 2

I DREAMT THE BOMB: that's my first thought. Then I realize that I can still smell the smoke, still feel the grit in my swollen throat as I start coughing.

When the spasm finishes I gulp down some water from the bottle they gave me at the station. I get out of bed and pull open the thin curtains, to see the view I hate. Today the station is cordoned off and the square in front is full of police vans. It's transformed from the usual gray emptiness to a mosaic of tiny colored figures. There's nothing to show the horror of what happened yesterday. Behind is the Old City, the turrets of the Brotherhood Meeting Hall dominating the sooty buildings that sprawl up the hill to the woods beyond. Far to the north, the roof of a stone mansion shows through the tree branches.

I can't face school today. But I can't bear to stay in here, on my own, so I'll go.

Yesterday's clothes are in a heap on the floor, still giving off that horrible stench. I pull on clean black jeans and a gray shirt, then slump back down on my bed. It's so tidy in my halfway house room, like nobody lives here. Maybe it would feel more homey if I stuck up some photos. But I don't have a single photo. Not even one of my parents. Grandma didn't like to be reminded. She wouldn't talk about them either, so all I have are their names, John and Jane Child: short, honest citizen names like mine.

I bundle the heap of stinking clothes, even my winter coat, into a plastic bag, and shrug on my summer jacket instead. On my way downstairs I have to stop in the brick stairwell to catch my breath. When I reach the lobby, I stuff the clothes into the bin and wait for the receptionist behind her glass partition to release the doors for me. She doesn't even look up and we don't know each other's names. At least in the children's home some people smiled at you. Head down, I huddle into the thin black cotton of my jacket and walk quickly out into the square.

Then I stop. I don't want to pass the station. I look around me. There are Brotherhood men in their checked shirts—Brotherhood women too, with checked scarves or red ribbons around their hats, long skirts swishing. I know they're just people rushing past on their way from the bus depot. But do any of these anxious strangers know who planned the bombing? Could one of them have another device nestling in their coat or secured in their backpack? Under their hats, are those women secretly pleased? But their faces look closed, revealing nothing.

I thought I could go to school today, but now I know I can't. I could walk around the far edge of the square to the cafe. But this is my town. Why should a Brotherhood bomb drive me out of it? I make my feet walk right past the cordoned-off entrance, and I fight down the nausea and force myself to look. On the newsstand the headlines scream: BROTHERHOOD SUICIDE BOMBER ON TRAIN. The police are mostly in uniform but some are wearing leather jackets and black jeans like the young man who rescued me yesterday. He's not there, though. Three brown-and-white spaniels wait beside a van, tense and alert, tails wagging.

Across the road there's a coffee stand under an awning, with nearly as many police crowded inside as there are at the station. The air crackles with walkie-talkies.

I think about the people who died in the train, deep underground. Under their coats and hats, some of them were citizens and a few of them Brotherhood, just like the people crossing the square with me now. They thought they were going to work, or school, or somewhere normal, that day. Yesterday. It could have been me. I think of the little boy. Why couldn't someone have stopped it? Nothing has changed after all these years since the Strife ended. Grandma said they would always be waiting for a chance to destroy the fragile peace, to destroy us. And now that the Reconciliation process has started, will they destroy that too? Was she right?

The cafe is lit up, a little boat on a gray sea. In the glass door I see my own thin and anxious face, my black hair scraped any-old-how behind my ears and flicking over the collar of my jacket. The door dings as I push it open, and the smell of coffee greets me. I feel better. Safe. The cafe is back to normal, not a medical post today. Fred is emptying the coffee machine. The TV is on as usual, blaring news of the bomb, same as yesterday.

Fred pours me a cup of strong tea. No sugar this time. I sit in my corner and pick up a magazine.

"Mind if I sit here?"

I look up. It's him: the guy from yesterday. He's wearing his leather jacket and jeans, like the detectives outside the station. Everything about him shouts, "Undercover!"

I only realize I'm smiling when I see he's smiling too. "Hello again."

I reach over and yank my bag off the opposite seat.

He sits down, puts his coffee down in front of him. His police ID badge falls from his hand onto the table. *Oskar Reynard.* I pass it back to him.

"Horrible photo." He makes a face as he takes it from me. "So, how're you doing this morning?"

"OK." My voice comes out in a croak. It's not just nerves; I still keep coughing all the time.

"It's a shock," he says. "Easier for me to deal with, because I'm busier than usual."

"Mmm." I look at him, and his gray eyes meet mine. I wonder what horrible things he has had to look at, whether he is the one who has to tell people their loved one has died.

"I'm Oskar," he says.

He's not an ordinary stranger, he saved my life. "I'm K. Just the letter."

He smiles. "Just K? That's cool. Nice name." He nods at the notebook sticking out of my bag. "No school today?"

"Not for me." What's he going to do? Arrest me?

But he just nods. "Are you feeling better now?" He takes a long swig of coffee.

"I'm fine. A cough, and a few cuts and bruises—but they'll go." I pick up my cup. Even though I'm toasty warm in here, my teeth have started chattering. Why is that? I set the cup down, but Oskar has noticed.

"Don't worry; it's just aftershock. Being so near the station again has probably brought it on." He leans forward. "So, what do you want to do, when you finish school?"

He's only doing that thing where you keep someone talking until they feel better, but all the same I try to answer. I don't want to tell him that I have no idea, that I hate school. Instead, I give him the answer I gave Grandma when I was five: "I want to be an artist." I wait for him to tell me that's not a real job.

But he leans back, stretching his arm along the back of the other chair. "Then you should do it."

There's a little silence, but not an awkward one.

"It's all starting up again, isn't it?" I didn't mean to say that, but now I keep talking. "They'll keep killing, won't they?"

"Who knows, K?" The corner of Oskar's mouth creases in a little half smile. "The Brotherhood wants to blow up the entire Reconciliation process." His face grows serious. "We're bending over backward in the name of peace, even removing the oath. But they have their grievances."

"Why? Nobody's stopping them from becoming citizens."

Oskar laughs. "You really don't know much about the Brotherhood, do you? They'll never swear the oath of allegiance to the State. It's 'against their religion,' as the saying goes."

"Everything's changed, hasn't it? Nothing will stop them."

"The police—" begins Oskar.

"The police? What do they know?" I push my mug away so hard that it crashes into the salt shaker. "They didn't see this coming, did they? They couldn't stop it, could they? *You* couldn't stop it! I saw all these Brotherhood guys at the station yesterday, but no one even asked them what they were doing there."

Oskar doesn't answer. He looks steadily at me. Then he smiles that warm smile that reaches up into his eyes. Once again it makes me feel safe, just like it did yesterday. He doesn't say sorry, or make a fake sad face. Instead he says, "Your parents must have been worried about you yesterday."

"My parents were killed in a Brotherhood bombing when I was two: the bomb that started the Strife thirteen years ago." Over his shoulder and through the cafe window, I see the bleached granite of the station building, the sky so clean and matte behind it today, free of smoke. "It was at Central Station too."

I wait for him to say, "I'm so sorry."

Instead he says, "My father too."

We gaze at each other for a long moment.

"I'm sorry." I look away. "I can't remember my parents."

"I remember," says Oskar. "I was nine. My dad was a policeman." He looks away too, staring across the square. "Yesterday must have been terrible for you. They know how many people died now. Forty-nine."

I think of all the other people whose lives have now been ruined. It must be hundreds. It's too hard to talk about yesterday.

"I don't remember the Strife," I say instead. It ended when I was six. "Only things Grandma told me." She didn't tell me much, because we never talked about my parents and now there's nobody to ask. And when I looked them up online, I couldn't find anything. But even so, the Strife has always been just behind my shoulder, the reason why Grandma would freeze if she saw an abandoned bag lying on the pavement. And why she hated fireworks.

Oskar smiles at me. "So you live with your grandma."

"No. She died when I was ten. I've moved around

a lot since then." I'm guessing that's a good way to end the conversation.

But Oskar says, "And now . . . ?"

"I live in a halfway house near here," I say. "I haven't been there long. It's not the nicest place."

Oskar's eyebrows go up.

"My social worker moved me there because I'll be sixteen this year and out of care. It's nowhere near the children's home so I had to move schools as well."

I wait for that look that means he thinks I'm nothing. Just another stray, washed up from the Strife. But instead he leans forward and says, "Where did you live with your grandma? Here in Gatesbrooke?"

"No." Although, technically, Yoremouth is a suburb of Gatesbrooke. I look closely at him. Why is he so interested? I'm not going to tell him where Grandma and I lived. I've only just met him, after all. Although he seems genuine, and I like the tiny chips of gold in his eyes, which look gray-green today. "By the sea," I add. I think of the nights when I used to sneak out of the window and run down to the shingle beach in the wind and the darkness.

"Just the two of you, eh?"

"Yes. I didn't go to school, she taught me." I don't know why I'm telling him all this. Only my social worker knows my story. "Maybe that's why I don't like school."

He laughs, and then there's a silence between us.

It's nice that he didn't pretend things are OK, when they're not.

It's nice that we understand each other, without needing words.

CHAPTER 3

THE DAYS PASS. I don't go on trains or buses anymore, so I haven't been to school since the bomb. Instead I wander around the New City or read in Fred's Cafe. Sometimes Oskar's there too. I delete the texts from the new social worker who came to see me after the bomb. And the messages from school. It's no big deal because none of them really care anyway. This afternoon, after passing a lonely day in the gray New City library, I picked up a free newspaper on my way out, scanning the headline before tucking it into my backpack: CAN RECONCILIATION SURVIVE?

The words prey on my mind as I walk home along the river, watching the seagulls wheeling overhead. When I turn the corner into the square, it's crowded with people. A stranger's elbow softly bumps against my arm in the crush, and suddenly I feel even more alone than ever. This isn't just the normal crowd of rush hour. I hug my bag against my chest, my heart starting to thump. *Not again.*

But there are no sirens. No smoke.

I take a few deep breaths and walk across to the station. About a hundred people are standing in front of the entrance, in silence. Each of them holds a candle, and there are more candles standing in jars and cans in a circle on the pavement in front of them. In the gathering dusk they glow with a friendly light, flickering as the wind skates by. I stand still for a moment, counting the candles in the circle. Forty-nine. One for each person who died. The people all have their heads bowed. They almost look like statues in their dark coats and scarves and their stillness. It's a vigil.

Are these the relatives? I need to pass them to get to the halfway house, but it feels disrespectful to just walk by. Grandma and I used to light candles when we were sad, or if someone died. I'd light one now if I could. I stare into one of the glowing pools of light, watching the wick stoop into the pool of oil.

Then I hear chanting in the distance. I turn, looking around to see who's doing it. A mass of protestors pushes its way along the main street, their Brotherhood clothing vivid red in the fading light. The marchers' chant cuts through the city's rumble.

What are *they* doing here? Can't they even leave people to grieve in peace? As they get nearer I see that some of them are holding placards, black and white against the red check of their clothes. I read the words, but can't take in their meaning. How can they do this, here, and now?

NO CURFEW
NO OATH
NO SEGREGATION

Movement ripples through the people at the vigil, faces turn in shock. At first they remain silent but then there's a shout and the orderly crowd of mourners breaks apart as some people hurl themselves toward the marchers, while others slip away.

I want to run toward them too, rip the placards out of their hands. But instead I stand frozen, smelling the smoke again, seeing the man with the suitcases, his head resting on the edge of the platform, his lips forming soundless words.

Sirens . . . I really can hear them. Police vans tear across the square from all sides, surrounding the Brotherhood protest. In the stampede a candle jar smashes at my feet. I try to turn and leave but the press of people pushes me toward the Brotherhood protestors. Beside me a hand reaches down to grab a jar and it whizzes through the air over our heads. A woman from the vigil sinks to her knees in the broken glass, but when I try to pull her up, she shakes me off.

The chanting is all around me now, and screaming too and the screech of sirens. But there's a gap in the crowd. I duck under a raised arm and weave through the people, tearing away in the opposite direction from the station.

I keep running uphill toward the Old City, head down, hood up, so that I crash into a man on the curb in front of me.

"Hello, stranger." He grabs my arms to steady me.

It's Oskar. He's wearing glasses today, fine gold-rimmed ones.

"Did you see it?" I try to catch my breath.

He stares over my head, down to the square, and I turn and look too. The vigil has broken up and the police, shields and batons in front of them, are arresting Brotherhood rioters. Sirens pulse over the shouting and the smashing of glass.

"Mmm." Oskar smiles. "Busy times."

"Don't you have to go down there?" I lean forward, my hands on my knees, sick from running and the lingering smoke and grit in my throat. If I let myself start coughing, I think I'll throw up.

"That's not what I do." He waves a hand toward the square. "This isn't a big deal. It'll all be over in a few minutes."

I sink down on the curb. "What *do* you do?" I ask. "Do you have to stop people and ask them if they saw anything? Is that why you're here?"

Oskar takes his glasses off and rubs his eyes. "K," he sighs. "You must realize I can't discuss my work?"

I feel my face flush. "Sorry."

"No, it's all right. I can see why you'd want to know." He sits down beside me and puts his glasses back on. "I didn't mean to snap. My day hasn't gone too well."

I look up at him. "Same here."

"Something wrong at school?"

Everything. "Not really." And then, because he's looking so kind, and so interested behind his unfamiliar glasses, I tell him that I haven't been there since the bomb.

"But you'll have to go back." Oskar frowns. "What about your exams?"

I shake my head. "I've skipped too much school. I think I've messed it up."

"Come on, K," says Oskar. "You can't just give up. What about your social worker?"

I make a face. "I don't take her calls."

"Ask her to go and talk to them. Explain why you haven't been there."

I think about social worker Sue Smith with her neat black suit and businesslike smile. I can't imagine her going into school to try and plead for me. "You don't know her." I shake my head. "She doesn't like me. She isn't on my side."

"So what?" says Oskar. "It's her job to support you." He stands up. "I'll walk you home, shall I?"

That would be OK, wouldn't it? The halfway house is on the other side of the square and it would be nice not to have to go near the station on my own. "All right." I stand up and we start walking. The river Gate rushes alongside the road, high with rain and the coming spring tide.

"You know something?" Oskar looks sideways at me. "Not everything about my job is secret."

"No?"

"The police can't fight terrorism without the public," says Oskar. "All kinds of people are involved, one way or another." He stops, looking over the wall down into the churning water.

I lean against the rough parapet, its damp chill spreading through my thin jacket sleeves. "Then how do you keep it secret?"

He laughs, tapping the side of his nose. Then his face turns serious again. "Because each person only knows what they need to know."

We start walking again, toward the bridge. A tram rattles over it, full of standing Brotherhood people going home from their jobs in the New City. On the other side—their side—a Brotherhood bar has its doors wide open, in spite of the cold, and people have spilled out on to the riverbank, their clothes bright red against the monochrome of the concrete bridge and the dark river. An angry murmur rises from the crowd. They look like they're gathering to head down to the square.

"Let's cross the road," says Oskar, his voice quiet beside me. He takes my elbow and leads me to the other side.

We turn into a narrow road away from the trouble, and Oskar starts speaking again. "It's a network of informants, K," he says. "We need all kinds of people, all ages, all backgrounds." He looks into my eyes. "But there's one thing they all have in common. You know what it is?"

I don't say anything, because I'm not sure what he means.

Oskar leans closer. "They all have a reason." His voice is low but full of feeling. "Like you and me. People who'll go the distance. If we don't stop it, who will?"

My heart starts beating faster again. How far would I go to stop the Strife from coming back? Is that what he meant? But why would he think I could do anything?

We walk in silence until we reach the blank and ugly face of the halfway house. I wish I didn't have to admit to Oskar that I live here. "This is it." I stop. "Thanks for walking me back."

Oskar smiles his kind smile. "Good luck," he says.

"Don't look so worried. I think things are going to work out for you."

"Thanks." I hesitate. I don't know how to say good-bye. I wait to see if he'll say anything more.

He says, "There's something about you, K. You'll go far."

But he's wrong. I'm nothing but a loner and a loser. What can I do to change anything? I can't even get myself to school. Nobody cares what I do.

"Listen, K." Oskar puts his hand over mine before I can press the entry buzzer. "Why don't you meet me tomorrow? Outside Central Station at two o'clock?"

"Central Station?"

"It's just that there's a parking lot there. And I've got to go away soon. But if you'd rather not . . ."

"No," I say quickly. "I'll be there." *Don't go, Oskar, please don't go.*

I press the buzzer and wait for the doors to release. Oskar turns away, walking briskly toward the station. I watch his back disappear.

Then I turn back to the door and step inside, only to see my social worker, Sue Smith, watching me through the glass of the inner doors. Too late to backtrack. The street door behind me has clicked shut already.

"K," she says, opening the inner doors. "We need to talk about this." She waves a folded piece of paper.

She waits for me to collect my key and then passes me the paper. It's a printout of my attendance record. I crumple it up in my hand, shrugging.

"K." Sue's voice is brisk. "I've tried to fight for you, but unfortunately you missed an exam." Her teeth flash in a smile. "You're obviously an able girl, but things just haven't worked out. And I'm sorry, but I'm being taken off your case, so there's really nothing I can do. Why not forget about staying in school and start thinking about finding a job? After all, in five months' time you're going to be sixteen. Your government funding will run out. You'll have to leave this halfway house and pay your own way."

Panic flutters around me. I open my mouth to speak, but then stop and look at her, in her black office suit, her short hair as tidy as a doll's. She throws me another mechanical smile. What's the point in saying anything? I turn away, and I'm through the swing doors to the corridor before she has time to speak. She doesn't follow me.

—

I RUN UP to my room and throw the newspaper I picked up outside the bus stop on to the bed. It falls open on a double spread about the Brotherhood bomber. I turn over and forty-nine faces look back at me. I sit down and spread it out, read each name. Some of them are wearing Brotherhood hats and checked shirts. The bomber even killed his own. And then I see it. The little boy's daddy, on his face the same expression he wore as he picked up the bag of cupcakes.

After that, I can't look at the pictures anymore. A trapdoor below me has opened, and I need to shut it again before I fall in forever.

I open the drawer where I keep my father's paintbox and a pair of folding scissors that were my mother's, and I fold the sheet of newspaper carefully and put it in there too. Because they're not really strangers, are they? Not in their own lives, to the people who love them.

CHAPTER 4

I KNEW I'D go to meet Oskar, even though I haven't been back to Central Station since the bomb last week. Yellow police tape still encircles the entrance and only one door is open. Next to it, I see Oskar leaning against the wall, wearing a motorcycle jacket. Does that mean he's going away right now? I almost turn around, run away rather than have to watch him leave. But I can't let him go like that. If only I didn't have to say good-bye.

I wait for the traffic lights to change. What will I do, in the long days, without the hope of seeing Oskar again?

He sees me and saunters toward his motorbike.

I hurry to reach him. "Are you leaving, Oskar?"

"Not exactly," he says. "But you could be."

He wants *me* to go away? I stop.

"It's only a proposal. You can always turn it down." He fastens his helmet under his chin, smiling at me. "I want to take you for a ride. OK?"

"All right." I've never been on a motorbike before, but it looks fun.

Oskar pulls the spare helmet over my hair, silky from washing. He leans down to adjust the catch. I can smell his aftershave and the mint on his breath.

"That should do," he says. "I want to show you something."

He straddles the bike and I climb on, desperately gripping the bar behind me as we shoot forward.

Oskar brakes and twists back toward me. "If you try and stay upright, we'll go over," he shouts above the motor. "It's easier if you put your arms around my waist and lean the way I do. You can put your hands in my pockets, if you like."

I can tell from his voice he isn't flirting with me, just looking after me. I put my hands on Oskar's leather sides, and he's right, it feels much safer. But it's hard to hold on to the smooth leather until I push my hands inside his pockets. It's warmer too, with my face pressed against Oskar's back. Now when the bike veers to the side, so do I. The wind sucks my breath away, whipping the ends of my hair against my neck.

And now we're roaring up the hill away from the square. But Oskar doesn't turn left at the bridge. He slows down and drives on to it, straight into the Old City.

"Oskar!" I shout. "Where are we going?" But the wind steals my voice away.

I've never crossed the river before. In spite of its name, so many buildings here are new. Half-crumbled tenements sit next to hastily built blocks whose wooden paneling runs green with mold. Only the Meeting Hall rises proud against the heavy sky, its turrets and spire black with soot, sharp as thorns, like the evil twin of our Town Hall.

We're on the wrong side of the river. Am I imagining hostile glances from people on the pavement as the bike slows down for traffic lights?

It doesn't take long to get out into wooded hills, hazy with the greenish fuzz that promises leaves. *You could draw them with a fine pen, against a watercolor wash*, I think. We're getting farther and farther away from the New City. Where are we going?

"Not far now!" Oskar shouts. "Look to your left."

We purr along, past a stone mansion fleetingly glimpsed through the trees. It's the building I can see from my room, I realize suddenly. It has a huge sign, proudly announcing *The Institute*. I've heard of the Institute because it's the oldest school in Gatesbrooke. Everything about it seems to shout "Keep out!" from the high perimeter fence with its loops of barbed wire to the cameras trained on the road. It's nothing like the school I went to. Of course, I've never been to a Brotherhood school. They keep themselves apart, in the Old City. We've had five hundred years to practice being separate, and only months, since the Reconciliation process began, of trying to integrate.

Oskar pulls up on a path leading into the forest and turns the bike around. "That's what I wanted to show you!" he shouts over his shoulder. "We'll go somewhere we can talk now."

Before I can reply, we roar off back downhill toward the Old City. I turn my head as we pass the Institute gate. From this side of the road I glimpse a long drive with high fences and another gate at the far end. A security guard is patroling the fence, behind a row of tall narrow trees. Beyond him tiny figures run on the grass, little splashes of red against the green. It looks like a place from someone else's life.

Oskar slows down as we approach the Old City. I wonder why they never clean their old buildings. Up close I can see that they're the same pink granite as ours, but black with grime. I hope we're not stopping here. But we shoot over the bridge toward the square and Central Station. Oskar turns left, following the river Gate as it passes Jubilee Park and the fish market and then widens out into the estuary. Ahead of us are the derricks and cranes of the port.

But we don't go to the port. Oskar swerves across the road and pulls up beside the gate into Jubilee Park. "We can talk in the Aquarium," he calls back to me as he climbs off the bike.

My face is so cold that I can't move my mouth. My hair smells of the helmet and the wind. We walk into the park toward the Aquarium, a low stone building near the gate. I follow Oskar inside and down the stairs into the first room. He stops in front of a tank full of seaweed. We sit down on a bench, Oskar's gloves between us on the light wood. Fronds of dirty brown seaweed twist and sway in front of us and the coarse sand shifts suddenly as a camouflaged flatfish stirs, only its black button eyes clearly visible.

"I won't be based at Gatesbrooke for much longer, K."

Oh, Oskar. You are leaving. "Where are you going?"

"I can't tell you that."

I stare into the murky tank. "But then, how can I . . . ?" I stop.

"Keep in touch?" Oskar smiles at me.

I look into his kind eyes that make me feel as if I've known him forever. But I can't tell him that he's my best friend, my only friend. That when I'm with him I feel as if my life matters. So I look away.

"K," says Oskar. "If you were one of us, things would be different."

One of us? One of who?

A family comes in, the two little boys running to get stools and clattering them down next to us. Oskar touches my arm lightly as he stands up. I follow him into the next room, where the light is dim. I stop in front of a gravel-floored tank full of dull green water. Oskar leans toward me, so that his head almost touches mine. "The Institute," he says. "How would you like to finish school there?"

"What do you mean? I'm not Brotherhood!" Surely Oskar doesn't think that?

"Of course not," says Oskar. "But what if you had papers that said you were? That gave you a Brotherhood identity? You could study Art at the Institute."

I know. The New City Art Gallery is full of old paintings from when the Institute was an Art school. In citizen schools Art isn't a subject, and I wonder what it would be like to be able to do it.

Oskar steps forward, resting his hand against the glass and letting his fingers spread out and relax.

He's remembered that I'd like to be an artist. He doesn't know that in my back pocket is the letter that came today, telling me that because of my missed deadlines and poor attendance I've been expelled from school. I won't even be able to take my exams.

And how would going to the Institute help me keep in touch with Oskar? I watch the sea grass waft in an invisible current. "I don't understand."

He lowers his voice. "We believe there's a cell of militant Brotherhood extremists at the Institute, maybe even linked to the Central Station bomb."

I feel my heart start racing again. How can Oskar ask me to go somewhere like that? "Who's 'we'?" I ask. "Why do you . . ."

"K," he says.

"OK, I know you can't answer that." I stare into the water and right at the back I suddenly see a small seahorse with its tail curled around a stem.

"That's where you come in. We want you to in-filtrate the Brotherhood cell. We need someone they'll trust."

"You mean . . . you want me to be a spy?" I stare at Oskar. Then I laugh, the sound harsh in this quiet place of humming pumps. "Me? That's crazy."

Oskar has seen the seahorse too. He's watching it move away, its gentle head bowed and the fin on its back whirring. Maybe he's a fantasist. I step back.

"No, no, no." Oskar turns toward me, holds my gaze with his eyes. "All we want you to do is go to the school, then just keep your eyes and ears open. You can feed back the dynamic of the groups: who's saying what, who's doing what, who's in charge. You might not find out anything at all. That's fine. We're playing a long game. But if you do, you might be able to prevent the deaths of innocent people."

"I don't know . . ."

Oskar and I both turn as the two boys run in. We move without speaking into the next room. The circular tank in the middle is full of bright fish swimming purposefully round and round. I stop in front of the glass and wait for a middle-aged couple to walk out through the other doorway.

"I don't know much about the Brotherhood." Grandma made sure of it. "I'd never be able to pull off a big lie like that."

Oskar rests his hand against the tank. The water is clear and blue, with tiny silver bubbles fizzing up from clam pumps. "It's a lot for you to think about," he says. "Of course it is. But K, we can make a new world, one where people will be safe. It has to start small, with people like you and me, because we know the real cost. We have to be determined and brave. And remember, you won't be on your own. You'll be part of something bigger." Between the cage of his fingers a yellow striped fish darts past.

He thinks I'm brave. Is that true? Will he be there for me? For always? I bump my finger gently against the face of a curious ultramarine fish on the other side of the glass. I wish I could paint it with colored inks, so that the colors would bleed into each other.

"And I can't stress strongly enough," Oskar says, "that you won't be a spy at the Institute. All you have to do is be there and establish yourself as a Brotherhood girl." He's trying to make it sound easy.

"I couldn't do that. I'd have to be, pretend to be . . . *Brotherhood*." I think of their long skirts and hats. Long hair for women, short for men. Getting married so young.

Oskar stays silent, watching the fish swim past.

"I'd be alone in the school."

"You're right." Oskar smiles his warm smile. "But you'll be part of the fight against fear and chaos. So you'll know inside that you're one of us."

"I am one of you." I turn to look into his face. I think how wonderful it would be to completely belong to something that important. To be that important. "But . . ."

"You can do it, K," says Oskar. "I'll help you. You've heard of Brer Magnus?"

I nod. He's always in the news making anticitizen comments.

"He's a Brotherhood leader but he's also the school director. He runs a student group and big meetings at the Institute. The police haven't been able to get him for anything yet. Someone will give him your cover story before you even get there—"

He puts up one hand to stop me interrupting. "It's based on the truth." He takes out a notebook. "Who are you? Verity Nekton. Daughter of Brotherhood activists sadly killed when the Strife began."

He stops and looks searchingly at me. His fingers tap lightly on the glass. "Where have you been?" he continues when I don't say anything. "In care since your parents died. No grandmother. It's not your fault you were raised citizen not Brotherhood . . ."

The yellow fish glides past again, its eye cold and black. I pull my thin jacket more tightly around me.

Oskar touches my arm in warning as the children run into the room. He guides me toward the door. The spiral stairwell beyond is empty and we start climbing. "You see, now you're nearly sixteen and old enough to make your own decisions, you want to return to your roots." His knuckles look yellow against the handrail. "That'll explain why the Brotherhood's new to you." He laughs shortly. "Everyone at the Institute will feel sorry for you. They'll want to help you truly be a Brotherhood girl."

"But why will they believe it?" I take two steps at a time to keep up with Oskar. "What will they do to me if they don't?" Why am I even thinking about this?

"Why won't they, K? Verity Nekton's social worker will visit. She'll have all the paperwork, birth certificate, and so on. And Nekton is a respected old Brotherhood name." Oskar stops when he reaches the landing. "And of course I'll keep in touch, all the time."

He's planned every detail, as if it's real, as if I'm part of it already. He must have been checking me out. But it was me who told him everything, wasn't it? I climb up the last flight of stairs. Why does Oskar think I would be able to do all this, when he doesn't even know me? Nobody else thinks I can do anything, not even the social worker who's supposed to help me. But this almost-stranger believes in me.

"Where would I live?"

"At the Institute," says Oskar. "It's not a boarding school, but some of the older students live there."

I don't speak, because I'm afraid that if I open my mouth I'll just say yes to him.

"It won't be that hard, K." Oskar walks toward the doors. "All you have to do is be there and keep your real feelings to yourself."

That should be easy for me. It's the one thing I'm really good at. Years of living with people you can't trust will do that. I smile at Oskar, and in the glass door behind him I see my eyes lit up, green and alive again, not dull and sad.

"Take all the time you need, K." Oskar isn't smiling now. "You'll do the right thing. You know what's at stake." His eyes hold mine. "We both know we have to do everything we can to prevent the Strife starting again."

I look back into his eyes. Since Grandma died, Oskar is the only person I've known who understands a loss like mine. And now he's offering me a way to do something about it. A chance to set my own life aside and work with him to stop our country from plunging back into war and chaos. Oskar opens the door and an icy wind cuts in.

—

As we roar uphill back toward the station I make two lists in my mind:

If I say yes, I'll be working with Oskar. Isn't it true that an individual, weak and helpless on their own, can become strong when they are part of a bigger whole? Doesn't the possibility of saving even one person make it worth trying? This might be my only chance. It's now or never. And I could study Art, for the first time.

If I say no, I'll never see Oskar again. I'll still have my room at the halfway house, but only until I'm sixteen. I can't go back to school. I will have thrown away the opportunity, however slim, to finally do something to stop *them*. Maybe one small piece of missing information could have stopped the bomb at Central Station. Just like one person's observation could have saved my parents thirteen years ago.

Am I as brave as Oskar thinks? Could I really go that far?

—

OF COURSE I'M not going to do it. It's crazy, unreal. I have no idea how to be a spy.

Oskar pulls up in the train station's parking lot and I climb off the bike.

But as my fingers fumble with the helmet strap, I hear myself say: "I'll do it."

What am I doing? But I can always leave, can't I?

Oskar lifts his helmet off. "Good. Good." His face breaks out into a smile.

It'll be OK.

He pulls off his gloves and unclasps my helmet strap because my fingers are too cold to do anything except fumble. "I knew you would." His friendly eyes smile into mine. "We'll get together in the cafe tomorrow, sort out your Brotherhood ID." He pulls a folder out of his crate.

He has it with him. He knew I would say yes.

"Here. This will tell you everything you need to know about the Brotherhood. Don't let anyone see it. Keep it with you always. Oh, and don't get a haircut."

"OK." I take the folder.

"Hey." He pulls me into a sudden bear hug. "You're not alone. Not now." He lets me go and laughs into my face. "Don't look so solemn."

But I don't feel solemn at all. I watch Oskar's bike roar around the corner. I know I'll see him again now that we're working together. The guilt that has been gnawing at me since the bomb lifts, just like that, and a wave of peace fills me. I think of the little boy with the cupcakes. "I'm doing this for you," I whisper.

I run back to the halfway house with the folder clutched to my chest. For the first time ever, it feels like going home.

CHAPTER 5

I STAND OUTSIDE the gate of the Institute, my finger pressing the buzzer. On the other side of the road, Oskar is watching me from the woods, which are dark in the dull afternoon light. Once I cross the threshold, there's no turning back, just as there was no going back after I walked out of the halfway house without saying where I was going. I look at the graffiti scrawled over the low stone wall in front of the fence: *Hoody Scum . . . Murderers.* It wasn't there when we drove past before.

Nothing happens, nobody comes. I could still turn back, run across the road to the clearing up the hill where Oskar parked the car. I could tell him I've changed my mind. But am I such a coward as that? *You might be able to prevent the deaths of innocent people.* I made up my mind and I gave my word. I press the buzzer again.

This time the gate swings open immediately, and before I have time to think again I walk in, pulling the new red suitcase Oskar gave me. The gate clangs shut behind me, and suddenly everything is different. I'm in a world controlled solely by the Brotherhood. My heart starts leaping about under my blouse.

A high barbed-wire fence borders the drive, with another locked gate at the end, trapping me in, under scrutiny. *Murderers . . . murderers . . .* My feet walk to the beat of the words as I approach the second gate. Beyond it there's a lodge, and behind that the stone mansion, with its leaded windows and crooked roof, squats solidly against the white wintry sky. Other old buildings sprawl around and behind it.

I refuse to be afraid to walk into the Institute, even though my feet are sending me an urgent message: *Turn around, go back!* The cameras perched above the barbed wire swivel to track me. I feel the wool bag drag on my shoulder, and my pumps skid on the gravel of the drive. I don't look like me, in this red-checked skirt that grabs my ankles as I walk and the floppy hat over my hair, still way too short for a Brotherhood girl. But I know that I'll see Oskar in a week when we meet in the woods, so I make my feet keep walking.

I won't think about what Grandma would say if she could see me now, dressed as a Brotherhood girl, with a Brotherhood name, walking into a Brotherhood school. Because if Grandma could see me, I wouldn't be doing this, would I?

I stop when I reach the second gate and the caretaker's lodge. On the wall I see the faded Gatesbrooke Council sign: *One City, Two Ways.* Above the sign, carved into the stone in weathered letters, is *The Institute.* It seems to mock the sign. *I was here first,* its crumbling stone says, *before your State.* Oskar's Manual explained the period of Brotherhood rule hundreds of years ago before we won the first civil war: our

Bloody Century, their Golden Hundred. I don't want to walk under this arch, which has always been here.

The parking lot only has a few cars in it. But this evening, Oskar has told me, is the Institute's big Spring Meeting. That's why he wanted me to go in today. The security guard comes out of the lodge and walks toward the gate, his walkie-talkie crackling in the quiet afternoon.

"And you are?" he barks.

"Verity Nekton." My voice sounds loud and clear, as if it's true. My heart thumps.

I hold out the letter Oskar gave me and the guard studies it. A brown-and-white spaniel walks up behind him and sniffs my hand through the rails. It's not much of a guard dog. It gives my knuckles a quick lick. The gate slides open, then clangs shut behind me.

I'm alone now. The Brotherhood don't trust television or computers. But they seem to have no problem with security cameras and signal-blocking technology. Even if I had a cell phone, I wouldn't be able to use it in here. Oskar feels very far away already. I must remember his warning about sticking to my story: *You're in real danger if they find out, K. You're pretty isolated in there.* I focus on the dog to calm my breathing. The white line down to its nose gives its chocolate eyes a sad and thoughtful look. Its tail wags slowly but hopefully. It's going to be OK. And at least I won't have to read or hear about terrorist threats every day. They don't do news here. You see, Oskar? I did read the Manual.

Even before I walk through the glass doors into the lobby, I can see that this is nothing like any school I've ever been in before. The smell hits me first, an ancient reek seeping from the oak paneling and the worn flagstones. Lavender polish too. A staircase with scrolled wooden banisters sweeps up to the floor above. It's so quiet that I can hear the solemn ticking of an ornate clock over the high-backed bench against the wall. Then I see a boy standing by the door opposite. All my calmness vanishes and I freeze. *It can't be*, I tell myself. But I look again and it is: it's the boy I collided with at the train station, before the bomb. Does he recognize me? Nausea floods my throat. *Get a grip, K.* I look up and our eyes meet. His are chestnut brown, I see now, and surprisingly warm. But they flick over me without recognition. I let myself breathe out.

"Are you all right?" He's so sure of himself, entirely at home, while I am on foreign ground.

Pull yourself together, K! I manage to nod.

"You are Verity, aren't you?"

I nod again.

He shrugs. "OK, well, Brer Magnus asked me to show you to the Sisters' house." He steps forward to hold the door open and reaches out his hand for my suitcase. "Shall I take that?"

"No!" I say. Then I remember what Oskar said: "*Be friendly, K.*" I take a deep breath. "Thanks, though."

He shrugs again, and turns away. "Sure."

I follow his red-checked shirt out of the lobby and across a grass quadrangle in front of a canteen with long glass doors. The Institute isn't one building at all, but rather a series of jumbled buildings connected by walkways and paths, everything hidden behind a wall or glimpsed through an archway. I know why they wear red check. It was the pattern favored by the Brotherhood leader, Antonius Nekton, on his battle standard four hundred years ago, when they last won control of the country. He was a nice man who burnt non-Brotherhood citizens at the stake.

I hurry to keep up, bumping the suitcase over cobbles, struggling with my skirt. This doesn't feel like a school to me, more like an old stately home. I wonder what it's like during the day, when the pupils are all here. The boy's dark hair is cut in the Brotherhood style, so short that I can see the lighter skin where it's been shaved at the back of his neck. I think of Oskar's blond hair that comes down to his collar. The boy stops outside a stone cottage in another grassy courtyard, and I almost walk into him, putting my hand out to stop myself so that my suitcase tips over on to its side.

He steps smartly back. "This is it," he says, opening the door for me. "Your room's upstairs."

I pick up the suitcase, but somehow it gets caught in my check skirt and almost tumbles on to the grass.

A flicker of a smile crosses the boy's face. He's laughing at me again. "I won't offer to carry your bag up for you."

I feel my face flushing, but I concentrate on what Oskar told me. *Friendly . . . Nice.* "Thank you," I say—with dignity, I hope. I don't look back to see if he's watching me bump the case inside and up the narrow stairs.

As I thump it down onto the landing at the top of the stairs, a door flies open.

"Hi!" A smiling girl bounds out. "I'm Serafina. You must be Verity."

Yes, I must.

"That's such a pretty name," says Serafina. She pulls me toward her, knocking my hat off and burying my nose in her curly brown hair, which smells of grapefruit. "Oops!" she laughs.

Oskar said they hug a lot, but this is way too much. Nobody has hugged me since I was little, and I hope she can't feel how tense I am. I pat her shoulder awkwardly until she lets me go. Was that friendly? Maybe not.

"Um, I like your perfume," I say.

"Thanks." Serafina picks up my hat and the suitcase and carries them into the room, setting the case on a bed to the right of the door. There are three beds. One is a jumble of clothes, files, and makeup bags. "That's Celestina's bed," says Serafina.

Their names are so long. Mind you, K is short even for a citizen.

She points to the bed beside the door. "This is yours," she says. "There isn't much space, I'm afraid. Only a few of us live here."

She bounces herself down on the bed opposite mine. Hers is covered in stuffed animals, like a five-year-old's bed. She sits there watching me and jiggling her foot in its flowered slipper. Her skirt fits her perfectly and her top wraps prettily around her shoulders. None of her clothes are red-checked except for a little scarf knotted loosely around her neck. She doesn't look drab at all.

I put my case on the bed and pull out long skirts, horrible ruffled blouses, and a candy-striped dress that looks like a deck chair. It's almost the only thing that isn't covered in red checks. I don't think Oskar went to the same Brotherhood shop as Serafina. I've never seen any of these things before. There aren't any jeans or pants or shoes I could run away in.

Serafina jumps up and puts the deck-chair dress on a hanger. "Brer Magnus said you've just rejoined the Brotherhood?" She gives me a quick sidelong glance. "So does that mean that before, you had to wear, well, men's clothes?"

"Men's clothes?"

"You know . . . pants?" She gives an embarrassed little laugh.

"Oh. Pants. Well, yes."

Men's clothes! I must be careful that the real me doesn't seep through my Brotherhood clothes. Perhaps Serafina already knows my cover story. At least then I won't have to show her the Certificate of Infant Initiation for Verity Nekton.

Serafina hasn't finished. "But why weren't you brought up in the Brotherhood?"

Maybe she doesn't know my story after all. "My parents were killed by a bomb when I was two," I say. "I grew up in the system."

Serafina is silent. Does she believe me? *It's the truth*, I tell myself—just not in the way she thinks. "Well." She brightens. "It must be great for you to finally get to be with your own people."

This almost makes me laugh. "Oh. Yes, great," I say quickly. I carry a bundle of clothes over to the wardrobe and fish out some hangers from the empty bit that they've left for me.

Serafina jumps up and comes over to help. "It's so nice to have someone new. And you're so lucky, your first day. It's the Spring Meeting."

Lucky me. But Oskar thought it would be a good idea to throw me straight in. "Keep your eyes peeled, K," he said. "It's one of their major events of the year, an ideal opportunity to recruit young people to the cell. We'd like to know what goes on there, who turns up."

"It's a really big thing," says Serafina. "Not just for the school, lots of other people come as well. It's quiet now, but give it an hour or so and everyone will start to arrive. You've got time to unpack, though—shall I get you a cup of tea?"

I say yes so that I'll have a few minutes alone. When I can hear her footsteps clattering down the stairs, I cross the room and look out of the window at the front of the cottage. Lights have gone on in the long windows of the canteen and I see people moving around, putting out trays of glasses. The bedroom runs the whole width of the house, but from the back window all I can see is a willow tree and a grassy lawn leading to woods. It would be easy to climb down the drainpipe and drop from the porch roof, I note.

Serafina comes back in, two mugs of tea in her hands. But she isn't alone. Behind her is another girl in a long green dress.

"This is Celestina," says Serafina. She puts the mugs down on her bedside table.

Celestina stops in the doorway, her long black hair swishing over her shoulders. She's slowly twirling a hat with a thin red-checked band, watching me.

"This is Verity," says Serafina.

"Hello, Verity." Celestina stares me out.

Did she say my name with a question?

Her eyes are the green of new ivy leaves. Her emerald dress makes her look like a model. She doesn't come closer to hug me. I wish my heart rate would slow down. She's looking at me as if she can see right through me. But Oskar said to stay calm. I give her a big fake smile.

Celestina doesn't smile back and I look away first. She's won the first round.

"Let me help put your things away," says Serafina. "You can have these drawers."

I wonder suddenly if they've had to move their stuff to make room for me. I've never shared a room before and already it feels like it's closing in on me. Maybe Celestina doesn't like a strange girl suddenly crashing in, making everything more crowded. She's sitting on her bed, carefully touching up her makeup, even though it already looks perfect to me.

It doesn't take long to put my things away. I sit on the bed—my bed—drinking tea and listening to Serafina chat. I don't have to say much. It's as different as possible from my room in the halfway house. All the quilts are different colors and the walls are a soft cream, so that when Celestina switches the light on, the room seems golden. It's getting dark when Serafina jumps up. "Time to go!" She throws a cardigan over my shoulders. "Here, have this. It's cold now."

"I'll catch up to you." Celestina is still sitting on her bed, doing her hair. Watching me.

CHAPTER 6

I FOLLOW SERAFINA downstairs and out into the grassy courtyard. It's enclosed by weathered old walls on three sides, but to the right there's a stone arch and a path leading down the side of the house into a rhododendron grove.

"What's down there?" I ask Serafina.

"Nothing really, just woods. And a pool—for brothers."

We walk back toward the canteen building, which is full of people, milling around, greeting each other, holding glasses of wine. There are children there too, dodging under arms and weaving around to the table where the cookies are. Serafina half-turns to me with an excited little laugh. "People are arriving!" she says.

We walk past the canteen and along the walkway to the main building. "There's a lot of security." I point at the caretaker's lodge through the glass doors of Reception. Immediately I wish I'd kept my mouth shut. That sounded just like the sort of thing a spy would say.

"We can ask to go out when we need to, though," says Serafina. "Mr. East opens the gate. It's just for our protection."

"Protection?"

"Yes." She gives me a second uneasy look. "We're not exactly flavor of the month."

And why is that? I wonder. *Could it be because you blow people up?*

The door of the main building is wedged open and now it's crowded with people coming through from the parking lot, so noisy with the rise and fall of voices that you can't hear the clock at all.

Serafina pulls me over to a table in the corner, covered in a gold brocade cloth embroidered with birds and flowers. A book is open on the table, with a pen lying on it. Serafina signs her name in round swirling handwriting. She passes me the pen.

But as I touch it to the creamy paper, my mind goes completely blank. *K Child.*

"Just sign your name, Verity."

I write it quickly then, because there's a line forming behind us. *Verity Nekton.* It doesn't look like a signature at all. I should have practiced.

"The Meeting Hall's upstairs," says Serafina.

The banister is smooth from centuries of hands running up and down its oak curves. It would be perfect for sliding down. I look down at the crowded lobby below, now a sea of red Brotherhood check, and a wave of nausea washes over me. What am I doing here? Isn't it glaringly obvious that I don't belong? *Calm down, K, nobody will notice you in all this crowd.*

I glance at our reflection in the stairwell windows as we go up the turn in the stairs. Serafina and Celestina wouldn't be seen dead in a skirt as shapeless as mine. Under my black hair, my face looks pale. My heart lurches. My hat! I'm the only girl I can see with an uncovered head. Serafina has tied her scarf over her head. I watched her do it and I still didn't remember the hat. But I think of what Oskar said: *Smile. You have to look friendly.* Like Serafina. How much will it matter, not having a hat?

The upstairs lobby is buzzing with people, and outside, the long drive is dotted by headlights as a line of cars creeps toward the parking lot. All Brotherhood. All the women and girls in hats. Beside the door two little girls have sat down to take off their shoes before going into the hall. I almost jump when I see the boy from the station standing in one of the doorways into the hall. His hair is wet. As we get closer, I smell chlorine.

"That's Gregory," says Serafina.

She squeezes my arm, and I stop myself from pulling it away.

"He's great." She gestures over to the other door, where a boy with corkscrew curls and a friendly smile is handing out candles. "He lives here because his family is overseas. And that's his friend, Emanuel. He lives here too. But you'll meet them later."

I think she likes Emanuel. I fake-smile at Serafina. "I already met him—Gregory."

I follow Serafina's lead and put my shoes next to hers in the shoe rack beside the door. The boy called Emanuel is standing on one side of the doorway, and a ginger-haired boy on the other. I can't see Gregory. We file in with everyone else and Emanuel gives Serafina a candle, but the ginger-haired boy on my side of the doorway ignores my open hand. He looks me up and down, for too long.

I stare back at him. I don't think I look friendly. Sorry, Oskar.

"That's Jeremiah," whispers Serafina. "He lives here as well."

I follow her in. Under other circumstances, I would love this room. Although it's so old, it's very simple, with huge windows that go from floor to ceiling. Outside, I can see a row of fir trees. Inside, there is nothing but carpet with a path through the middle that leads to a high table where their huge Book lies. Women and girls sit on the left side, men and boys on the right. Serafina clutches my arm as we sit down.

"I'm so sorry," she whispers. "I didn't notice your head's not covered. We don't have to wear hats indoors, but we do need something. That's why Jeremiah couldn't give you a candle. Now you won't be able to come up and receive the blessing." Her face has gone pink under her red-checked scarf.

Sure enough, all the girls and women are wearing hats or scarves. I try to look like I care. "Hey, that's OK. I can just watch you get yours."

But then I start to think what it's going to look like when they all go up to the front, leaving me alone in a carpet sea. Grandma would be pleased I wasn't taking part, at least. I feel a grim smile twist the corners of my mouth, not the sort of smile Oskar meant. And he said not to draw attention to myself. And soon I'll be sticking out, all on my own. I should have remembered the stupid hat. How could I have been so careless?

I jump as a red-checked shape leans over my shoulder. It's Gregory, the station boy. He's so close that his chlorine smell overwhelms Serafina's perfume. He opens his mouth as if to say something, but then reaches over me to pass a scarf and a candle to Serafina instead. Does this mean he can't even speak to me if my head's not covered in the Meeting Hall? He stands up and hurries away.

Serafina turns to me, beaming. "Typical Gregory. So thoughtful," she whispers. "Now you can go up too!" She holds out a candle, and the scarf.

"What?" I want to push her hand away, but I stop myself. At least he's saved me from having to sit on my own.

Serafina's face clouds a little. "Come on," she murmurs. "Look, he even got one that matches your blouse."

I look down. The scarf is navy, with tiny pink flowers like the ones on my top. Serafina's gazing at me with puppy eyes.

"OK." I take the scarf from her. "Thanks."

I tie the headscarf in a knot under my chin, not prettily at the back like Serafina's.

—

IT'S NOT WHAT I expected. Nobody sings, and nobody speaks, and in the deep hush I watch the sky turn from indigo to black. Who are all these people? I wonder. Who here is in the cell? Which of these quiet people could be a bomber? Then Brer Magnus comes in, a red cloak swinging behind him. He strides down the corridor between the men and boys and the women and girls and there's a rush of movement as everyone scrambles to their feet. He stands behind the table with the Book, staring around the room with fierce blue eyes beneath the gray wing of his comb-over. The room is stilled into an expectant hush. Brer Magnus doesn't speak as his eyes scan the room, searching every face. *Oskar has told me all about you.* I remember what he'd said: *Who knows how many pupils he has radicalized?*

Just thinking this seems to draw his eyes to mine. I stare back. I'm not looking away first. What would happen if he guessed I wasn't really Brotherhood? If I was here to "infiltrate a cell." A tap on the shoulder followed by an "accident"? How easily I could just disappear. After all, I'm Verity Nekton now, an imaginary person. How would Oskar even know? It's hot in this crowded room so I slide my borrowed cardigan off, letting it slip to the floor.

Brer Magnus raises his hands and we all sit down again. "Brothers and Sisters, welcome to the Spring Meeting," he says. "We are here to hold fast in these days of change! To protect our Brotherhood heritage even as our very existence is threatened by those who want us to sit at table with nonbelievers." He raises his voice. "To force our children into mixed schools. To compromise our Brotherhood heritage." His eyes sweep the room. "Brothers and Sisters, we must do everything in our power to preserve our separateness."

Everything in our power? A wave of panic floods me, but I make myself breathe calmly, staring out at the fir trees feathered against the sunset. We could be on top of a forested mountain instead of in a school. I let his voice roll over me like background music while I fix my eyes on the silhouette of a black crow until I forget where I am.

Brer Magnus talks and talks, and nobody else says anything at all. At last his voice changes, becoming lighter. "And now we will light our candles of purity," he says, "before we eat together. I hope that everyone will join with us in this time of fellowship."

A grateful ripple waves through the room and we all clamber stiffly to our feet, taking the candles up to the table. Brer Magnus still stands behind it, his hands spread wide on the gold cloth beneath the Book, the red check of his cloak glowing. He fixes his piercing gaze on each person as they approach. He makes my flesh crawl. I stand next to Serafina, clutching my candle, panic beating in my chest. I look over the top of his head as he lights my candle. But when I put it down in front of the Book with the others and see all the little lights glimmering together, the memory of the vigil strikes me. I wish I was wearing the floppy hat, so that I could hide my face. Instead I lower my head.

—

AFTERWARD I LOSE Serafina. There are so many people thronging around Brer Magnus in the lobby below the Meeting Hall that I can't see her. Maybe Brer Magnus is standing by the door to make sure that nobody leaves early. That boy Jeremiah seems to have his whole family here. They all look like each other and they're all hanging on to Brer Magnus's words with glowing faces. Have they come just to hear him speak? I edge closer in the crowd.

"I wish I could go too," Jeremiah is saying. He indicates the boy standing next to him. "This is my cousin."

Brer Magnus smiles, puts one hand on Jeremiah's shoulder. "You're nearly old enough." He turns and nods at Jeremiah's cousin, who steps eagerly forward.

"You'll meet interesting people there when you come," says the cousin. "People who will make them sit up and take note."

Them? Does he mean "us"? Citizens? My heart starts beating faster. I dig my fingernails into the palms of my hands, pretending to look around for Serafina.

Out of the corner of my eye I see Jeremiah eagerly nodding.

"They live like animals, without rules," he continues. "But they need to know we haven't forgotten."

I try to look as if I'm in the line to sign the visitors' book, still on the little table in the corner, rather than listening in. I'm glad for the scarf now. It seems to make me almost invisible. Maybe that's its purpose.

"I want to do more," says Jeremiah.

The other boy steps even closer to Brer Magnus. "Talk to them in the language they understand, if you get what I mean." He turns to Jeremiah. "You should join."

Brer Magnus laughs and pats Jeremiah's shoulder. "It's wonderful to see the passion you young men have." His voice takes on a note of warning. "Just don't get carried away." Then he turns to someone at his elbow.

I can't believe what I've just heard. They weren't even talking quietly! I look over to the stairs and my eyes meet Gregory's. I wonder if he noticed me listening. I look away, cursing myself. I'm no good at this—why would Oskar think I could do it? Why would anyone?

People are beginning to disperse now, across the grass toward the canteen block. As I reach the cold air in the doorway, I remember Serafina's cardigan. I run upstairs to fetch it. It's empty up here now. I slip off my shoes again, just in case, and kick them to the side of the door. In the Meeting Hall, only one lamp still shines, above the closed Book and the snuffed-out candles, and suddenly I need to see it for myself. What does it say in their Book that makes them want to kill strangers?

I can see the cardigan lying on the carpet. After I've picked it up, I glance over my shoulder, but nobody is there. I pad over to the table. I can hear my own breath, loud and quick. I am going to look at the Book. I turn it around and open it, letting the heavy pages fall back. I think of all the times I tried to peer through the Brotherhood Meeting Hall doorway in Yoremouth while Grandma dragged me quickly past. And here I am actually leafing through their famous Book for myself. I'd better be quick, though.

I'm expecting to find incendiary prose about killing nonbelievers, but all I find is a long poem about fish in a lake.

That's when I feel eyes boring into my back. I turn to see Gregory standing there, frowning. I didn't hear him come in.

"What are you doing?" His voice is grim.

"Reading?" I hide my flash of anger. Who made him judge and jury? And I want to ask him what he was doing at the station that day.

I wait for him to tell me that Sisters have to keep their polluting hands off the Book, but he hesitates for a moment and then half-nods. "It's there to be read." He waits, like a dog guarding something.

I close the Book carefully. "I'm done now," I say, turning to leave. *Be careful. Be friendly.* "I left this." I hold up my cardigan. "I'm Verity, by the way."

"I know. And I'm Greg," he adds.

"I know."

He waits behind me as I shuffle my feet into my pumps back outside the Meeting Hall. Then he follows me down the stairs. The foyer is empty. Through the stairwell windows I see that all the people are in the canteen, eating and drinking. Fiddle music drifts across the courtyard. I glance back when I reach the door.

Gregory's still standing at the foot of the stairs, watching me. *I think he knows, Oskar. You feel so far away. You said I wouldn't feel alone.* But I do.

CHAPTER 7

I LIE AWAKE in the darkness at the end of this long first day. The bed is comfy enough, warm and cozy, but I can't relax. I never thought I would miss the four stark walls of my room at the halfway house, but hearing a stranger's sleep-breathing is so odd that it's keeping me on edge. Serafina has been sleeping for a while when the bedroom door creaks open and Celestina slips in. She nearly trips over Serafina's stuffed giraffe and swears softly. Where has she been? I wait until she's in bed. She can't sleep either. It's ages before she stops shuffling about and her breathing slows down. Then I get up.

I have to get outside now, before I lose it. I can see I'll never be able to be alone here. We eat together, study together, even sleep in the same room. And all the time there are the watchful eyes of Greg and Celestina, waiting for me to give myself away.

I put my clothes and shoes back on, and the long woolly cardigan Serafina lent me. She won't mind. She seems to like giving me things. I've been given keys for the Sisters' house, two for the front door and one for the back, and now I put them in the cardigan pocket. Upstairs there's just our room and a bathroom. I tiptoe downstairs past the kitchenette and Georgette the cook's apartment and open the front door, letting it click shut softly behind me. Oskar wouldn't like this. Guilt stabs at me. Am I being reckless? I pause for a moment, under the porch. But Oskar doesn't have to live here.

The air is cold and clear, sweet with night dew. It's colder here than in the city. I feel my spirits lift as I run down the path to the rhododendron grove. Free! I can hear an owl, and foxes barking in staccato calls. We have foxes in the city, but I haven't heard owls since I was little. Sometimes I could hear them call from the woods behind Grandma's house. It's very dark here, because there's only a thin crescent moon tonight. But through the trees I see something gleam—a pond, surrounded by trees. As I get closer I see it has a wooden platform by the edge. The water shines in the sliver of moonlight. *I'm not afraid of deep, dark water.*

I know it's way too cold, but even so I climb onto the deck and pull off my clothes. It can't be much colder than the sea at Yoremouth, which faces the open ocean and is almost never calm. And however cold it is, at least I will *feel* it. Maybe it will wash away Verity Nekton, just for a few moments.

I stand on the edge of the platform and leap in, and then I'm whooshing up for air and gasping, gasping with the ice-cold water crackling inside my head and tingling my skin. I swim as hard as I can across the pond and then back, splashing up white spray in the moonlight. Then I stop, treading water; I'm making too much noise.

Maybe I can survive here if just now and again I can have a swim in this magic pond. It's not that bad, after all. I've gotten through this day. Tomorrow for the first time ever I'll have an Art lesson. Serafina is kind and the food's great.

Twigs snap near the edge of the trees. In the weak moonlight a shadowy figure shifts.

Is it security? What was I thinking? I am naked in a Brotherhood pond!

I duck under, holding my breath, but can't stay submerged for long. I surface and tread water as softly as I can. I can't see anyone in the inky shadow of the rhododendrons. Did I imagine it?

I listen and peer into the shrubbery, my ears and eyes straining. The cold is gripping me. I can't stay in here much longer. I swim breaststroke back to the platform, skirting the side of the pond, trying not to go too near the weeds. I have to get out, even if someone's lurking there, waiting.

I heave myself up. There's nobody hiding in the shadows after all, so I must have imagined it. My teeth are clattering together and I'm shivering, but I feel like me again. I won't give up after just one day. I rub myself dry with Serafina's cardigan—hopefully it'll dry before morning—haul on my clothes any old how, and jog back through the trees. Moonlight silvers the edges of the buds.

Then I hear footsteps thudding on the path behind me. A jolt of fear charges through me. I leap into a rhododendron bush and crouch down in the dark, my arms hugging my knees. I'm so cold that my whole body is shaking.

The footsteps slow down and stop. I hold my breath. An owl hoots above me. The footsteps move on.

I wait until I can't hear anymore, and then I slip out of the bushes and onto the path. Too late I see the waiting black shape of someone. I crash into him, he grabs hold of me and we teeter together for a second before I regain my balance enough to try and pull away.

"Verity?" It's Greg.

I jerk myself free, panting. "What are you doing, sneaking up on me like that?"

"I didn't look," he blurts out.

So he did see me in the pond. I feel my face turning bright red and I'm so glad it's dark. He sounded just as uncomfortable.

"What were you doing, swimming on your own in the middle of the night?" He sounds outraged. "I'll walk you back to your house." I hear his frown, in the darkness, and under his breath I hear him mutter, "What an idiot."

Who does he think he is?

He starts taking off his jacket. "Here, have this," he says. "You must be freezing."

"No, thanks," I say. "How would I explain why I've got your coat?"

"Oh," he says, his jacket half on and half off. "But you look so cold."

"I'm fine," I say. "But thanks for not watching."

"I'm not a perv."

I can't help liking him a little bit then. "Of course not, I know that." Because there are different kinds of spies, aren't there? I should know. "Sorry."

We stand there awkwardly for a moment. Then he says, "You must really like swimming." I think I hear a smile in his voice. A friendly smile.

"I do. But you're right. It was a bit too cold." What would Oskar think if he knew how I've risked everything? "You won't tell anyone, will you?"

He laughs. It was a sneering smile after all. He really does think I'm an idiot. And I am.

"I'll just run the last bit," I say, taking off. I can't afford to be so careless again. This time Greg doesn't follow me.

But he did follow me before. He must have been hanging about near the Sisters' house. I look back as I slip through the front door, under its ancient stone porch, but there's no sign of Greg. That doesn't mean he isn't there, though. What was he doing out in the middle of the night?

Then I think about Celestina coming in late too. Were they together?

I'll ask Oskar what he thinks, when I see him. Maybe the cell is right in front of me.

CHAPTER 8

THE NEXT MORNING the Institute is transformed. At breakfast, the few boarders rattled around in the empty canteen. But by half past eight, buses are lining up in the parking lot and the corridors are already full of hurrying pupils. Still, it's not like my last school. There aren't any bells, for one thing, or a uniform. Just a lit-tle bit of red check on everyone. Apart from me—I'm covered in it from head to toe. Thanks, Oskar.

Everything is different. Here, the library isn't a gray glass facility for computers and hidden books, but a wood-paneled room with alcoves and nooks, squashy leather armchairs, and glowing lamps. The books fill floor-to-ceiling bookcases in a jumble of color. There's even a common room for the older students that looks like a sit-ting room in a family home—paintings by students on the walls and inviting couches around a coffee table.

My first full day here is confusing and busy. As well as finding my way around, I have to remember how to act, what to conceal. I can't ignore the curious staring at my too short hair and over-the-top clothes. Walk-ing into the canteen at lunchtime on my own is the worst moment. So I'm glad when Serafina finds me as I leave History.

"There you are," she says. "Brer Magnus always talks to us after school, in the auditorium. Come on!"

Not another dose of Brer Magnus, so soon. But it's good, isn't it? I'll have more to tell Oskar.

The auditorium is at the bottom of a classroom block, near the library, and I'm surprised to see that it's an actual movie theater with seats that tip up and armrests for your drink. I'm sure Brotherhood schools in the Old City aren't like this—my citizen school wasn't either.

There's no sign of Brer Magnus on the stage. In-stead, the curtains at the back of the stage have been pulled back to reveal a screen.

"It's a film today!" Serafina says. "It must be because of the Spring Meeting yesterday."

I won't have to sit through another of Brer Magnus's talks, wondering whether his eyes will fix on me. Serafina grabs my hand and pulls me to the back of the auditorium, past the seats full of pupils, while I try to ignore the staring as we climb. She seems to want to look after me. And if she's not around, Greg is. Jeremiah steers clear of me, though, so I haven't gotten anything else to tell Oskar. I'm glad for the dark. At least I won't have to guard the expressions on my face.

Celestina, Emanuel, and Greg are already here.

"Hello, Serafina. Verity." Emanuel jumps up to let us pass. I slide past Greg's knees to sit between Celestina and Serafina.

I guess the school has its own theater because they don't want any of the kids to be contaminated by going to the one in town where they might have to sit next to a citizen, or "nonbeliever," as Brer Magnus calls us. Unless they sit next to me here and now, of course. In the half darkness there's a buzz of chatter and the rustling of candy wrappers. I relax into my chair.

Greg reaches across Celestina. "Popcorn, Serafina? . . . Verity?"

I reach into the bag, but Greg almost drops it, grabbing my fingers through the paper. I tug them away and he lets go, sending popcorn flying out over Celestina. Greg stares at me. Then he laughs. So far I don't think he's told anyone about the swimming but I can't thank him, not with everyone listening.

Celestina swipes the popcorn off her skirt. "Idiot," she says.

I don't think she means Greg but she punches him lightly on the shoulder. They seem to have a comfortable friendship. I'm sure Greg smiles more when Celestina's there.

The lights go all the way down, and the screen flickers into life.

"It's a romantic comedy," Serafina whispers, her curls brushing my ear.

But it isn't.

The screen goes black, and then white, and then block letters appear: THE GATESBROOKE MASSACRE. My heart starts thumping. They're going to show footage of the bomb. I want to get up and run out, but I'm frozen in my seat, eyes fixed on the screen.

For a moment there's a still image of the Gatesbrooke town square. I steel myself for the explosion. But something is different—there are cars crossing the square, when it's only for pedestrians. It takes me a moment to realize that this is an old film. My heart lurches, my breath seizes up. They're going to show the bomb that killed my parents! Grainy shapes spill into the square, hundreds of people . . . No, this isn't the bomb after all. I start to breathe again. And then I see that the station name is "New City Station" and that makes me remember: a black-and-white photo in an old green history book, with the caption, *The Brotherhood Rebellion at Gatesbrooke was successfully contained, ending the Strife and allowing the establishment of the Peace that we enjoy today.*

Grandma made me copy it out, to improve my handwriting, she said. So I'm watching the screen, but in my mind I'm sitting at the dining table with my hand resting on a lined composition book, and the sound of Grandma clinking pans in the kitchen.

The photo vanishes. I crunch into the toffee crust of the popcorn. Then I really see what's on the screen.

It's footage from twelve years ago. Music crackles in a solemn dirge. Figures run across the screen. Some are running away, and some are chasing them. It takes me a few seconds to realize that all the people running away are dressed in Brotherhood clothes.

Government soldiers—citizen soldiers—shoot everyone who moves. They pitch their bayonets into children. One holds up fingers, grinning, keeping score. The soundtrack laments.

"Rebellion at Gatesbrooke . . . successfully contained . . ."

Not a rebellion. A massacre. There was nothing about this in Oskar's Manual.

Serafina's staring at the screen, chewing popcorn. She doesn't look shocked at all. I'm glad it's dark, because I can sense Greg leaning forward, as if he's trying to look at my face, to see my reaction. I move back in my seat.

The music fades as the camera pans jerkily closer and closer, until it finds the wound, the still body, the face with a silent scream.

The popcorn is a sticky clump in my palm. I make myself swallow the bits in my mouth.

Greg leans farther forward, around Celestina. I look to see if he's going to speak. His eyes gleam in the light from the screen, but he doesn't say anything. I turn away to see Serafina looking up at Greg. Then at me. Her hand flies to her mouth. She covers my hand with hers and squeezes it.

"I'm so sorry, Verity," she whispers. "I forgot they show that. It must have been terrible for you, seeing it for the first time. We'll go, if you want?"

I shake my head. I don't want to get up. I want to stay here, in the darkness. Serafina presses my hand again. She seems so concerned. I know she thinks I'm thinking of the bomb that killed my parents. And she's right. But now there's something else to think of too.

All around us is the sound of popcorn. Then the screen flickers and the main film begins. I don't really watch it. I make myself relax because Serafina is still holding my hand. What am I doing here? Now it feels wrong. I didn't think this through. I need to see Oskar. But all of a sudden I can't even remember what he looks like. His face has blurred into just his familiar gray eyes, smiling from behind his dirty-blond fringe. And I have to wait for a whole week before I can meet him.

In the darkness, from the corner of my eye, I can see Greg's and Celestina's profiles lit in colored flashes from the screen. I've never felt so alone.

After the film finishes, Greg waits at the end of our row, until I reach the steps. "Did you enjoy it, Verity?" he says. He looks at me as if he knows something, as if he's caught me out.

I can't believe I almost thanked him for not telling anyone about my swim. "Um," I begin.

He looks right into my eyes. "They always show

that," he says. "Before every film. We've all seen it hundreds of times."

I just nod.

Greg's eyebrows lift. "So we don't forget."

You can't forget something you never knew.

CHAPTER 9

"Verity," ms. cobana says. "What's wrong with your picture?" She pushes her black-framed glasses up her nose and taps the drawing board.

I look at my sketch, pinned to the board. The whole class is waiting, gathered around Ms. Cobana's desk while she dissects the week's work. This is the first portrait that I've ever drawn. I wish she'd put my other picture up—fish in a colored-ink aquarium. I stare at the charcoal Greg. The real one is frowning at my drawing. His sketch was perfect, like all his other work. Ms. Cobana has just spent ten minutes praising it while Greg sat there looking pleased with himself.

A girl called Melissa leans forward, but Greg speaks first. "My head's too big!"

You said it, Brother.

Ms. Cobana makes Greg stand at the other end of the Art room, so that we can all hold up our pencils and measure how many times his head goes into his red-checked shirt. Not that many. Ha!

"OK, then." She hooks a wild strand of salt-and-pepper hair behind her ear. "Your head goes about eight times into your body, less if you're sitting down. Get back in your pairs and have another go."

So I have to go with Greg again and that means I'll have that feeling that he's watching me. He disappears into the supply closet, and comes out with two pieces of drawing paper and a box of charcoal. Even though I've been here a week, I still can't believe that this is an actual school subject that people think is important. Or that they have a whole closet full of everything you could possibly need.

"Drawing boards?" Greg says to me.

I open my mouth to tell him what to do with his drawing boards, but stop myself just in time. I glance at the clock. Only five hours to go, and I'll see Oskar.

So I go into the closet to fetch the boards. The doorway darkens as Greg blocks it.

He holds something out to me. "D'you want this?" He places a paintbrush in my hand. It's an expensive one with a wide bit for painting a wash but also a fine dot of a point.

"Thanks." I stroke it across the back of my hand, and the fibers spring back. "Was it in the closet? I haven't seen any other brushes like this in here."

Greg half-turns toward the Art room. "It's an old one of mine." He takes the drawing boards from me. "You can keep it if you want. I don't paint much."

Light floods back as he moves away from the doorway. I look at the brush. On the glossy black wood there's a sticky patch from the price label, and it looks new. Did he buy me a paintbrush? What's he up to?

Greg is already sitting on the stool, grinning at me. He has carefully placed his hands on his knees so that the perspective makes them even harder to draw. I can't stop looking at his smile, and it's hard to stop myself from smiling back. He's a Brotherhood boy, I remind myself. He was at the station on the day of the bomb. How do I even know that he didn't have something to do with it?

"How about you turn and face the closet?" I suggest coldly. I refuse to like him. "And put your hands under your legs?"

He laughs at me. "Nice try, Verity."

I shrug. "Suit yourself."

Ms. Cobana is watching, so I shut one eye and position the pencil end in the air where I see the top of Greg's dark brown hair, which lies smoothly on his head like a seal's. He has good cheekbones. Then I slide my thumb down the pencil to the edge of his chin. How many of those into the whole of Greg? I move my thumb mark on the pencil down his red-checked chest, his blue jeans, and then his legs until they meet his sneakers. Greg's eyes are wide open and staring straight at me. He holds mine a moment too long, but I pretend not to notice.

I mark two almond shapes over the eyeballs, then add the pupils, very large. I darken them with a soft pencil, leaving a little bit of white to make them come alive. Greg's eyes are chestnut brown, with golden-brown lights, when you look closely, so I mark the irises with tiny fanning-out lines. I put in his eyelashes with tapered strokes . . .

"Time's up!" calls Ms. Cobana. "Change over now."

Everyone is swapping places, taking the chance to look at each other's work. I scribble in the rest of Greg, so that at the end his eyes jump out with a dark intensity. It's not bad.

Greg stands up and stretches. "Pins and needles," he says. He comes over and looks at my drawing. "Is that what I look like?"

"Not really." It's obvious that I spent far too long trying to capture his eyes. "I'm no good at drawing people."

I hop up on the bench. There's so much space here. In my old State school there were thirty students in every class, but here it's about half. "So, how come everyone calls you Greg, not Gregory?" I ask. Maybe I can start to find out the truth about this boy. And why he's buying me brand-new paintbrushes and then lying about it. "Everyone else has long names."

Charcoal splinters out from behind Greg's easel. "It's what my little sister used to call me."

"Oh. It's quite short, that's all."

"So, what about your name, then?"

My name? K? My fingers grip the wooden edge of the bench. I stare back at Greg.

"*Verity*," he says. "Would you have picked it, if you could have chosen?"

"Yes." No. But I can imagine new parents choosing "Verity" for their baby girl. Not like "K."

"So . . . you know what it means?" He's still splattering charcoal shards.

"Of course I know what my own name means." *Careful, K. Don't take the bait.* "So, what do you want to study next year?" I ask quickly, changing the subject.

The charcoal shower pauses. "I'm going to take Science subjects. For Medicine."

"I thought you'd want to study Art." I try to keep still.

"My parents are doctors, and I always thought I'd

be one too." He starts drawing again, even more wildly than before. "I wish I could study Animation, though."

"Then you should," I say. "It's your life."

Greg doesn't reply. Maybe I've annoyed him.

"OK." He steps out from behind his drawing board. "I'm done."

I jump down and walk around the easel. The picture's not like me. This girl's hair is behind her shoulders. Has he made it look longer? She's staring far into the distance, but she looks like someone you'd want to be friends with. She's . . . pretty. "Does it look like me?"

"I think so," Greg says.

I thought his picture of me would make me look somehow suspicious. But it doesn't.

Ms. Cobana walks over and looks at the drawing of Greg over my shoulder. "Come here, everyone!" She holds up my portrait. There's an appreciative little buzz as people stop to look at it. I think of the secret drawings I used to make when I was little, of Grandma finding one and ripping it in two. Ms. Cobana is still talking about my work, as if it's important. It's the first time anyone has ever liked my pictures. For the first time, I feel as if they're looking at the real me.

CHAPTER 10

WHEN HE DROPPED me off a week ago, Oskar showed me where to meet him, from the other side of the school grounds. Of course we didn't know about the afternoon indoctrination sessions then, so I'm going to have to miss today's talk.

At lunch, when we're sitting at the table by the

long glass doors, I turn to Serafina. "I'm not feeling too good," I say. "I've got a really bad headache. So after Math I'm not going to the talk today. Don't bother waiting for me."

I can see that Greg is listening, because his fork has stopped in midair. Celestina carries on eating, but I'm sure she's paying attention too. Jeremiah is eating at another table with other friends.

"Oh, poor you." Serafina touches my arm. "Why don't you go and lie down now?"

"No, it's OK," I say quickly. "I can't afford to miss Math." If anyone finds out and asks me later why I didn't go to the Sisters' house, I'll say I went for a walk to clear my head.

Nobody is around as I walk into the woods after the day's last lesson. They're all in the auditorium, so maybe it's good timing after all. The fence runs alongside the Gatesbrooke road and all I have to do is follow it downhill through the woods in the Institute grounds. Oskar said he would wait by the huge oak. After about ten minutes of quick walking, I get there.

It's very quiet here. The mist threads silver beads along the fir needles.

"K?"

I jump. Oskar appears behind the wire mesh, in his leather jacket and pointed tan boots. He puts one finger to his lips and gestures with a pair of wire cutters toward a hole in the fence.

My long skirt snags as I crawl through the cut wire, which scratches a line along my thigh as I stand up. Oskar nods toward the woods and I follow him across the road. His motorbike is parked a little way up a forest path. I wonder where we'll go. His spare helmet is strapped to the passenger seat, ready for me.

He waves the wire cutters at me. "Result! This way nobody will know you've even left the grounds." He smiles. "So no need for anyone to follow you."

It's so good to see him. His sandy hair is flattened by the crash helmet. His eyes are grayer than I remember. I feel like I did the first time I met him; as if I've known him always. I stand beside the motorbike, trying to stop smiling.

Oskar drops the wire cutters into the motorbike crate. "Everything OK?"

"Not bad," I manage to say.

He sits down on a granite stone, and pats the space beside him. I thought we'd be leaving straight away, but I sit down too.

"How's it going? It must be difficult pretending to conform to their beliefs?"

I shake my head. "They don't really talk in their services." I pick moss off the rock. "Except Brer Magnus, in his afternoon talks. Every day. Endlessly." I fix my face into Brer Magnus's stare. "Nonbelievers!" I deepen my voice. "They corrupted our heritage and stole our country!"

Oskar doesn't laugh. "Just be on your guard," he says. "Don't forget, K, they're fanatics."

I think of Serafina, and Greg. "Well," I begin. But then I remember Brer Magnus and Jeremiah's family.

Oskar looks at me earnestly, kindly. "They'll try to get inside your head," he says. "So keep your wits about you. I don't expect you've heard anything yet . . ."

"Actually . . ." I stop. I was going to tell him about Celestina and Greg being out late at night. Only Greg didn't tell on me for swimming, and Celestina—I can't make her out.

"Any little thing, no matter how small," says Oskar. "Something that seems like an insignificant detail to you might be the missing piece of a bigger picture."

"There's a boy called Jeremiah. Jeremiah Elyard. He was at the Spring Meeting with his family, I think."

"Ah." Oskar turns to look full into my face, and I see then that his eyes look worried. "The Spring Meeting. Go on."

"It's only that they were talking about . . ." I try to remember exactly what I heard. "How they want action, and they're tired of words."

Oskar smiles into my eyes. "That's very good, K," he says. "I didn't expect you to have anything so soon." He takes out his phone and notes something down. "Jeremiah Elyard. Well done. Now," and he puts his phone back in his pocket, "it's funny you should mention the Spring Meeting, because I want you to get me the list of names of everyone who attended."

"They had a visitors' book . . ." But before I have time to ask him more, his phone rings.

Oskar leaps up. "Hello? Col? One second, K." He walks toward the trees, his voice trailing away.

I stand up and pull my jacket around me, because fine rain has started to fall. It's heavier than it looks, so I move toward the shelter of the trees.

I can hear Oskar talking now, his voice low and urgent. "Not Mona?" His voice cracks. "Mona Talbot?" There's a long silence. Then his voice, very low. "Yes. Yes. I know. Bye." Twigs snap as he walks back to the clearing. But he doesn't appear immediately.

When he does, his face is drawn and gray. "K." Oskar reaches into his jacket pocket to replace his phone, but it falls to the ground. "I'm sorry." He stoops to pick it up, grabbing his helmet and jamming it onto his head. "Got to go. There's been another incident. A bomb scare. At a school in the New City." He tries to smile at me, but his eyes keep roving toward the road. He looks back at me, as if he's seeing me for the first time. "K . . ." His gaze travels down my Brotherhood clothes, my wool shoulder bag, and my shoes.

I glance down. Everything is right. I remembered the hat.

"Now, this is important." His eyes stare into mine, full of sadness.

"OK. Oskar?" I want to ask him what's wrong.

"Next time we meet, someone called Ril will come, OK? She's your 'social worker.'" He makes speech marks in the air.

I nod. "Ril." At least I won't have to see Sue Smith again.

"You remember?" Oskar seems so worried. Or maybe he's tired. "She's the one who went to see Brer Magnus before you joined the Institute."

I nod again, ignoring the hard lump lodged in my throat.

"I'll be in touch very soon too." He gives my

shoulder a warm pat. "OK?"

I can't believe I've only been with him for a few minutes. "Oskar," I begin. "I really need to talk to you . . ."

He moves his hand under my elbow. "You're doing great, K. Don't forget the list. I'll see you soon." He propels me across the road. "You must stay strong. Ril will be in touch. Soon, very soon."

I swallow my disappointment. It isn't Oskar's fault that he has to go. I know I can't ask him, but something has clearly gone badly wrong. I'm sure it's more than the bomb scare. It's certainly something urgent, maybe dangerous. Something he couldn't share with me.

He watches me scramble back through the fence into the Institute's grounds. I wish he'd made the hole bigger. Oskar pulls the wires back together so that you can hardly tell they've been cut. He raises his hand in a silent wave, mouths the word "Ril," and runs lightly into the trees on the other side of the road. I wait until I see his motorbike roar out and away down the hill toward Gatesbrooke.

I don't know what to do now. I was counting on talking with Oskar. I was so sure that he would help me see things clearly again. I wanted to ask him about the Gatesbrooke Massacre, why our soldiers did those terrible things. In the quiet woods all I can hear is the dripping of the leaves.

Then I hear the throbbing of engines, growing louder up the Gatesbrooke road. First a motorbike appears. *Oskar!* I think, for one glad moment. Then another motorbike roars past, and another. Then a car crammed full of people, windows open, shouting. And a minibus, its windows filled with yelling faces. Not Brotherhood—that's clear. Citizens. But where are they going?

I wait by the fence until they've all passed and the engines have faded into the distance. Then I see a bicycle, its rider plugging up the hill, head down against the drizzling rain, standing up on the pedals. It's a moment before I recognize Serafina. Where has she been? She must have left long before school ended. She doesn't see me, hidden behind the fence in the trees, and I don't call out to her, because then she might spot the damaged wire.

She has disappeared around the corner when I hear the shouting begin, far up the hill near the Institute. And now all those cars and buses have stopped. They're angry citizens. And Serafina's going to ride straight into the middle of them!

If I try to run after her on this side of the fence, the dense undergrowth will slow me down too much. I tear at the wire to find the broken bit, and yank the flap open again. This time as I scramble through the hole, the jagged edge grazes my other leg. But I don't stop to look at it. I don't look around to check whether anyone could be watching me. I start running up the hill behind Serafina.

I hope she gets off and pushes her bike as the hill gets steeper. Then maybe I'll be able to stop her before she rides into the middle of the angry crowd.

But all I can think is that I'm on the wrong side. I'm running into danger to save a Brotherhood girl from my own people.

CHAPTER 11

IT'S HARD RUNNING uphill in pumps that slip and slide on the wet road. Brotherhood girls are supposed to walk, like ladies. Instead of team games on the field, we have to do dancing in the gym. I still can't see Serafina. I thud around the corner where the road straightens out before it reaches the Institute. There she is, next to the last of the cars parked roughly up the grass verge. She is standing beside her bike, hesitating, because of the noise coming from the direction of the Institute: the shouting and chanting and glass smashing. *Come on, Serafina, turn around!*

I keep on running. I'm too far away to shout. We're on the wrong side of the perimeter fence. I think of the graffiti outside the gate, and now this. Maybe it happens all the time. No wonder they have such heavy security.

Serafina begins pushing her bike slowly toward the last bend, then stops again.

Now we can both see the mob at the gates in front of the bikes, cars, and minibus. So many people crammed into so few vehicles. The chanting sounds like hundreds: "Hoods! Hoods! Murderers!" They are rattling the outer gate, and some of them are assaulting it with crowbars. Others lob bottles over the top. An alarm rings frantically. Where are the police? Huge, dripping red letters already cover the walls—more graffiti. Any moment someone will turn around and see us, Brotherhood girls alone on the wrong side of the wall.

Serafina turns and sees me at last. Her face is rigid with fear.

"Serafina." I grab her arm as I reach her. "Go back! Quick!"

She nods and starts to maneuver her bike around to face downhill, her hands clumsy with terror. That's when some of the protestors see us. In their dark pants and jackets they look as if they're in uniform. More faces turn to look, and they all wear the same expression. It's half revulsion and half a kind of angry joy, because they've come here for a target and Serafina has given them one. It makes them all look the same: parts of the crowd rather than individual people.

"Hoods!"

Then more voices, a chorus of voices. "Hoods! Hoods!"

A stone whizzes through the air and hits Serafina's bike.

In spite of the danger we're in, I feel anger surging up through me. What did she ever do to them? A bit of me wants to pick up the stone and hurl it back. They're as bad as the Brotherhood!

Serafina has straddled her bike. "Get on the back!" she shouts.

I clamber onto the crate rack, sidesaddle because of my long skirt, and we begin to wobble down the hill. We start to build up speed. If we can get around the corner, maybe we'll be able to hide in the bushes until they've gone. I cling onto the rack with my fingers. Behind us, footsteps and shouts thud down the road.

We're almost at the place where Oskar waited for me. The bike is whirling down now, faster with my extra weight. I lean toward Serafina's ear to tell her to turn to the left, when something shoots over me and smashes into Serafina's head. Glass shatters into the road. The bike wheel twists sickeningly to the left as Serafina slumps sideways. Then we're falling, the bike skidding away from under us. The road rushes up to meet me.

I can't move straight away. When I can, I sit up and look behind me for Serafina. She's lying on the ground with her head in a hawthorn bush and her hair over her face. A thin line of blood trickles down her neck. From up the road comes the buzz of a motorbike.

Oskar!

But it's coming from the Institute gates—the wrong direction. I don't even have time to stand up before the motorbike appears and swerves around to stop several feet away from the twisted bicycle. Serafina lies still. I kneel in front of her, hoping they won't see her.

The black-clad passenger on the back of the motorbike climbs off. It's a woman. She laughs an expectant, excited little laugh, which is much worse than the cry of "Hoods!" Her head turns toward me, eyes invisible behind the darkened visor. Behind me a blackbird calls urgently in car-alarm rings. She takes a step toward us. Her boots are black leather with gleaming silver toe caps.

I look up at the visor. "Don't hurt her!" I cry.

But she smiles. She draws back her foot. It's not Serafina she's looking at, but me.

"Stop! I'm one of . . ."

Her foot shoots out and kicks my chest. As I fall sideways, she pulls my hat away, catching at my ear. Then she carefully raises her visor and spits into my face. I feel the warm glob ooze down my cheek. I'm struggling to catch my breath.

"Dirty Hood." A flash of silver glints as her boot moves back again. I cover my face with my arms.

From downhill a van growls toward us.

But from the motorbike a man's voice calls. "Get back on. Police!"

She doesn't go immediately. She bends down to me. "I'll be back." Then she turns and throws her leg over the motorbike. It roars away in a torrent of skidding and engine whine.

I crawl back to Serafina, gasping for air. "Serafina! Come on, I can get us back inside."

But she doesn't say anything. I pull her hair back but her white face stays still, tilted to the side, her curls tangled into the thorns. The van is almost level with us, but it isn't the police. It's an old white van, its cab full of Brotherhood people, yelling and screaming, getting ready to join the fight at the gates. I can't tell if they've seen us. I turn back to Serafina.

I pull her hair loose. I feel as if I'm moving in slow motion. There's no time to be gentle, but Serafina doesn't notice anyway. Her forehead is beaded with tiny drops of sweat, but I can feel her breath on my cheek. Relief flows through me. I lift her up a little and she slumps against my shoulder.

"It's OK, Serafina," I say. "I've got you, it's OK." Her weight throws me back against the bank. Her arm falls against me, and she groans.

The noise up the hill is getting louder. At any moment they could get here.

"Serafina? Serafina!" Maybe if I can wake her up, I can help her walk across the road and through the hole in the fence.

I try to take the weight off her arm because it's

hanging loosely from her shoulder and I think it's hurt. "Serafina!"

Serafina groans again, without coming around. Then I hear someone calling me. "Verity! Verity!"

It takes me a moment to realize that's my name. I twist around, my chest aching as I move. There's nobody on the road.

But then I see a figure standing on the other side of the fence.

Greg.

CHAPTER 12

OUR EYES MEET across the road and through the wire diamonds of the fence. There's no time for our usual wariness. Carefully I lay Serafina down against the bank and climb to my feet. I run across the road toward Greg, calling as I go.

"Serafina's hurt. We were attacked. They're coming back." My eyes search frantically for the hole, but I can't see it. With a sinking heart I realize that this isn't the place where I met Oskar after all. Greg is looking up at the fence to see if he could climb it, but it's too high, and there are rolls of barbed wire along the top. "There's a hole," I say, still breathless, "it's by the big oak."

I run down alongside the fence, my breath gasping in my throat. On the other side, Greg crashes through the undergrowth. Then I see the oak towering above the other trees. "There it is!" But where's the hole? I search frantically by the long grass.

Greg barrels out of a bramble thicket. "I can see it!" He crouches down in front of the hole. "You got through here?"

"Yes."

It's hardly big enough for him. I start pulling the wires toward me, away from Greg. It's difficult, with my right hand wet from the blood on Serafina's neck. I wipe it on my skirt.

Greg starts clambering through.

"Bend it out," I say, clutching at the wires. I try to hold them back but they tear into his jeans.

He stands up, panting. "Where is she?"

I point uphill. We both run across the road to where Serafina lies in the ditch, still unconscious. Greg kneels down beside her.

"She needs an ambulance," he says. "We'll have to take her back through the fence and carry her up to the school."

I shake my head. "There's no time, and it's too far. The rioters might be coming back."

Greg looks behind him into the undergrowth. There's a large laurel bush, vivid yellow in the gloomy light. "There?" He slides his arms under Serafina and half-carries her into the middle of the laurel. I follow him inside, bending her knees so that her feet are hidden under the leaves. Serafina starts groaning again.

Greg sits in the leafy cave of the laurel bush with Serafina cradled in his arms. Her head is lolling down and I put out my hands to support it. Over Serafina's wild brown hair, dotted with tiny white raindrops, our eyes meet again the way they did in Art this afternoon. Greg's eyes are very dark, just as I drew them. He's breathing fast, trying to be quiet. His breath puffs against my face. We both stay very still, listening. *Please stop groaning, Serafina.*

If they come back, they're certain to find us.

I can feel Greg's arm vibrating as he struggles to hold Serafina without moving. His breath has stilled.

He didn't tell anyone about the swimming. I want to trust him. He lets out a long hiss of air. He has a little scratch down his cheek. It's not bleeding, but the skin is red and drawn up into a row of bumps. I find myself thinking I should have used pen and ink instead of pencil to draw him this morning, because of the clean lines of his cheekbones.

Serafina's head feels very heavy. I don't like the snuffly, snoring sound she's making.

I peer out through the wet leaves. The road is empty. Dark clouds are stealing the daylight.

"We should call an ambulance." Greg has a phone to keep in touch with his family overseas.

He frowns at me.

"With your cell phone."

"You can't get a signal in the Institute grounds," he says.

"Not in there," I say. "But out here you can."

He shakes his head. "I never get a signal outside the gate."

Oskar's phone worked here. But I can't tell Greg that. "Come on, Greg—just give it a try!"

He stares hard at me. Then he gets out his phone and punches in the emergency number. "Ambulance," he says. He listens to the twittering voice. "On the road out of Gatesbrooke, a few minutes downhill from the Institute." He pauses again. "They can look for the bike by the side of the road."

I hold Serafina up until he's finished the call.

"You were right." His brown eyes bore into mine as he tucks the phone back into his coat pocket. "Now we just have to wait."

I look away. He must know I met someone here today—someone who cut a hole in the fence. Maybe he was watching. Maybe he saw Oskar. Anyway, it's too late now to worry about what he'll do.

I meet Greg's eyes. I'm not going to beg for his silence. I have so much to lose, but I look steadily at him.

He stares back at me. His hair has gone black in the rain. There's no future or past, just this moment, the two of us trying to save Serafina.

But the ambulance doesn't come. We lay Serafina down on the earth. Time ticks by.

"Call them again?" I suggest.

Greg gives a short laugh. "What for?" he says. "They won't come, will they? Not for us."

From up the hill there's a sudden bang—an explosion that makes me scramble to my feet. Then an engine roaring down the hill. What if it's the woman on the motorbike again?

I pull the laurel leaves apart. But it's the white van I saw before. It screeches to a halt next to Serafina's bike. The passenger door opens and a Brotherhood boy gets out, looking up the bank toward us. I freeze, but Greg clambers out into the road.

Serafina groans, so I don't hear what Greg says to the boy, but when I look up again, they are both running toward us, pushing the leaves aside.

"It's OK," Greg says. "They're going to take us to the hospital."

I look over at the van. The back doors are open and inside I can see Brotherhood men and one girl sitting silently, watching us from the benches on either side, tension crackling off them. They're all wearing balaclavas or scarves wrapped over their faces. Greg and the other boy are already carrying Serafina over to the back of the van.

"Greg?" I begin. "Is this a good idea?"

I don't think he heard me. They lay Serafina down in between all the feet. I follow them and put my hat under her head so that her hair isn't resting on the floor of the van, and climb aboard myself, squeezing in beside the other girl. The doors bang shut and then the only light is from the sliding window into the front. The van shudders into motion.

It careens around the bends much too fast, and I'm thrown against Greg more than once. Under the seat, wooden bats and other weapons roll against my heels. A gasoline can and bottles. Who are these people? What was the explosion we heard? We're in a van full of Brotherhood activists. Who knows what else they've done? I look at Greg, but he's just staring straight ahead. Does he know them? Is he one of them?

"Got to hurry," says the boy who helped carry Serafina. "The police will come, now that *we've* shown up."

I can still hear the explosion ringing in my ears. What will the police think if they stop us? How will Greg and I be able to prove that we weren't fighting the protestors too?

WE DRIVE IN silence. When we stop, the man from the front seat opens the doors to reveal the back of a hospital where bins are lined up behind a screen. I see the Gatesbrooke logo above the door.

"You're on your own now," he says to Greg. "Gotta go. We always drop off here, no cameras. Take her through that door . . ." and he points to a fire door wedged open with a brick. "There's usually some wheelchairs just inside. Follow the green line."

He helps Greg lift Serafina out. I grab my hat and follow. He's right about the wheelchairs. Greg pushes Serafina through the corridor and I keep one hand on her shoulder to stop her falling out. When we reach the waiting area, a passing nurse in green clothes sees Serafina's unconscious blood-streaked face. He immediately takes the wheelchair from Greg, pushing it toward the swinging doors while we hold them open.

But before we can follow, the woman behind the reception desk snaps: "Not you!" Her eyes run over our Brotherhood clothes as we turn back. "You can give me the details."

We wait at the counter while she goes out to the room behind. I hear her say, "Hoods." Then she picks up the phone.

I look at Greg in shock. Even here, in the hospital?

He shrugs. "What did you expect? She's probably calling the police. I'll call Brer Magnus."

That will really help, I think. I can't say anything.

"You can wait over there," the woman says as she comes back out.

What if Serafina doesn't regain consciousness? I imagine waking up in the morning and seeing her neatly made bed, instead of the usual hump of blanket and the flinging off of sheets and fluffy animals. Even in the short time I've known her, I've realized Serafina is never still.

I let my hat fall over my face and press my knuckles hard under my nose. Greg gets up and goes over to the vending machine, his phone in his hand. While he has his back to me, I wipe my eyes and blow my nose and push my hair behind my ears.

He comes back carrying two plastic cups. "Hot chocolate," he says. "I know you like tea, but it looked really orange."

"Thanks," I say, though I like orange tea. He's trying to be kind.

He sits down beside me, and the sleeve of his shirt brushes against mine. It's nice. I want his arm to stay there.

"I phoned Brer Magnus." He pauses when I don't reply.

What can I say, when I don't know what to think? Suddenly I blurt out: "Was that a bomb? I heard a bang. Was it them?" When he doesn't answer, I carry on: "I saw the bottles and the gasoline can."

Greg drinks some hot chocolate. "They torched one of the cars," he says. "Nobody was in it." He balances his cup carefully on the sloping seat beside him. "Brer Magnus said not to say we were there. He's coming, to explain that we're just students who were out of school at the time. Otherwise . . ."

I nod. I glance at his troubled face.

He turns to me. "You did a good thing."

I look at him, but his brown eyes just look serious.

"And it's good you were there," I say. "I couldn't have carried her."

But what was he doing there anyway? Close behind me again. He should have been in the auditorium.

We wait. Greg's arm is still against mine, but that's OK, because there's not much room in this row of chairs. I'm starting to get warm now and it's quite nice not to feel alone. We look like two Brotherhood kids, and some people give us the evil eye as they pass. I eye them back from under my hat.

—

"Gregory. verity."

I look up. Brer Magnus is striding across the waiting area.

Greg springs to his feet, so I stand up too, suppressing the little shiver that Brer Magnus's presence always gives me. I wish I'd asked Greg not to tell Brer Magnus about the hole in the fence. But now it's too late.

"So, Verity." He fixes me with his ice-blue gaze. "Mr. East only opened the gates for Serafina. How did you get over the fence?"

Before I can reply Greg speaks. "Verity found a way out."

Here it comes. I dig my fingernails into the palm of my hand. It's over.

"There was a gap," Greg continues. "Somebody must have cut a hole in the fence. The rioters."

I look at Greg, but he's staring straight ahead at the reception desk.

"I'll get Security to look into it," says Brer Magnus. "We can't leave the school unprotected. Not with the increased threat from the *majority*."

The doors to the treatment room open and the nurse in green walks toward us.

Greg still doesn't look at me. His fist is clenched on his knee. There's a dark smear on the denim that I think is blood from the wire. Why didn't he give me away? Is he angry now, because he lied to Brer Magnus? This is the second time he's covered up for me. Why? I'm sure he doesn't trust me, and I don't even think he likes me. Does he want something in return?

Brer Magnus goes to meet the nurse. After a short conversation, he beckons me over. "Verity, Serafina is conscious now." His eyes sweep over me. "She's asking to see *you*."

—

I FOLLOW THE nurse through the doors. Serafina is in a cubicle with green curtains. She's sitting up, leaning against a pillow. Her head has a huge white dressing on one side, but her face breaks into a smile when she sees me.

I sit on the plastic seat beside her bed. "Are you OK?"

Serafina grabs my hand, and I find myself squeezing back.

"Yes, yes, I'm fine."

She may be Brotherhood, but now that I know she's all right, relief floods through me. "What about your arm?" There's no plaster, so it can't be broken.

"I dislocated my elbow. They put it back in its socket." She makes a face. "That's what woke me up."

"Ugh. Poor you. Does it still hurt?"

"Not so much." Serafina lowers her voice. "But Verity, there's something I want to ask you. A favor."

"Of course."

"It's . . . I've got . . ." She stops, and looks anxiously toward the corridor. "Open the curtain a bit so I can see if anyone's coming."

I do that.

"I have a secret," whispers Serafina when I sit down again. "It's about my boyfriend."

"You have a boyfriend?" Emanuel's face flashes into my mind.

"Shh. Yes. I was coming back from meeting him. And my parents will be here in a minute, and I don't want them to know."

They must live pretty near if they can get here so quickly. Why doesn't Serafina live at home? I'm intrigued now. "Who is it?"

"Nobody," she says quickly. "He's not at the school. He isn't even Brotherhood." She looks at me, her forehead creased in a frown. "You're shocked, aren't you?"

"I'm not shocked."

But I am. Not because Serafina's boyfriend is a citizen, but because she has a secret. At the Institute they all seem to follow the rules.

"I guess I thought maybe you wouldn't be," says Serafina sadly. "Because you had to grow up with them and everything."

Them. My mind starts racing. If Serafina knew

who I really was, would she maybe understand? Then we could be real friends.

"Everyone has secrets." I lean in closer. "I might tell you mine too." I shouldn't have said that out loud.

Serafina's voice cracks. "I had to talk to someone, before I end it." Tears gather in her eyes. "Of course it's got to end. I can't let my parents know. They'll disown me if they find out."

I lean back.

"Surely they'd come around, Serafina?"

But she shakes her head, and then stops, wincing. "No. They could never, never accept it. They would never even allow a nonbeliever to cross their doorway." She pulls a tissue out of the box on the side table and blows her nose. "I'm going to break it off."

Serafina's parents sound like Grandma. "Couldn't you keep seeing him secretly?"

"It's impossible." Her voice catches. "Especially after today." Tears spill from her eyes. "They hate us so much, Verity. There's no future in it. It's oil and water."

My heart chills. If she thinks that, then she's not the rebel I imagined. I hope she wasn't listening when I mentioned I had a secret too.

"Does anyone else know?"

"Just you," says Serafina. "It was easier to tell you, because I haven't known you for so long."

"Don't worry," I say. "I won't tell anyone."

"I know you won't," she says. "But there's something I have to ask you. It's a big thing. It would mean you'd have to lie."

"What is it?" I should be able to manage one more.

"Can I tell my parents that I was meeting you? In case they ask why I was outside the school? I could say I was going to show you the Trembling Rock."

I smile. "Of course. Is that in the grounds near where you fell?"

She smiles back. "Thanks, Verity." She hesitates. "No, the Trembling Rock's outside the fence. It was OK telling Mr. East I wanted to go for a bike ride but my parents are way too suspicious. Anyway . . ." She makes an effort to brighten her voice. "What's your secret?"

My thoughts race. What can I say? I'm a secret citizen, an enemy agent? I'm oil to your water?

"It's OK," says Serafina. "I've guessed it anyway."

My heart starts thumping and my mind goes blank. If I get through today without giving myself away, it'll be a miracle.

The curtain jerks open, and the nurse appears. "Serafina? Your parents are here."

CHAPTER 13

I'M WITH THE others at our table by the long canteen windows, watching Greg, Celestina, and Emanuel getting ready to leave. Every week they go to a State school in the New City—Math lectures for gifted pupils. It's part of the Reconciliation process to integrate schools. Brer Magnus hates the idea of integration, but if he doesn't want his school closed down he has cooperate. It suddenly dawns on me—was Greg at the station on the day of the bomb because he was going to his advanced Math class? Maybe I'm just looking for reasons to trust him.

"Can I come with you?" I ask suddenly, as Greg picks up his tray, ignoring me. "To Gatesbrooke, I mean?" Maybe I can find Oskar there. I have so many questions.

"Why not?" Emanuel smiles at me. He's been very friendly since I helped rescue Serafina. He obviously doesn't know about her boyfriend.

But Greg pauses, tray in hands. "You'll have to ask Brer Magnus." Greg's kept away from me since the hospital, as if he doesn't know what to think of me. He didn't tell Brer Magnus about the hole in the fence, but now he seems angry.

"I'll go and see him." Of course I have no intention of actually doing it, but Greg walks out of the canteen with me.

"I'll come with you," he says. "I need to see him too."

We cut across the grass to the main building in silence. Brer Magnus's office is down a wood-paneled corridor by the stairs that lead to the Meeting Hall. I glance up as we pass. Is there any chance the visitors' book is still there? Greg knocks on the door, but when Brer Magnus calls "Enter," he stands back to let me go in first. The room takes up the whole width of the building, so that through the two windows Brer Magnus can see both the gates and the canteen.

"Yes?" Brer Magnus peers across his desk.

"I wanted to know if it's all right for me to go to the city this afternoon." I hate having to ask permission just to get out. I think longingly of the hole in the fence.

"Why do you want to go?"

"I've got some shopping to do. I don't have lessons

this afternoon." I'm supposed to do dance though, so he'll probably say no.

"I don't see why not," he says instead. "Gregory?"

Greg glances at me. "I'll catch up to you," he says, staring at me until I take the hint and walk out of the office, leaving him alone with Brer Magnus. It's as if rescuing Serafina together never happened.

I've got my bag, and I always have the hat with me now, so I go through Reception and out to the parking lot where Celestina and Emanuel are waiting. Mr. East, the groundskeeper, lumbers out from the trees, with a bag slung across his body and a roll of heavy wire under one arm, his spaniel beside him. "The fence is done," he says to me, letting the wire fall to the ground in front of the lodge. "Just the graffiti now."

So that's my escape route gone. The dog ambles toward me, tail wagging slowly from side to side as I walk up. At least there's a dog here.

"What's his name?" I say to Mr. East.

"Raymond."

"Hello, Raymond." I stroke his floppy ears. "Can I take him for a walk sometimes?" If I can do that, maybe it'll be a way of getting out of the Institute.

"Why not? Mind you, if you start, you have to keep going."

"That's fine. I can come at lunchtime." It'll be nice to have an excuse to get away on my own.

Mr. East looks toward the road. "Is it safe to go to Gatesbrooke, after what happened the other day?"

Celestina's mouth sets in a hard line. "We have to carry on as normal," she says. "Otherwise they've won."

Raymond licks my hand, and I stoop down to stroke his silky ears again. Through the Reception doors I see Greg running across the quad toward us. Celestina presses a button next to the gate, which swings open. Would it open like that for me? The camera follows us along the drive.

The bus stop is across the road, but it doesn't have a timetable posted on it. Maybe I can find one in town. When the bus comes, it's quite full, so I head for the back, where there are enough empty seats for all of us. But Celestina and Emanuel perch on the high seats next to the luggage rack in the middle. Greg swings himself on just as the bus is pulling away. He stands in front of them with his backpack hanging off one shoulder, leaning down to laugh at something Celestina's saying. I don't know why he minded me coming with them, because I'm on my own anyway. Outside, rain begins to fall from the dense sky.

The bus rumbles through the Old City, over the bridge and into the terminal, which is on the edge of the Central Station square.

"Where are you going, Verity?" Emanuel asks me as I climb down, holding my long skirt up.

"I'm going to see if there are any letters at my old halfway house," I improvise.

Emanuel pauses. "You'll be OK? Things aren't good at the moment . . ."

Celestina grabs his arm. "She'll be fine!" She throws me a smile. "She can look after herself, can't you, Verity?"

"Yes, of course I—"

Greg interrupts. "Come on! We need to go."

And they're gone, with just a "Bye, Verity!" from Emanuel.

I jot down the times of the buses, in case I can get out of the Institute again. Last week the others came back on the latest service. But that could have been because there was another bomb scare. I don't have to go back with them anyway. *They're not real friends*, I tell myself. They're just people I happen to live with while I trick them by pretending to be somebody else.

I feel a touch on my shoulder.

It's Greg. "Forgot my Math file." He leans forward to catch his breath. His jacket is wet from the rain already.

I look up at the bus. "That's not the one we were on."

He runs off again, calling over his shoulder, "We're getting the six o'clock bus back, OK?"

I don't have to get that bus just because Greg said to. But at least he didn't ask me where I was going.

I cross the square with my bag bouncing against my side. I've grown to like it, with its tassels on the corners and the wooden fastener that holds it shut.

I can't help smiling when I see Fred's Cafe. The windows are cozy and yellow, all steamed up. Even if Oskar's not there, I'll have a cup of strong orange tea and get warm. I can read the newspaper. I'll remember the first time I talked with Oskar and the couple of afternoons we spent poring over the Manual, chatting and drinking tea. I've never told anyone else the things I told Oskar; something about the way he listened drew out my life story.

I push the door open, and the smell of fried bacon and coffee greets me. And then I remember too late that

Fred will be surprised to see me dressed as a Brotherhood girl, from my hat to my pumps that let in the rain.

But it's all right, because I don't know the man who is filling the coffee machine behind the counter. He looks up, and his smile hardens.

"No Hoods!" he shouts. He edges out from behind the urn. "I said no Hoods." He fixes his eyes on mine.

Of course he means me. Look at how I'm dressed. He steps forward.

I slam the door shut behind me and run from the cafe so that I don't have to look at the cold hate in his eyes. After a few minutes I force myself to walk, while my heart hammers against my ribs, and my wet skirt slaps against my legs. *It's not really me he hates; it's not me*, my feet pound. But when I reach the other side of the bus depot and look back at the yellow lights of the cafe, I know that it is. I am the stranger he wanted to hurt. I catch my breath under a bus shelter. A "Hood." It's as if I'm not a person.

I didn't even have time to look for Oskar. The rain is slashing into puddles now. Where can I go? I watch a tram rattle over the bridge and into the Old City. I've never walked there before. But why not? I'm dressed in the right clothes for it. I feel a spark of excitement as I cross the road to the bridge and climb the steps.

In front of me the sooty stone of the Old City's Meeting Hall rises against the dull sky. I walk over the bridge and stop to look around. On the other side of the road a boy in a baggy gray jacket and baseball cap darts into a cafe: The Pelican. It would be warm and dry in there. But the memory of Fred's

Cafe sends a stab of fear into my stomach. Instead I walk around to the front of the Meeting Hall. It's almost as grand as the Town Hall. I look up at the entrance with its arched doorway and double staircase the width of the building.

Beside it is a rundown shopping center, and when I wander through it I come out alongside a canal basin with houseboats and barges moored up against neat walkways. The water is murky green, pitted with raindrops. I stand on the strip of grass at the edge of the water looking at the boats. The oldest-looking one has been painted with swirling flowers in bright colors against its chipped green paint. Each petal is a single free brushstroke. But I'm too cold and wet to stand still for long so I walk down the service road that goes around the shopping center. The Meeting Hall towers above me.

I look up at the entrance again. Why shouldn't I go inside? I'll fit in here. Through the glass in the door I can see that the lights are on. I have to clasp the door handle with both hands because all the blood has drained out of my fingers and left them waxwork yellow. I don't go into the grand wooden cave of the main hall, which smells like the Reception at the Institute. I follow a small corridor ending in a glowing frosted-glass door.

I can hear cups clinking and voices from inside. "It's not us it would help," says a soft voice. "It's the young ones."

I push the door open. It's a kitchen. Three old Brotherhood ladies are sitting around a pine table, with a teapot and green cups and saucers, and a plate of chocolate chip cookies. All the women stop speaking and look up.

"Hello, dear," says one. "Would you like a cup of tea?"

I think I know what they see: a nice Brotherhood girl to look after.

"Sit down." One of the women gets up and fetches another cup and saucer. "Oh, you're wet through." She smiles at me as she sets it on the table. Her eyes are the same color as the cornflowers on her apron. "What's your name?"

"Verity Nekton." It just comes out.

"Nekton." She nods, and smiles at me again. "That's a good name."

I curl my fingers around the cup and take a long warming sip of tea. My fingers are beginning to turn red as the blood returns.

Her friend pats my arm. She has rings on all her fingers and curly hair dyed a purply shade of brown. "We're just talking about the Identity Cards, dear."

"Identity Cards?"

"Yes, dear. What it would mean not to have cards for all us Brotherhood."

Suddenly I think of Grandma. What if she was sitting with her friends, in her community center, drinking tea with a Brotherhood girl dressed in citizen's clothes? I can see her face change to horror and disgust.

My cup clanks back on to the saucer. I look at the woman with the washed-blue eyes. "I'm sorry, I've got to go." My chair grates on the linoleum tiles as I stand up.

"But you haven't finished your tea, dear." She pauses, her hand on the teapot.

I pick up my cup and gulp the rest. "Thank you so

much. You've been very kind." Then I turn to the door.

As I walk down the corridor, I hear her gentle voice. "I think we frightened her off!"

I close the door quietly behind me as I step back out into the rain.

—

I HURRY OVER the bridge, splashing through the puddles because I can't feel my feet anymore in these shoes, which are thinner than slippers.

"Stupid useless shoes," I mutter out loud. "Wish I had my boots."

Where can I warm myself for a couple of hours? Department stores, the library, the shopping center? I walk through Jubilee Park toward the main shopping center. The cherry trees have just burst into flower. They splash pink against the gray lid of the sky.

I thought I'd feel more comfortable here in the New City, but it's the opposite. I hear footsteps round the corner of the ice-cream stand. Is someone following me? When I look back down the path I see the boy I saw on the bridge. His gray jacket collar is hunched up around his neck and his cap hides his face.

And maybe there is a security camera trained on me now as I walk through the park in the rain in my Brotherhood clothes. I even have a bag to keep a bomb in. I run toward the gate, looking behind me. But the park is empty.

The New City shopping center is shiny glass and marble, not gray cement and fading special offer signs. I go to the bookstore, where even a Brotherhood girl can sit and read for as long as she likes, and I pick up the free newspaper someone left on the table.

RECONCILIATION AGREEMENT THREATENED

Critics Call for New Laws Targeting
Suspected Brotherhood Terrorists

I scan through the measures listed in the article. Some of them are familiar to me from Oskar's Manual but the curfew for all Brotherhood people is new. I flick through the rest of the paper but I can't find anything about the attack on the Institute last week. I put the paper down and get a book instead.

At last it's five thirty. I can meet the others soon, if I want to. It might be nice not to be alone. Passing the register I notice a box of paintbrushes like the one Greg gave me. Maybe he bought it here. I pick up a putty eraser and a charcoal pencil. The sales assistant puts them in a pink-striped paper bag.

As I leave the bookstore, I look around. I can't see the boy in the baseball cap. I don't think anyone is following me now. But it's hard to tell because of the crowds surging toward Central Station.

The others aren't at the bus stop. I huddle into my jacket under the shelter, watching darts of rain slant down. In a puddle beside the curb, a rainbow gleams in the grease.

Maybe they've left without me.

CHAPTER 14

WHEN I SEE the three of them coming toward me across the concourse, I can't stop the grin that spreads over my face.

As I climb the bus steps, my bag slips off my shoulder. Greg is behind me and his hand reaches around me to catch it. Celestina and Emanuel share a seat because they're still worrying about their Math problem. I sit in the seat behind. I don't expect Greg to sit beside me, but he does. He doesn't seem to mind me being with them now. Maybe he was worried about his class before. He reaches down and puts my bag on the floor beside my feet.

The bus grinds through the Old City, past the cluttered shops and featureless office blocks and the houses with their golden lights. Each house looks like a warm haven. I know they may not be. It's just how they look to me, with my face pressed against the glass and my teeth chattering.

"Verity." Greg touches my arm.

"Mmm?" Why is he suddenly friendly again? I can't work him out.

"You look very cold," he says. "You want my jacket?"

"No, it's OK," I begin, but Greg takes his jacket off anyway and wraps it over my shoulders. It's like his checked shirts, red plaid, with wool on the outside and padding on the inside. "It'll get wet," I say.

"Doesn't matter." He tucks it around me, under my chin and behind my shoulders.

His jacket's still warm. It's heaven.

"Thanks," I say. "Was your Math class good?"

"Yeah, yeah." Greg leans down to rummage in his backpack. He takes out half a bar of chocolate and offers me some. The chocolate melts around my teeth. I didn't realize how hungry I was.

Greg breaks a piece off and passes the rest through the gap in the seats in front.

I tuck my arms into the soft cotton of his jacket and close my eyes. I want to sleep, not think, but as soon as I shut my eyes, thoughts jostle for attention; the man in the cafe, the footsteps behind me . . . I push them away.

I'm warming up. Tears of rain run down the glass. Greg leans forward to argue with Celestina. I listen to them until I drift off, my head *bump-bumping* against the pane.

The bus is growling uphill when I wake up. My head has fallen the other way, against Greg's shoulder. I stay very still, pretending to be asleep. I can feel the warmth of his arm against my cheek. I can see his hand, holding an open book. It was so simple when Greg and I were working together to hide Serafina under the laurel bush. Just for a moment I close my eyes and imagine I'm who they all think I am. I know Greg suspects me of something. But for this one moment, I'm pretending he doesn't.

"Verity," says Greg.

I sit up and move away from him.

"We're nearly there."

Outside I can make out the dark shapes of the fir trees that surround the Institute.

I reach down for my bag and feel the rustle of the paper bag from the bookstore. I take it out and hand it to Greg. "I got this for you."

"Oh!" he sounds shocked, but peers inside. "Yeah. Thanks. That's cool." He tucks it away in his backpack and gives me an uncertain smile.

I look straight into his eyes. He seems suddenly . . . doubtful, and that makes for a nice change.

"No problem," I say.

I reach back down to get my bag, but it's fallen open and my purse has slid out onto the floor. I fish around, the blood rushing to my head.

When I pull the bag up to my knees, I see why it's open. "The button's come off."

"I'll look for it." Greg gets down on his hands and knees and scrabbles about under the seats. He even gets out a little flashlight on a key ring. He has to wind it up first.

I stop myself from laughing.

"Nope," he says as he comes back up. "Nothing there."

He takes out the paper bag I gave him and looks at the charcoal pencil and the putty eraser. "Great." He takes out the eraser. "I needed one of these." He smiles at me, a warm, friendly smile.

He's never smiled at me like that before.

CHAPTER 15

WE TRUDGE UP the gravel drive. A dark silhouette stands behind the glass door into Reception. Brer Magnus. He waits, unmoving. As we go through the gate, he opens the door.

"Ah, Verity." He steps back to let us in.

The sight of Brer Magnus wipes away the memory of my friendly bus ride in an instant.

"You've got a visitor."

I can't read the expression on his face. It could

be disapproval, or even pleasure in catching me out.

Celestina gives me a knowing look. Greg pauses in the doorway. He isn't smiling at me anymore.

Is it Oskar? Surely that's too risky?

"I've put her in the waiting room," says Brer Magnus. "It's your social worker." There's no hiding the disapproval in his voice.

My heart slows down again. It must be this person called "Ril." Just as Oskar said. Maybe she will take me to him. I push the door open. A slim woman in a black pants suit stands with her back to me, looking out at the lawn that leads down to the parking lot. She's not Brotherhood.

"Hello." I step into the room.

She turns, her tidy brown hair staying still, and I stop. It really *is* my social worker. Sue Smith. Is she here to tell Brer Magnus who I really am? Has she already told him?

But before I can say anything, she puts her finger up to stop me speaking.

"Hello, Verity," she says loudly. "Remember me? Your social worker, Ril."

I stare at her.

"Well," says *Ril*. "Shall we go?"

She doesn't speak again until the door has swung shut behind us. "I thought we'd go out for dinner."

As we cross the parking lot, I glance back. Greg is standing looking out through the glass door. When our eyes meet, he turns away.

———

"I TAKE IT you went to the cafe to see Oskar?" Ril flicks a sideways glance at me.

I don't ask her how she knows this, or even how she knows Oskar.

"He couldn't come tonight," she says. "He's very sorry. But we know it must be really hard for you. I thought we could have a meal."

"OK." I am quite hungry.

Oskar knows she's here, then. My feet are numb with cold again. I wish I still had Greg's jacket wrapped around me. I think of the evening I thought I'd be having: lovely hot shower, snuggled up in a Brotherhood tea-cozy sweater, dinner in the canteen with the others. I realize I was actually looking forward to it.

We stop outside a small hotel and go into a lounge where vinyl armchairs huddle around a flickering fire. The fire is one of those jumping gas ones with no real heat. I curl up in a chair with my feet tucked into my skirt. You couldn't do that in pants. Ril orders food for us both.

"So, how's it going?" She sits back in her chair.

Who are you? I wonder. *Sue Smith? Or Ril Somebody?* Did Oskar set Ril in place before I'd agreed to help the police?

I shrug. "Some of the subjects are different," I say. "History—you'd think it was a different country. And Devotional Studies. Art, of course. But the teachers are really good. I think I might pass some exams now." I give her a hard stare. *Like you care.* "I told Oskar everything I know. It's just a school. They're just kids."

"Of course." Ril nods. "You're doing great, K. You're doing everything we need you to do—just being there."

We. When did Sue Smith and Oskar become "we"?

"What about Sue Smith?" I blurt out.

But instead of answering me, she smiles briskly. "Now, have you got the list?"

"The list?"

"The names of everyone who attended the Spring Meeting. Oskar asked you to get it for him. We want to follow up on your first lead—Jeremiah?"

I don't want her to see that I forgot all about that. "Where's Oskar? I need to see him."

Ril sighs. "I told you. He couldn't come, but he said to tell you he'll see you soon, next week. We'll all go away for the weekend."

Why do you have to come? "Oskar will be there too?"

"Of course." She smiles. "You can bring the list then."

I think of the visitors' book that everyone was lining up to sign. Even the children.

Chicken and fries arrive, and we eat in silence.

"I nearly forgot." Ril puts down her fork. "We thought you might like your boots back. I've got them in the car."

I nod. I'd wondered what Oskar had done with my old clothes.

"I'm really tired," I say. "Could I go ho—er, back now?"

She gives me a sharp look, but she doesn't say anything.

—

WE DRIVE TO the Institute and Ril idles the car inside the gate. She reaches behind her. "Your boots." She pulls a bag over the hand brake.

I peer inside. "You've cleaned them up."

"They were a bit battered, so I got them reheeled too." She stays in the car when I get out, with the engine running and her eyes glancing up at the security cameras.

I'll ask Oskar about Sue Smith.

As I walk past the canteen, I hesitate, listening to the laughter. The door is ajar, and I can see Georgette at the counter. She makes watery cocoa for us in the evenings. Everyone is there, even Serafina who is back from the hospital. Greg throws his head back and laughs at something Celestina is saying.

I want to join them. But I imagine all the questions I'm not sure how to answer. Instead I go back to the caretaker's lodge and ask Mr. East if I can take Raymond for a walk.

"Just in the grounds at this time of night, though." He clips on Raymond's leash.

—

RAYMOND TROTS ALONGSIDE me, looking up at me every so often. We walk alongside a line of cherry trees that haven't quite come into blossom yet. The grass is spongy from the rain.

"At least I have my boots back, Raymond," I say, rustling the bag at him as if that will help him understand.

He rests his head against my leg as I reach down to stroke him, giving me one of his brief upward glances.

Weird that I was thinking about my boots all day, as my feet got wetter and colder, and then Ril gave them to me. Eventually I take Raymond back, and trudge up to the Sisters' house.

There's no one in the bedroom. I put my boots under the bedside table, get into bed, and lie staring into the dark.

I'm tired but I can't switch off. So I make a list of all the beds I've ever slept in. This one, then the narrow, hard bed at the halfway house. Then the single beds in foster homes until I get back to the lumpy mattress on the iron bed frame at Grandma's house. I could hear the sea there, on rough nights, rocking me to sleep.

The door opens and Celestina comes in, late as usual. "Verity? You awake?"

"Mmm."

"You should have come to the canteen," she says.

"I wasn't sure you'd still be there when I got back," I lie. "I suppose you and Emanuel were still arguing about your Math thing with Greg?" Greg is studying for three different Math exams to prepare for Medicine at college.

"Greg." Celestina snorts. "What would he know? He didn't even come to the lesson this afternoon! I've no idea where he went."

I think of the boy in the gray jacket and baseball cap, and my sense of being followed. Could it have been Greg? I should have recognized him, but I've never seen him without his red checks. Thinking about it, I'm not even surprised. Following me is what Greg does, isn't it? He stopped for a private talk with Brer Magnus before we left. It's like he's my watcher.

Now I really can't sleep. I don't want to think about Greg following me all around Gatesbrooke. Is it because he doesn't trust me, or because he's part of the cell? And what about Ril? Or is her name actually Sue Smith? Even Oskar is becoming a big question mark. I don't want to think about them either. I wish I could just be me. A girl with no secrets.

I want to go to sleep jolting with the bus, my ear warm against Greg's checked shoulder; I want to go back to that moment before I fully woke up, when we could both pretend we hadn't noticed how close we were. But it's not real.

I can't believe that Greg's in the cell. I'm sure he was unhappy with the Brotherhood activists torching the rioters' car. I can't see him being violent.

I want to go to sleep as Verity. Tomorrow I can go back to the hard task of being K. Or is it the other way around?

I have even less of an idea who to watch than when I first came in. How can I make friends with people only to spy on them, when my gut feeling is telling me that we're looking in the wrong place? I push away the thought that I could be horribly wrong, that I could be right in the middle of the hornet's nest.

No, I can't do this anymore. It's suddenly so clear that I sit up straight.

When I see Oskar next week, I'm going to tell him I made a mistake. We'll have the whole weekend, so there will be time to talk, and Oskar will understand. He'll make it OK.

I want my old life back. I want to be K Child again.

CHAPTER 16

SCHOOL'S OVER FOR the week and those of us who board are relaxing on the couches in the common room, when the loudspeaker cuts over our conversation: "Verity Nekton to Reception."

Greg looks across the coffee table, one eyebrow raised. Celestina puts her book down. "Where are you going, Verity?" She gives me an innocent little smile, but I'm sure she thinks I'm up to something.

"Um, I don't really know." I put my sketchbook down on a cushion and it falls open to a drawing of the view from my halfway house room.

"If you don't know, why are you going?" Greg leans forward.

Always so suspicious. But that's it, isn't it? It's that *he* doesn't trust *me*. Within the Institute or the Brotherhood. His suspicion masks his worry. He thinks *I* might be an activist. Oskar is wrong about there being a cell here. I'm the cell, the citizen cell.

"I'm going away for the weekend with my social worker," I say. "She didn't say where."

Greg smiles. He's put me in the wrong again.

Celestina picks up my sketchbook. "Hey, this is good," she says. "There's the station, the square, the Town Hall. And even"—she passes it back to me—"the Institute, up at the top."

I take the sketchbook from her, seeing it suddenly through her eyes. The river, bisecting the picture, and the Old City Meeting Hall so small compared to the Town Hall in the New City. "I'd better go." I pick up my file.

"Have a nice weekend, Verity." It's a relief to have Serafina back from the hospital. There's nothing knowing in her voice. She really means it.

And then I realize with a pang of sadness that I might never see any of them again. But I feel relief too, because I'm not going to harm them, or lie to them anymore. I look at Serafina, beaming at me. Emanuel smiling at her.

Celestina half-turns, her hair falling over one shoulder. "Bye, Verity."

"Bye, Celestina." I wish I could have gotten to know her properly.

Jeremiah looks up and nods. That's ultrafriendly, for him. I feel a stab of guilt because I don't even think Jeremiah's suspicious now.

"Good-bye, Verity." Greg fixes me with a stare.

I look back at him. "Bye."

I go to the Sisters' house to fetch my things. I didn't pack much, because Ril said she'd bring my own stuff. I swing my bag over one shoulder and pause in the doorway. My eyes fall on the miniature zoo of stuffed animals scattered across Serafina's bed. I will never see this room again. That's what I want, isn't it? To leave? But still, it's gnawing at me, inside my chest. I didn't say good-bye properly.

—

RIL IS PACING the Reception when I come in. "You were a long time."

"Sorry."

We walk to her blue car in silence. She brakes at the caretaker's lodge, waiting for Mr. East to open the gate.

"Ril? Can you hold on one second? There's someone I have to see." I jump out and run around the back of the car to the lodge. Raymond comes out, tail whirling. He doesn't know that I will never take him for another walk.

I crouch down and gather him into my arms.

Raymond's tail lowers slowly as he realizes there's no walk today.

Ril smiles when I get back in. "I thought for a minute there you weren't going to come." She glances at me.

"I'm here, aren't I?"

Ril drives away from the Institute and turns off the road onto a forestry path. She parks next to a shiny black four-wheel drive, jumps out, and opens the back door. "Come on!" She tosses my bag inside, and peels off her stylish jacket. Underneath it she's just wearing a black vest. She puts a khaki jacket on and pulls off a wig. No wonder her hair was always so neat! She runs her fingers through her short auburn hair, spiking it up. "That's better!"

Who *is* she? Not my social worker, that's for sure. She looks like a different person, a pretty one. I look down at my clothes. I'm wearing the deck-chair and Serafina's pink hooded cardigan, which I now remember I forgot to ask to borrow. The weird thing is, I also feel like me.

"Why don't you change too, K?" says Ril. "I've got some things for you here. You won't want to look too Brotherhood where we're going."

I look in the backpack she's holding out. "These aren't my things. You said you'd bring my own stuff."

"I know. Sorry." She goes around to the front and gets into the driver's seat. "Just wasn't possible for this weekend."

I pull the jeans on beneath the dress. They almost fit. I tug the deck-chair off over my head and put on a black T-shirt instead of the lemon one I was wearing under the dress. Then I shrug Serafina's pink cardigan back on again. There's something comforting about it. I climb into the passenger seat. Ril sees me look back at the blue car.

"Don't worry about that." She starts the engine. "It'll get picked up." She glances down at my feet, in their friendly boots, and she smiles. "You got the list? From the visitors' book?"

"Not yet."

She frowns.

"Where's Oskar?" I know I sound like a child.

"He's there already."

I'm not going to ask her any more questions. I'll wait until I see Oskar. I wish I had a bottle of water. I bet Greg would have brought one. He'd probably have a bar of chocolate too, and his wind-up flashlight and a compass. I smile.

I thought we were going somewhere far away, but Ril heads for the Old City and the ring road that leads to the coast. And then we're going uphill, fields on either side of the road, and I know what I'll see as we come over the crest.

Below, the green arms of the hills circle the valley. The little stone town curls around the bay, and the sea stretches to the sky, touched with fingers of pink and gold.

Yoremouth.

I stare up at the sunshade to stop my tears. This is the first time I've been home in almost six years, since Grandma died.

"Ah." I let myself breathe out. "You didn't say we were going to Yoremouth."

"I know," says Ril. "Poor K! And you didn't even get to bring your bucket and spade."

I look at her. But she's smiling a friendly smile.

We follow the seafront, under the ruined castle and around to the south bay. Ril parks outside a row of fishermen's cottages, the ones on the pebble beach where I used to swim.

She turns off the engine and spikes up her short hair with one hand while checking her phone with the other. "Oskar's with some friends," she says. "We'll go straight there."

We walk briskly through the back streets away from the promenade. Groups of students are going out for the evening, gathering in the street outside bars and restaurants. I want to go slowly, take in all the things that are different and yet familiar. We stop at an inn in a narrow street. I follow Ril up the wooden stairs, and as we reach the landing a door opens and Oskar appears.

"Oskar!" I step closer.

"K." Oskar puts his arms around me in a bear hug.

I hug him back, not wanting to let go. His leather jacket feels warm under my hands and he makes me feel safe again, just like he did on the day of the bomb. Everything will be OK now.

His long hair flops over one eye. "Look at you." He smiles at me, giving the back of my cardigan a friendly tug. "Little Hoody!"

He's only joking.

I follow them into the bar. I'm with Oskar for the whole weekend. It'll be such a relief to talk to him about what's been happening. To tell him I want to leave. I look at him as he stands beside a table. He looks older than I remember. He glances at me and smiles easily, right up into the amber flecks of his eyes.

It's very crowded in here, and everyone seems to know each other. A girl on the bench beside me moves over to make room, so I sit down. Ril goes to get drinks, but the man on the end, with a stubbly beard and spiky dark hair, jumps up to get them instead.

"Thanks, Col," says Ril. She sits down opposite me.

Oskar sits beside her, too far away to talk to me. Are he and Ril partners? And if so, what kind? I don't like to think of Oskar being with Ril. She's just too shifty. Oskar turns quickly as Ril speaks to him.

She smiles at me across the table. She's clearly not a social worker. But I can ask Oskar everything tomorrow.

Col puts a beer in front of me. I'm so thirsty that I drink it very quickly. I look up at the TV screen, which has rolling subtitles: *TWELVE CHARGED DESE-CRATING VIGIL . . . THREE MORE SUSPECTED TERRORISTS SENT TO TRANQUILITY SOUND . . .*

Col's eyes follow mine. "They seem to worship death. They have no respect, K."

I jump when he calls me "K," and glance at Oskar. But he doesn't see me. He's leaning forward to listen to Col.

"They're not living in the same century as us, and they treat women like servants. Though I suppose you know that from the Institute," Col continues.

Oskar nods. Ril props her chin on her elbows.

They. I think of Greg and Emanuel. "They" have never treated me like a servant and "they" certainly don't worship death. But then I think of the man who blew himself up at Central Station. That's who Col is talking about. Col walks back with us, because it's his house we're staying in. It's dark now, and fog is rolling in from the sea.

Even that fills me with a sense of peace, because I'm in the only place I've ever been at home. It's nice not having to pretend to be a Brotherhood girl, to feel part of a group without tricking anyone. Oskar must live here too, because he unlocks the cottage door, which leads straight into the front room. It smells of wood fires and damp. There are newspapers on every surface. It's strange to see them now. Maybe I'll read one. Maybe we'll eat at last.

But Ril says, "You must be tired. I'll show you to your room."

I pick up my wool bag and the backpack she gave me, and follow her up to the attic. The room has a sloping ceiling and a bow window looking out to sea.

"Good night, then," she says in the doorway. It's like a dismissal.

I get into bed hungry and lie there for a while, alone with the sea, my head thrumming. Oskar must think that Ril and I ate on the way. I'm sure I could go downstairs and find something, but I don't want to seem like a child getting out of bed to get a drink of water, and I can't hear if they're still up because of the crashing waves. From the Gatesbrooke Sound a foghorn echoes. The wind has risen and the sash window rattles in its pane. I don't have to think of anything but the swishing of the waves. I should have gotten a glass of water from the kitchen. I lie in the dark, my mouth dry as crackers.

—

"K? K! OSKAR wants to talk to you."

I snap awake. Ril's footsteps run down the stairs.

Sunlight sneaks around the edges of the curtain. I drag myself up. My head feels as if ants are crawling under my scalp. I pull on the jeans and a brown T-shirt from the bag Ril gave me. There's a gray long-sleeved top too, so I leave Serafina's cardigan on my bed, even though it's warmer. When I look in the little mirror, I see that my hair is a little too long for a citizen now. I tie it up to make it look shorter.

There's a delicious smell of toast in the kitchen, where Oskar and Ril are sitting at the table. Ril lays her newspaper down, and I read the headline: RIOTS AFTER RECONCILIATION BILL.

Col is in the living room, sorting through papers on the couch.

"K." Oskar leaps up. "Let's go for a walk." His eyes follow mine to the plate of toast on the table.

But before he can speak Ril says, "You can have breakfast later."

Outside, the breeze blows away the sun's warmth. Oskar strides toward the harbor, and I hurry to keep up. We pass beach huts painted lemon and rose and mint. After a while they give way to the old blue and white huts that I remember. Their paint is cracking into blisters and their iron doors are crusted red. They each have a padlock securing the door. They used to be easy to force open, though; half of them were so rusted that one good knock would break them. I used to spend cozy times hiding inside, drawing in peace where Grandma couldn't see. Not a bad place to go if you ever needed somewhere to lay your head.

We reach the end of the promenade and sit on the harbor wall with our legs dangling over the edge. I need to get all my questions straight and in the right order. And then to tell Oskar he's wrong—there's nothing at the Institute, no sleeper cells or terrorists, not even Jeremiah. And that because of this I want to leave.

The fishing boats dip on the white caps of the waves and the breeze makes me shiver. It's hard to concentrate with the sun dazzling my eyes and Oskar's leather arm against mine.

I look sideways at him. He turns to smile at me, and it's such a warm smile that it makes me forget all the questions I meant to ask. Where should I begin?

Oskar looks away, across to where the sea churns around rocks at the end of the harbor wall.

I want to ask him who Ril is. And tell him that I made a mistake. I look at him again. The breeze lifts his sandy hair. I promised him I would do this. I'm letting him down. My heart begins to hammer as I open my mouth to speak.

But Oskar speaks first.

"K," he says, shifting sideways so that he can look straight at me. In the glittering sunlight his eyes look green. "There's something I have to tell you. It might come as a bit of a shock."

Is this about the list? Or have they found something? Not about Greg? I feel the blood drumming in my ears.

"It's about your name," says Oskar. "K Child. Your real name."

He pauses, and I don't say anything, so he goes on.

"The thing is," he says, "we've had to get rid of K Child."

My hand grasps the metal railing.

"K Child is . . . gone," says Oskar.

"What do you mean?" My voice is thin and dry.

Oskar's hand skims my back. He looks into my eyes and smiles. "K Child is dead."

CHAPTER 17

EVERYTHING GOES STILL. All I can hear is the pulse deep inside my ears. *Dead. Dead. Dead.* The sunlight glints off the waves and into my eyes. I let myself breathe out, very slowly. The only thing that feels real is the metal railing I'm gripping.

"What do you mean?" I say again. I'm surprised how clear my voice sounds. "Dead?"

Oskar keeps his eyes on mine, but now his expression shifts. He looks relieved. "A girl was found," he says. "Drowned. She was identified as K Child."

"By 'Sue Smith'?" I can't hide the hostility in my voice. "Or by you? What have you done? Who do you work for?"

Oskar puts his hand on my arm, stopping me from getting up. "No, actually," he says, "it was staff from the halfway house, initially. You were registered missing. Sue Smith confirmed it. And you know who I work for, K." He hesitates. "You have to remember the body was in the sea for a while. Decomposed beyond recognition."

"Whose body?" Below us, green water swirls around the harbor supports.

Oskar shrugs. "Who knows? Just a girl. Nobody was looking for her. It was simply good timing."

I try not to think about that girl, who has taken

my name to the grave. But I can't stop myself from asking. "What happened to her?" I don't care that my voice is shaky.

Oskar stares at me. "What?"

"Her body. What happened to it?"

Oskar looks out across the harbor. "It—she—would have been cremated. I suppose they scatter the ashes in the crematorium if nobody wants them." He puts his arm across my shoulders and pats my back. "You're shocked," he says. "Of course you are. Let's go back and have breakfast."

"I don't want to be Verity Nekton anymore." My voice is high and small, not like my voice at all. I can barely breathe.

"You don't have any choice," says Oskar quietly.

"What if I find someone who remembers me? What then?"

Oskar takes hold of my arm. I can feel his fingers and thumb on either side of the bone. I stare into his eyes, and in the glare his pupils have receded to dots. He's going to push me off the harbor wall!

Then he laughs, and pulls me toward him. "It's not very likely," he says. "You've got no papers—not anymore; Ril has seen to that. You hardly went to your school in the New City. You've moved around a lot, and we confirmed as part of our initial background check that your last foster parents emigrated to the southern hemisphere. The staff at the halfway house have changed since you left. Who else is there?" He jumps up. "Come on, let's go and get breakfast."

I'm not hungry anymore. And my hand is fastened

around the railing. Frozen in place. It takes me a moment to uncurl my white knuckles. I twist my legs around and over, and slide down from the wall. Of course Oskar wasn't going to push me in. All the same, the trust we had feels broken.

I walk beside Oskar back along the promenade. Seagulls swoop and shriek over the nets on the mudflats. I wish I had Serafina's pink cardigan wrapped around me. The jeans are too big, and as I walk they crease into ridges behind my knees.

I stop beside the path that leads up to the castle. A dull ache grips my forehead. "Why did you do it?"

Oskar looks down at me. "Do what, K?"

"Take away my name," I say. "Why did you take away my name?"

Oskar puts both his hands on my shoulders. "It's only a name." He turns me to face him. "Bigger things were at stake. The Brotherhood are trying to destroy our whole society. And you agreed to it. Don't you remember, K?"

I shake my head. I don't remember anything now. But I see that I don't matter much in Oskar's world.

"I explained it all to you. You read the Manual about the Brotherhood so you'd know how to live like one."

"But not forever!" I cry. "I thought it would only be until school finished!"

"You can't have thought that." Oskar's voice is slow and patient. "What would be the use of that? You have a Brotherhood identity now; your finger-prints are in the Brotherhood database."

"What?" I pull away from Oskar. "I never agreed to that!"

Oskar steps closer. "Yes, you did, K. Remember, in the cafe, when we got everything ready for your new ID card? We did it then—together."

I cast my mind back, trying to remember. Did I read about the fingerprint database in Oskar's Manual? I don't know anymore.

Oskar puts his arm around my shoulders again. "The whole point is that you are now a trusted member of the Brotherhood. You've infiltrated the Institute—just as you were supposed to. And now you carry on until we need you." He lets go of me and starts walking up the castle path.

I watch his back as he walks away. Then I run to catch up to him. I think of the suspicious way Brer Magnus looked at me in the hospital. I think of Greg following me. All the details I should report back to Oskar like a proper little spy. But I don't say them. I don't want Oskar ever to hear Greg's name.

"They might not let me stay on at the Institute," I say when I reach Oskar. "What will happen then?"

He puts his arm back around me. "K," he says. "Do you think we won't look after you? You're one of us now. Of course we won't leave you on your own." He pulls me closer, into a hug. "You worry too much. Hasn't everything happened that I said would happen? Ril came to the school, and here you are now."

Ril. "That's another thing." I stop walking. "Who is Ril? Is she really a social worker?"

Oskar laughs. "I thought I explained it all before," he says. "We don't operate within normal boundaries. Let's just say Ril's a talented computer programmer."

"But then you planned it all before you even asked me!"

"Of course we did." Oskar looks amused. "We're good at what we do."

My special friendship with Oskar shatters into pieces. He just needed a girl who nobody would miss.

We walk on in silence through the castle playground, past children swinging and shouting in the bright spring sunshine. Then we cross the road and come out into a square where a tall building blocks out the sun.

It's Grandma's community center. I stare up at the oak door until I've eaten my tears. Oh, what would Grandma say, if she knew that I'd taken a Brotherhood girl's identity? I walk up the steps so that Oskar won't see my face.

A Brotherhood girl's identity.

Horror rushes through me. What if they killed the real one? Can the police do that? Maybe they can if they're antiterrorism? I feel myself become very still. Frozen, again.

"You're a bit quiet," says Oskar.

I turn around. "The girl who drowned."

Oskar has to lean forward to catch my whisper. Suddenly I feel scared again. What else might he be capable of? But I have to know.

"Was she . . . was she the real Verity Nekton?"

He stares at me in blank astonishment. Then he bursts out laughing. "No!" He splutters again. "No, no, no!"

"Why are you laughing?"

Oskar stops himself. "Sorry. Sorry." But his eyes are still dancing. "It's your face." He puts his arm around me. "*You* are Verity Nekton. Or nobody is. It's just a name, that's all."

"Not hers?"

"No!" He gives me a friendly shake.

Is he telling the truth? There are no twitches or tells of a liar. The terror evaporates.

"But I've lost everything." I can let myself feel angry with him now. "My name. My things. My future. I don't know who I am anymore. And the Institute's not like I thought it would be either. It's pretty normal, really. It's just kids and teachers. They don't believe in violence. They're too busy trying to be good." I kick one foot up and down the step, and wrap my arms around myself.

"K." Oskar looks at me earnestly. "I told you it would be like that. But who knows what they're hiding?"

"But what's the point of me being there?"

"There *is* a militant cell linked to the Institute," says Oskar. "You know there is. You gave us the name, Jeremiah Elyard—you'll give us the list of names from the Spring Meeting. They're the enemy within, you must never forget that. And maybe you'll be able to find something out now."

"I don't know for sure that Jeremiah's involved in anything! I'm not a detective. I don't know how to do it."

"It's early days, K," says Oskar. "All you have to do is point out to me anyone you might suspect. No matter how trivial. Just indicate who to watch. We'll do the rest. If someone had done that before the Gatesbrooke bomb, think of how many people would still be alive."

I go up a couple of steps so that he has to look up at me. "I don't know."

"It's not for long."

"How long?"

Oskar pauses. Then he says, "A year. Just one year."

A year sounds a lot different from forever. I could plan my own future when it's over.

"And then I wouldn't have to be Verity Nekton anymore?"

"Absolutely not. You could choose a new name."

People do that, don't they? Change their name. It's not *that* unusual. Look at me, I've already had two.

"What about my fingerprints?" I ask.

"Well," says Oskar, "I'm sure Ril could find a way to get them removed from the database."

I step down on to the pavement.

Oskar stays on the steps. I let my life run past me in a slide show of losses. The bomb that killed my parents. Grandma dying. Being moved when foster parents got sick or had a baby. I can't lose Oskar too. He saved my life. I can never forget that.

The only thing I chose to do myself was to go to the Institute. If I go back, I'll see them all again: Serafina, Celestina, Emanuel. And even Greg. I know we can't really be friends. But maybe it could lead to me being an artist. Maybe it could still be OK.

Oskar waits, smiling patiently.

"I don't know," I say.

He comes down the steps. "Would it help if you could contact me whenever you want? I'll get you a cell phone you can use." He touches my shoulder. "What about some breakfast first?" His eyes are alight with concern.

"OK." I look back up at the community center. Why did Grandma go there every week but never take me? She never took me anywhere.

We pass through an alley that leads to the yard at the back of the cottage. Oskar stoops to take the key from under an upturned fire bucket. When he opens the door, the scent of sizzling bacon makes me feel almost faint with hunger. I follow him in.

Col is sitting at the kitchen table working through some papers. He looks up inquiringly at Oskar, who half-nods with a look of relief. In the front room the TV is blasting out the news channel. Oskar goes through the arch between the two rooms and sits down on the couch.

Ril is at the stove. "Tea, K?" She passes me a mug.

"Thanks." I hover by the table. On the news they're showing another Brotherhood demonstration. Close-ups of chanting faces, and angry shouting that masks the actual words. I bet they never even filmed the citizen mob outside the Institute.

Col walks over to the archway to look at the TV. "Hoods." His voice rises, competing with the television. "They always argue that they've been around for longer. That's true. But what they don't realize is that makes them obsolete. Like all life forms that don't evolve, eventually they'll just wither away." He crosses the room in a couple of strides and turns off the TV.

I suddenly think of Fred, that day after the bomb: *Hoods—they'd kill us all if they could.*

I take a sip of tea. If it wasn't so hot, I'd gulp it down in one go. Col doesn't seem to need a response.

Ril drops an egg into the pan. In the new silence it makes a soft hiss.

"Want some help?" I ask.

"The more the merrier," says Ril. She looks young and pretty here. She smiles as she passes me a white sliced loaf. "You can put the toast on."

"Any more tea in the pot?" calls Oskar from the front room. Ril takes it in to him on a tray, and that makes me suddenly picture Greg, carrying everyone's empty dishes after dinner.

Col hasn't finished. "I'm glad I don't live in the city," he says. "There are too many of them there." He sits back down at the table.

"But surely they're not all bad?" I say. "They're just people."

Col shakes his head. "That's what I used to think," he says. "But now I know there's something in them that can make them do anything. *Anything.* They think they're doing the right thing. That's why they're so dangerous. That's why you can never change them."

He sounds like Grandma.

"They'll just keep doing it," he goes on. "They're always out there, planning and waiting for their chance."

"Breakfast!" Ril starts putting the plates down on the table, fragrant and hot.

Oskar comes back into the kitchen as I sit down. "Why so serious, K?" He puts his arm loosely around my shoulders and gives me a little hug. "All you have to do for now is keep your head down, do your schoolwork, find me that list. And it's not for long," he whispers in my ear. "Not long at all."

CHAPTER 18

WHEN RIL DROPS me off after lunch two days later, the Institute feels empty. I forgot that this was the spring break long weekend. There are only three of us who haven't gone home: Greg, Celestina, and me. The office staff, including Brer Magnus's secretary, aren't here and hopefully Brer Magnus will be in his own house in the grounds. This could be the best chance I'll get to look for the visitors' book. If I do it right away, I can just forget about being a spy and get on with my life here. One more year.

The Sisters' house is empty. I decide to check out where the others are. And if I'm honest, I want to see them too.

They're in the library, sharing a table with their books and files spread out all over it.

A slow smile spreads over Celestina's face when she sees me. "Well, look who's come back," she says, tapping Greg's shoulder. It's almost as if she knew I'd planned not to.

Greg looks up too. "Hello, Verity."

I turn back to Celestina. "Did you stay here to study?"

She gives me a small smile. "Let's just say my parents like me better from a distance."

Celestina's never told me anything like this before. "I'm sorry," I say.

Greg breaks into the pause that follows. "Sit here if you want, Verity."

"Thanks, but I'm going to the Art room. I just came to say hello." I can't lose this opportunity. I run down the library stairwell and turn back toward the canteen and across the courtyard into the old building. I hurry up the stairs to the Meeting Hall. *No, slow down*, I remind myself. I can say I want to be alone there, to reflect. That's allowed, surely? Maybe the door will be closed. But it's half open already. This room is so bare and clear that I know immediately I'm not going to find the visitors' book here.

All the same, I go up to the table where the Book lies, closed now. It's the only book on the stiff gold brocade cloth. I resist the temptation to have another look inside, although if anyone comes, that's what I'll say I'm doing. I even look under the cloth, which hangs down to the floor. But there's nothing there. Nothing on the shelf at the back of the hall either, or on the little table where they placed the visitors' book for signing at the Spring Meeting.

My heart sinks as I walk down the stairs, wondering who might be watching me through these long glass windows. Since I didn't find the visitors' book in the Meeting Hall, I can guess where it will be. In Brer Magnus's office. At the bottom of the stairs I hesitate, looking down the paneled corridor. I don't know if Brer Magnus is in there, or even in the Institute at all. What can I say if he is?

I take a step into the corridor. This is where the lavender polish smell comes from. If he's there, I'll say I've come to ask if I can go to the city, to buy some pastels. It's very quiet here. His door is at the end. He has a gold name sign. I tap on the shiny dark wood.

There's no reply. I wait, knock again. It's all I have to do, Oskar said. Just get the list and they'll take it from there. I'm a tiny cog and this is my task to keep the clock ticking.

I turn the handle and the door opens, slowly because of the thick fawn-colored carpet inside. Brer Magnus isn't there, but the room is heavy with his presence. His desk is in front of the window that overlooks the canteen. I check for cameras, but I can't see one, so I take a last look down the empty corridor, then push the door wide open so that I'll hear if anyone comes. I glance at the window that overlooks the drive, but I think the vertical blinds are angled to stop people from seeing in. I pull my sleeves down to cover my fingertips before trying to open the desk drawers. Of course they're locked, except for the top middle one, which holds pens, a paper knife, sticky notes. And a half-eaten bar of chocolate. That stops me. I've never imagined Brer Magnus doing anything as human as eating a bar of chocolate.

Next to the desk there's a glass-fronted bookcase, also locked. I scan the books. They seem to be mostly yearbooks. And then I see it, on the bottom shelf, lying flat on its own, in a navy cardboard box embossed with: *Visitors' Book*.

It's only a flimsy door, easily forced open with something like a ruler. But then I won't be able to sneak the book back undetected. I rattle the doorknobs until I feel that there's an inner bolt at the top on the left-hand door. I grab Brer Magnus's paper knife and wiggle it up into the little gap between door and frame, catching it against the top of the bolt. It doesn't take long to ease it down, and then all I have to do is pull the doors toward me until the catch slips out of the lock. But I've been in here too long now.

I open the cabinet and take the book out of its box, which I replace before pushing the doors shut until the catch clicks and wiping everything I touched with my scarf. Should I copy down the names now so that I never have to come here again, or should I take the book with me, to copy in a less stressful place? If only there was a photocopier in this room, but Brer Magnus's office has no modern technology at all. It could be a couple of centuries ago in here.

The sound of the outside doors sends me scurrying back to the doorway. Nowhere to hide! I stuff the book into my open bag, swing it over my shoulder, then get myself outside the door and close it as silently as I can. There's nowhere to go. I turn my back to the Reception area and knock loudly on the door. I hear footsteps behind me. I hope it's not Brer Magnus.

"Verity?"

It is him. I turn, sick with dread. But my voice sounds clear. "Oh, hello, Brer Magnus. I was just coming to see you."

He walks slowly toward me. He opens his door. "You'd better come in."

What am I going to say? I open my mouth but nothing comes out. I stare at him while he goes and sits in his chair, behind his massive desk. His face falls into shadow with the window behind him.

"Yes?" He waits.

"I came to ask you"—and I feel my hands clasp themselves together in front of me—"if I could go into Gatesbrooke, into the city, I mean . . ." My mind goes completely blank.

He tilts his head back in surprise. He knows I'm lying.

"Because," I burble on, "I want to go with the others when they . . ." *Think, K!* ". . . when they take part in the . . . Reconciliation activities."

Brer Magnus puts his fingertips on his desk and gives me a long look. "Really." He carries on watching me. "I'll have to think about that."

I nod, much too vigorously. I force myself to be still.

"Was there anything else?"

I shake my head. The corner of the visitors' book digs into my hip through my wool bag.

"I must say I'm surprised," says Brer Magnus. "But I'll certainly give it my full consideration."

"Yes. Thanks. Sir," I add, since that's what Greg calls him. I edge backward toward the doorway.

But he hasn't finished. He makes a pyramid with the fingertips of his hands, under his chin. "Why do you want to take part in the Reconciliation process?"

Why would I want to do that? "Because the others are doing it," I say. "I'd like to go with them."

"You haven't known them very long."

He's right. I feel my face grow hot. I think of gentle Serafina. Celestina, with her knowing glance. Emanuel and his sweet smile. And Greg's one smile at me, on the bus.

I need a better reason. What would Celestina say? "Because things have to change," I say.

"Of course," says Brer Magnus. "I'd like to encourage

that spirit in our students. But . . ."

I don't know what more to say, so I keep quiet.

"But first," says Brer Magnus, "there's something else we need to discuss."

Here it comes. He's going to ask me about the visitors' book. It's all I can do to keep my eyes from flicking down to the bag at my side.

CHAPTER 19

"I WANT TO talk to you about your parents," says Brer Magnus. "I don't know if the other pupils have asked you about them?"

"No. Not really." *He knows, he knows all about me.*

Brer Magnus fixes me with his unmoving stare. "I was concerned that some students might have felt uncomfortable with your parents' role in the bombing—"

I interrupt him. 'My parents' role?'

"Yes." He gives me what I think he means to be a smile. "I just wanted to reassure you that I have nothing but admiration for your parents, whatever they did."

"Whatever they did?"

"Yes. Times were very different then. In a sense, it was a war."

He carries on talking, but I'm not listening anymore. It takes me a moment to remember that he isn't talking about my parents at all. All this is about Verity Nekton's imaginary parents. All the same, I need to be sure.

"Brer Magnus . . ." I interrupt him again. "Are you saying that you think . . . my parents . . . planted the bomb?"

"I assumed you would know." He leans back in his chair, watching me. "Who can say?" he says. "However, that's my understanding, yes. But I want you to know that I understand their motivation, their sacrifice. In no way does this make me think less highly of you. Far from it."

My mind is reeling. I want to run out of the room and keep running and never come back. I feel dirty. Is this why Brer Magnus let me into the Institute? Does everyone know? They all think my parents were terrorists? Does Greg know?

But Brer Magnus is speaking again. "And now about your boots," he says.

"My boots?"

"Yes. They're men's boots. I don't believe it's suitable for you to wear them here. It sets a bad example for the younger students. Girls should not dress like men."

I can't believe he's talking about boots after all he's just said. I'm so surprised that I start arguing. "They're not men's boots. They're way too small."

"Verity." Brer Magnus frowns. "It's not negotiable. The boots have to go. In fact, I'd like you to leave them here now." He reaches under his desk and pulls out a pair of pink flip-flops with big red roses on them. "You can wear these back to the dormitory."

I don't move but I can feel my face going red. If I was K, I would get up and walk out in my boots. But I'm Verity now. I put my bag down carefully, then pull them off one by one and hand them silently to Brer Magnus.

He places them beside his desk, next to the bin. But he still isn't finished. He stands up and looks down at me. "Verity, I had already decided to choose you and Gregory to represent the Institute at the Reconciliation youth event." I feel my mouth drop open.

Brer Magnus makes the face that I think is his smile. "There's going to be what they call a 'Reconciliation Rally.'" His mouth twists in distaste. "On the day before the Reconciliation Agreement is signed, in five months. This youth event is in preparation for that. It's tomorrow," he continues. "In Yoremouth."

There's a silence. Brer Magnus looks at me. "Well?"

I start to stammer an answer, but Brer Magnus speaks first.

"Good. That's settled, then," he says. "I've already informed your social worker. You can go now. I'll run through the arrangements later with Greg."

I watch him pick up a sheaf of papers and turn his attention away from me. There's nothing I can say. He's like a cat with one paw on a sparrow's wing, waiting. It's hard to look dignified wearing socks and flip-flops with massive flowers. I thought Brer Magnus was going to tell me to leave. But instead I'm even more firmly entrenched here.

I try to walk away slowly. Everyone will still be in the library so the Art room is the only place I can think of where I can be alone at this time of day, and maybe even find somewhere to hide the visitors' book. I should be worrying about that, but all I can think of is that Brer Magnus has chosen me to represent the Institute because he admires my "freedom fighter" parents. *How could you have given me terrorist parents, Oskar? Even fake ones?* But then I remember with a jolt what else Oskar has done.

—

"NICE SHOES," SAYS Greg as I push open the door of the Art Room.

I glare at him.

Greg smiles. "Where have you been, then, Verity? I thought you said you were coming straight here?"

On the other side of the room Ms. Cobana has spread folders across three tables and is scribbling in her grade book. She must be the only teacher in today.

"I went to see Brer Magnus." I take my Math book and pencil case out of my bag, keeping the visitors' book hidden, and put them on the bench. "As if it's anything to do with you." I concentrate on delving in the bag until I find my paintbrushes.

Greg puts his hands up in an exaggerated back-off. "Hey! I was only asking." He carries on drawing in his sketchbook.

Ms. Cobana goes over to the wall with some pictures and starts shooting staples into the board. I fetch inks and a sheet of paper from the closet trying to quell the panic rising up in my throat. I dip my brush—the one Greg gave me—into yellow ink and wash it over the whole surface. In the quiet my breathing is too loud and fast.

"Verity?" Greg has stopped drawing. "Are you all right?"

I get a grip on myself, and nod. Even shortish long

hair is useful for hiding behind at times like this.

"OK," he says. But under my hair I can see that he hasn't picked up his charcoal pencil again He pulls a stool over, next to mine. "Verity?"

I look up. The afternoon sun is gold on his face. His eyes have a navy circle around the brown.

"You OK?" he says.

I wait for him to ask me again why I went to see Brer Magnus. Or what's wrong. Wherever I go there is someone waiting to question me.

But instead he picks up my Math book.

I try to snatch it back, but he whisks it away. He opens it and looks at the fractions I can never remember. Now he'll think I'm a total moron. He is probably up to the kind of Math where you can work out time travel.

"I was thinking," he says.

"Oh dear. What will Brer Magnus say?"

Greg frowns. But he continues. "If you like, I could help you with your Math sometimes."

"You don't have time."

"It's OK," he says. "I could spare half an hour a week. If you want."

I think it over. "All right," I say. "But just stop if you change your mind."

"It'll be OK." He looks at his watch. "We could start now."

I don't feel like painting anymore. "OK."

Greg writes quickly on my book. "You do this one."

He looks at my answer. "Trial and error," he says. "That's no good." He starts breaking it down. His sleeves are rolled up and the fine hairs on his arms catch the late sunshine. If I was drawing his arm, it would make a nice curve.

"Verity!" says Greg. "Pay attention."

"Sorry," I say. I try to concentrate, because it would be good to pass. "Not everyone is studying Math, Honors Math, Advanced Math, Statistics, and Quantum Physics, you know."

Greg puts down his pencil. "Do you not want me to help you?"

"No. Yes. I do want you to."

"All right, then. Engage your brain."

I try to fill my mind with numbers. I watch them dancing on the page under Greg's pencil. Out of the corner of my eye I can see the shape of his shoulder, and the sunlit line of his cheekbone, and the way his hair has grown just long enough to fall near his eyebrows as he leans forward. I stare at the white paper and try to breathe slowly. But it's no good. I didn't feel like this when I was drawing him.

I close my eyes, because if I look at him, I want to reach out and touch him. Even so, his voice is too close to my ear, sending a current through me. No, no, no! I can't feel this for Greg. How did I let this happen? This mustn't happen.

"OK." Greg nudges me with his elbow. "You do this one."

I jolt away.

"What?" Greg looks at me.

I stand up. "Isn't it time for dinner?" I say, scooping my Math book up from under Greg's elbow and stuffing it into my bag. I start clinking ink bottles into the tray. "I'm going to the library first," I say. "I'll see you in the canteen."

—

THE LIBRARY IS empty now. I hurry to the Art section alcove and take down a large book. I kick off my flip-flops and curl up in an armchair, hiding the visitors' book behind the book while I write down the names in the middle of my art pad. There are hundreds. I glance at the clock. Dinner will be in twenty minutes. But at last I've got them all.

I stand up and hide the visitors' book behind the art tome and then push it back in. I'll have to return it to Brer Magnus's office soon, but for now it's safer here than in the Sisters' house. *Better borrow a book*, I think, *as cover.* I find one on printmaking and head for the door. When I open it I see Ms. Cobana coming up the stairs.

"Hello, Verity." She stops, glancing at my feet in their ridiculous flowery flip-flops. "Verity? I hope you don't mind," she begins, "but I couldn't help overhearing your conversation with Greg."

"Oh," I say. Here we go again.

"I was just wondering—you're not in some kind of trouble, are you?"

I pretend to consider her question. I'm still here, at least. "I don't think so."

"You've gotten very friendly with Greg."

I let my hair fall across to hide my face. "Not particularly Greg; it's the whole group, really."

She nods, as if I haven't spoken. "He's a lovely boy," she says. "Very thick with Brer Magnus, of course."

"Oh. Is he?" Like I haven't noticed.

She nods again, emphatically. It's almost as though she's trying to warn me about something. But then she says, "I'm glad you've made friends. I hope you get to stay on here with them all next year."

"I do too," I say. And I do. Don't I? Because I've never had friends like these before. And if I don't stay on, where will I go? Who will I be?

"I also hope you don't mind me saying," Ms. Cobana goes on. "It's just that you seem a bit . . . adrift. And I'd like you to know that if you ever need help, you can ask me."

"Thanks."

But now she's handing me a little card. "No, I really mean it, Verity." She frowns. "Here's my number."

I take the card.

"If you ever need help, I'll be there for you," she says. "OK?"

I look at her. She looks steadily back at me from behind her big glasses. There's something in her eyes that makes me want to believe she does mean it.

"OK," I say. "OK." I put the card in my wallet. "Thanks," I add.

It doesn't have her name on it, just a number.

CHAPTER 20

THE NEXT MORNING, Greg is waiting at the caretaker's lodge. His eyebrows shoot up when he sees me. "You look like Celestina."

I think that's a good thing, or is it? I look down at the clothes I've borrowed. A swishy skirt and a cropped jacket, and a silk scarf around my neck. And pointy pumps that are too tight.

Greg is in full red check. Red-checked jacket, red-checked shirt. But he looks lovely. "You're late. We'd better run."

But we miss the next bus into the New City and then we have to run across the square toward Central Station. There's no time to think about the last time I went inside. The first time I saw Greg. I expect our bags to be searched as we enter. But instead the policeman takes Greg to one side. He has to stand with his arms and legs outstretched to be frisked.

"Go behind there." The other policeman jerks his head toward a screen.

Now it's my turn. A policewoman runs her hands up and down my body, arms, and legs. She doesn't speak or make eye contact.

And then we find that we've missed the Yoremouth train after all and there isn't another one for an hour.

An hour is all I need to check out Oskar's story.

"Let's split up and meet back here," I say to Greg. "I want to go around the shops."

He looks at me with his usual expression of distrust. "Don't be late again," he says.

It doesn't take me long to walk to the crematorium. I stop at the flower stall outside the station and buy a white rose. Three black cars drive slowly through the stone gateway as I jog up to it. The gleaming black paintwork and the cloud reflections in the windows fill me with dread. I lean against the wall, catching my breath and waiting for the cars to disappear up the drive and behind some fir trees. I don't want to go in now. But I have to see for myself. So I slip through, past the stone pillars and the open wrought-iron gates. The Garden of Remembrance is on the left.

Trees line the path, their bark black with rain, silver drops dotting every leaf. They're poplars, like the trees beside the playing field at the Institute. Emanuel told me. He studies plants.

On my left there is a wall checkered with small brass plaques. Most only have a name, but some have messages too. I feel sick now. This is a place to come and remember loved ones. Each plaque has a metal vase below, some holding flowers and others withered remains. On the opposite wall I see a tap for filling the vases. I look back along the lines of new names, the shinier plaques.

I'm looking for it, but I don't really expect to see it, so when I do, it's as if it punches me in the chest.

K CHILD

There it is, in black and gold. The letters reach out and hold me. I no longer exist.

But I didn't come here for me. I came for the girl who ended up here in my name. I have to believe Oskar was telling the truth when he swore that she wasn't the real Verity Nekton. I do believe it. But all the same I'm so shocked that I can hardly breathe. What else would Oskar do to further the cause, if he thought it necessary? I was right to decide never to talk to him about my friends at the Institute.

This girl must have been someone like me. Someone who could disappear without anyone noticing. It could have *been* me.

I lay the palm of my hand against the brass. The flower vase below is empty, and I pour some water in and place the white rose inside. Then I wait until my tears stop before I leave the Garden of Remembrance.

I don't cry as I run back to the station because I'll have to face Greg in a minute. But there is a soreness in my heart.

—

GREG IS WAITING inside the station, looking at his watch.

"Sorry!" I pant as I run up.

He doesn't say anything; instead he makes his way toward the platform. I follow him, but as we reach the ticket barrier, my feet slow down. I can see the train waiting on the other side. It's going to leave in six minutes. It doesn't even look like the train that was bombed, yet I still can't make myself move forward. Greg stops and turns back. His eyes search my face. Then he reaches out and takes my hand. His clasps mine as if we always hold hands.

"You were there that day," he says. "Before the bomb." He gives my hand a little tug. "Ready?"

We jump onto the train just before it rolls out of the station. I look down at our hands and let go of Greg's. The blood springs back where I was gripping his fingers so tightly. "Sorry."

But he doesn't say anything. He gives me a little smile. It didn't mean anything, he was just being kind.

The train is full of young people, some citizens and some Brotherhood. Now that we've left the station, I start enjoying the trip. Celestina's shoes are biting my toes, so I kick them off and put my feet up under me on the seat. Greg's legs don't really fit in the space. His knees are wedged up against the seat in front. He opens his backpack and gets out two packed lunches in white paper bags.

A strong smell of boiled egg leaps out as I open mine. But that's OK. I like eggs, Grandma's favorite sandwich filling. "Very organized," I say. I can't imagine Oskar or Col making a packed lunch for anyone.

"I ordered them from Georgette last night," he says. He gets out his book, so we don't talk again until we get there. But I steal secret glances at him as he reads.

—

WE MAKE OUR way slowly out of the station, in the middle of the crowd. I see Greg glancing around him carefully at the citizens. It's different for me—I feel comfortable with both now. In any case, it's a nice crowd, with an excited buzz. Although I was here the other day as a citizen, I feel sure that nobody will recognize me under my hat. I still can't quite believe that after being gone for so long, I've come home to Yoremouth twice in just the past few days.

When we come out of the station into the gray afternoon, there's a bank of journalists waiting, cameras clicking. It's a breezy day. At the end of the road to the station, I know that the sea will be dashing pebbles against the promenade. The Reconciliation meeting is in the Yoremouth school, up the hill.

"This way," I say, pointing to the right.

"You know Yoremouth?"

"Um, no. I just thought we might as well follow everyone else."

But Greg is checking a map on his phone. "Well, you're right," he says.

It isn't possible to walk fast in this crowd. Greg is looking around him. He turns to me, his face lit up. "Everyone looks so happy," he says. "We should always be like this"—and he pauses as we inch forward—"together."

There's no way Greg would have anything to do with a militant cell. I'm sure of it. Even I feel excited now. For the first time I wonder if it could really work, if all these years of hate could end. But how can I ever forget that a Brotherhood bomb killed my parents?

Greg turns to me when we reach the school. "If we get split up, let's arrange a meeting place, OK?" He doesn't wait for me to reply. "On the platform for the seven o'clock train?" Then he adds, "You look nice."

We follow the crowd into the hall. Journalists line the entrance, filming and shouting out questions: "How do you feel about sitting with nonbelievers?"

"Could you go to school with them?"

"Are you worried that Brotherhood extremists will use violence against this meeting?"

We filter into the huge hall, where there's no girls' side or boys' side, no special seats for Brotherhood or citizens. Everyone sits down wherever they like.

—

GREG AND I do lose each other, because the youth event is not a speech. Instead, we are all split up into mixed groups to talk about the changes in the Reconciliation Agreement. How do we feel about mixed schooling? Should we be able to have normal social contact between Brotherhood and citizens? Would it be better if we didn't live in segregated areas? What do we think of paramilitaries on either side?

I can say what I really think and feel here, and for the first time since I became Verity Nekton that's the only lie I tell—my name. And then I think of the list of names I stole yesterday, how they're hiding in my art pad.

I can't find Greg afterward, so I go down to the station on my own. We shouldn't have arranged to meet so late. Almost everyone else from the Reconciliation event seems to have left already. There are two policemen outside the station but inside the station concourse it's quiet. I look at the clock. Six forty-five. Time to go to the platform. I hobble over in Celestina's tight shoes. I hope they don't have bloodstains in them when I give them back. There's no sign of Greg. The train is waiting, creaking and hissing.

Maybe I've been in the safe world of the Institute for too long. Normally I would be aware of who was around me. But this evening I'm busy looking for Greg, and I don't take notice. Until I hear a voice in my ear.

"*Hood.*"

I spin around. There are three boys, two behind

me and now one in front of me. They are all wearing baseball caps with the peaks shading their faces.

I step back, gripping my bag like a shield.

The boy facing me steps forward so that I'm backed up against the side of the train. I'm next to the open door, just where I was when the Gatesbrooke bomb went off.

I fight down the panic and ram my bag hard into him, twisting sideways to jump onto the train. In the train car I turn to see if they've followed me, but through the dusky glass of the window I see them sauntering off down the platform, toward the concourse. Where is Greg? I know he won't get on the train without me.

If any of the other passengers have noticed, they're pretending they haven't seen a thing. I stand watching through the window, getting my breath back.

There's no sign of Greg. I take out my ticket to see what car our seats are in. Maybe he thought I would go straight there? So I walk quickly through the train until I find our car. He's not there.

I step down onto the platform. The citizen thugs have come back this way. They're barging into each other, and there seem to be more of them. I work my keys into my hand, like I used to do walking in the city at night. Each key sticks out between my knuckles.

They're coming closer. I see something red in the middle of them. I peer down the platform in the fading light. Then I realize what it is. Greg's jacket. They've surrounded him and they're all shoving and pushing. I catch sight of his face for a second, and there's red there too. Then *I* see red.

"Hey!" I fly down the platform. "Leave him alone!"

There's a moment when they all look at me in surprise—Greg too. Then he sprints free of them, grabs my hand, and leaps into the train, pulling me with him. We run through the car and into the next one, our car. Greg puts his face close to the darkened window so that he can look out.

"Still there," he says. There's a thump on the window and a muffled shout. "Don't worry, they've stayed on the platform."

The train lurches and vibrates into motion. We sit down in our seats. We're the only ones at this end of the car.

Greg looks down at my hand, with my keys sticking up between my knuckles.

"Wow," he says. "Would you have used those? Where did you learn that?"

I uncurl my fingers and put the keys back in my bag. "I've never had to use them." I don't want him to think I'm a violent person. "The police came to my old school to teach some self-defense techniques," I say. "They said it would give you a chance to get away."

Greg is bleeding under his left eye.

"We need to clean your face." I take out a new packet of tissues and a bottle of water I had in my bag. Then I trickle some water onto one tissue and reach across to dab the blood away. It's only a small cut after all, right on the edge of Greg's cheekbone. He has nice cheekbones. I know their shape from drawing him. I must stop thinking like this. Concentrate on the task at hand. I wet another tissue. Now I'm cleaning the wound, so I lean across and put my other hand behind Greg's head to hold it steady. I can feel the bones under the softness of his hair. He's so close that his breath is warm on my face. He doesn't wince. The cut's still bleeding.

"Keep still for a minute." I press the tissue pad against Greg's cheek. We stay like that for a long moment.

"One of them punched me," he says. "I think he had a sharp ring." He looks at my hand with a little half smile. "Or a knuckleduster."

"Were they trying to mug you?"

"I don't think so," says Greg. "They were saying things."

"'Hood'?" I ask.

"And the rest." Greg looks into my eyes briefly.

I'm still holding the tissue against his cut, so our faces are close. Greg is still breathing quickly. So am I.

I lift the corner of the tissue. "It's stopped bleeding, I think."

I remove it slowly and take my hand away from the back of Greg's head.

"Aren't you going to kiss it better?" says Greg suddenly.

I look at him in surprise. He's joking, of course. I wish he wasn't. But I touch my fingertips to my lips and then to Greg's face, below the cut, very lightly. "There you go," I say.

The train is pulling into a station on the edge of the city. It's not really stopping here, just slowing down to roll silently past the platform. Greg stares over my head toward the far end of the car.

"Oh no," he says.

I look around. The baseball cap boys are coming into the vestibule outside our car.

CHAPTER 21

"VERITY!" GREG GRABS my hand and pulls me out toward the passage at the opposite end of the car. He yanks down the window and opens the door from outside, then leaps off, pulling me after him. We're traveling so slowly that we only stagger for a few steps, but we're very near the end of the platform. The train glides smoothly past and picks up speed.

We look at each other, gasping for breath, still holding hands. The sign over the platform says *Limbourne*. It's suspiciously empty.

I pull my hand away. Blood has started dripping down Greg's face again. I give him another tissue.

In the last light of dusk, I can see trees all around, just trees and more trees, with their branches full of new leaves. There's a waiting room in the middle of the platform, with a vending machine outside it.

Greg studies the timetable on the wall. "There isn't another stopping train until seven-fifteen tomorrow morning."

"Hmm," I say. "This wasn't one of your best ideas."

"And my phone's dead."

"You don't have a wind-up charger? To go with your wind-up flashlight?" I smile in spite of myself.

Greg looks sheepish. "Not with me."

We walk to the end of the platform, where steps lead up to a pedestrian bridge and the station concourse. But when we get there, it's clear that the station is closed for the night. Not only that, the doors to the street are locked.

"Looks like we're stuck here until morning. We'll be breaking the curfew." Greg frowns. "Brer Magnus will be worried." He notices me looking down at the track. "Don't even think about it. There might be a live rail."

There's a rush below us as an intercity train streams past. We go back downstairs to the platform. The waiting room is open. It's cold, but at least there are benches to sit on.

I shrug. "It's no big deal. We'll just wait, then. I like being out at night anyway."

"On your broomstick?" murmurs Greg. He raises his eyebrow, but now it looks teasing rather than disapproving.

"Hey!" I say. "I was trying to be positive."

"Have you got any food?"

I shake my head. "You?"

Greg holds up an apple.

"We'll have to eat chocolate."

We tip all our cash onto the bench. His fingers brush against mine as we sort the coins. I want to hold his hand again. But I don't think he noticed. There's enough money for just one bar and we each have a bottle of water from the Reconciliation event. The chocolate falls into the tray with a *thunk* and Greg is so pleased he laughs.

We go back into the waiting room. I sit down in the far corner. Greg shuffles up so that I am wedged right in. "Huddling together for warmth," he says. "It's what you have to do to prevent exposure."

"Crushing me to death, more like."

He moves away and I wish I hadn't said anything. Then he puts the chocolate bar and the apple on the bench. "Dinner." He takes a small penknife out of his backpack, and cuts the apple in half. I take the knife from him and pull open all the gadgets. It has a pair of scissors, a saw, a screwdriver, and a corkscrew.

"What's this for?" I tap a spikelike thing.

"It's for taking stones out of horses' hooves."

I nod. "Handy." I close it up and pass it back to him.

He opens the chocolate bar. It has five pieces and he gives me three. I break off one and try to snap it in two. But it's far too cold, so I bite it in half and stick the other half in his mouth. My finger touches his lower lip and I look away.

"Fair shares," I say quickly, to hide my embarrassment.

"If you could have anything you wanted to eat, what would you have?" asks Greg.

"A cup of tea," I say. "What about you?"

"Chicken and rice," says Greg. "Hot chocolate."

"Hot chocolate would be good."

"And one of those serious camping sleeping bags people use on mountains." He looks at me, smiling his half smile. "Two, I mean."

"And woolly hats," I add, feeling guilty. I left Celestina's hat on the train.

Greg shifts over and looks at me. Then he unties my scarf and knots it around my head and under my chin like a bonnet. I remember that's how I tied the scarf he gave me in that first meeting at the Institute.

But I sit very still and stop myself from putting my hands up and pulling him toward me.

He laughs. He's just messing about. "There you go," he says. "Woolly hat. Cover your ears."

"What?" I say, pretending not to hear.

"Very funny. Will you stay on at the Institute?" Greg asks me, more seriously.

"If I can." It's the only home I have now.

"What will you do if you don't?"

"I don't know." I don't want to think about that. "What about you?" I ask quickly.

"I'm changing schools. The Institute's really good for Arts, but not so great for Science. So if I want to be a doctor . . ."

"Oh yeah, you said."

Outside, the main lamp goes out, leaving just a dim maintenance light. In the sudden darkness I look sideways up at Greg. My hand reaches up and touches his face.

He turns toward me.

"Just checking," I say quickly, pulling back my hand and looking down. "The bleeding's stopped."

"Verity?" says Greg. His voice is close to my ear.

First my heart lifts, but then it sinks, because he's going to start with all the questions, all the questions I don't have answers for, and he's being friendlier than he's ever been, and it will be hard to put him off with flippant one-liners the way I usually do.

"Tell me about your family," I ask before he has a chance to speak. "How many sisters do you have again?"

"Two."

"And brothers?"

"None." He doesn't ask me back, because he already knows I don't have any.

"I'd like to have brothers and sisters," I say. I can't let him see how I feel about him, I shouldn't be feeling it. "You wouldn't be a bad brother. Maybe I'll borrow you."

Greg is silent. Then he says, "You *are* my Sister."

I don't know what to say. It feels like he accepts me.

Greg speaks again. "Angelina's nine, and Meredith is fourteen. They're abroad, with our parents."

"Do you miss them?" I'm glad the conversation has turned away from me and toward Greg.

"I'm used to it now. And I'm going this summer." All the same, his voice sounds sad.

"What's it like there?"

"Hot," he says. "Different animals, different plants. We don't have apples in our garden; we have pineapples and pawpaws and guavas."

"We had an apple tree," I begin. But then I stiffen, remembering that that tree was in Grandma's garden in Yoremouth. I can't talk about Grandma to Greg.

He turns his head toward me.

"Um, my old foster family."

But I'm thinking of Grandma's house, with its dark hallway and silver mirror. And how there were no pictures in that house, not even photos.

"You've had a hard life," says Greg. "But maybe it's made you strong."

I don't know what to say. "Mmm."

"Or maybe it's just made you snarky?" He gives me a nudge with his elbow.

"Huh!" I need to change the subject. "Did you always live abroad?" I ask. "Before the Institute?"

"Pretty much," says Greg. "What about you? Did you always live in Gatesbrooke?"

"Yes," I say. "Mostly in the New City. In fact, you know that time we went there? With Emanuel and Celestina, you had your Math lesson? That was the first time I went right into the Old City."

"To the Meeting Hall," says Greg.

A chill sinks through me. "Yes."

We sit there quietly for a while. *Why did you have to bring that up now, Greg?* I want to ask. But it's no surprise. I suspected he was following me that day, and now I know for sure. It's good that he's reminded me of how far from being friends we really are. I've known all along that these feelings have got to stop. Even if he liked me too, it could never work. One of us a liar, and the other a spy.

Greg's arm feels warm against mine, but the rest of me is getting colder and colder. I can't even feel my hands or feet anymore.

"What do you want to do, when you're older?" Greg asks me.

I think about this. I can tell the truth, because it's all just air. "I'd like to be an artist." I think of my walk around the Old City. "I'd like to live on a canal boat, with my dog."

"Let me guess," says Greg. "A scruffy brown-and-white spaniel?"

That makes me smile. Raymond. It's nice talking to Greg when I can't see his quizzical raised eyebrow. "What about you?"

"Maybe travel?" he says. "I might have a yacht and sail around the world."

"I'll come with you," I say. "I'd like to see the world."

"What about your dog?"

"He can come too. Dogs like swimming." I move my hands about to try and get the circulation going.

Greg picks up my hand. "You have very, very cold hands," he says, in his frowning voice. He cups both my hands in his and rubs them gently. His hands are so warm. He puts his arm around me and pulls me close. "You're shivering." He starts taking his jacket off.

"I'm not taking your coat again," I say.

"You're very stubborn." Greg pulls his backpack over. "Look, I've got my blazer in here. What about that?" He takes it out.

"All right." I stand up and put it on over Celestina's thin navy one.

Greg looks at me in the darkness. "Very elegant."

I sit down again, close to Greg, but only because it's warmer that way.

"You're still shivering," he says. "It's too cold to sleep."

"Mmm," I say. "Better not to try."

We sit there in silence for a while.

"Poor cold little Verity," says Greg at last. He puts his arm around me.

"Poor cold little Gregory," I say back. I can't believe how normal my voice sounds.

I don't move. I know Greg doesn't mean anything by it. All the same, when he pulls me close to his side I let myself slip toward him, so near that I can feel his face against my hair. I close my eyes, even though it's already dark. This is just one moment, that's all. I can have this one moment.

We sit in the dark tucked up in the corner waiting for the night to pass. I don't mind how long it lasts. My head is against Greg's neck. I can feel his breath in my hair. I wish. I wish I could tell him. I wish I could tell him everything.

"Greg?"

"Are you not asleep?" Greg says quickly.

"Night," I say.

"Night," says Greg. And something lightly touches the top of my head.

Did Greg just give me a good-night kiss? But I don't say anything, because if he did, it was only like my kiss-it-better kiss. A little bit of nothing.

CHAPTER 22

IT'S 9:15 IN the morning when we get back from Limbourne. We walk up the drive. Already the closeness of the night is evaporating. I look sideways at Greg, and a kind of pain takes hold of me. We walk carefully apart from each other. *Greg, the things I say to you aren't the things I think about you.*

Brer Magnus is standing at the window of his office watching us walk up the drive. He knows exactly who comes in and who goes out. I think Greg is nervous too.

Brer Magnus meets us in Reception and tells us to go to his office. But when we get there, he asks me to wait in the corridor. I look at Greg, but he accepts this and goes in. All the worry comes rumbling back. I'm supposed to meet Oskar in three days to give him the list of names. I'm so glad I put the visitors' book box back. But even so, it'll only cover me until they have another meeting. And isn't there one next weekend?

Brer Magnus closes the door, and I can't hear anything they say.

After a few minutes Greg comes out. He looks straight at me but he doesn't say anything. Our eyes lock together. Greg looks away first, and I walk into Brer Magnus's office, leaving the door open behind me. Being in here renews the worry that I haven't done anything about the visitors' book. What did Greg and Brer Magnus talk about?

"Greg has told me what happened," says Brer Magnus.

I nod.

"Well." He stands up. "I'm sure you want to get to your class."

I turn toward the door. "Yes. OK."

"Oh, and Verity?" he says. "You seem to be wearing Greg's jacket. Surely you remember what I said about girls wearing men's clothes?"

I look down. "Oh, yes." I take the jacket off. And feel myself turning red.

I can give Greg his jacket back at lunch. I go to the Sisters' house. It feels like a thousand years since I was here. I sit down on my bed, Greg's jacket still over my arm. It smells of the cold night at Limbourne station, and some other scent. Soap, deodorant? Something that Greg uses. I put it up to my face and breathe it in.

—

AT LUNCHTIME, GREG'S already in the canteen, sitting next to Jeremiah. I join the line for food and look over at him. He has a black eye. The cut on his cheekbone is an angry red but it's starting to close up. When I put my tray down opposite him, I feel a big smile spread over my face. I can't help it. But Greg doesn't look up.

"Greg?"

He looks at me briefly and smiles a businesslike little smile.

"How's your face?" My hand drifts up to touch my own cheek.

"Much better, thanks." He turns back to Jeremiah.

What happened in Brer Magnus's office?

"Hello, Verity," says Celestina, sitting down next to me. "What's this I hear about you two staying out all night?"

I look at Greg, but he's concentrating on his food. I turn back to Celestina and hand her the shoes. "I'm sorry I spoiled them."

Celestina waves the shoes away. "Keep them," she says.

"And I lost your hat. I'm sorry. I'll get you a new one."

"Really, Verity!" She gives me a stern look. "What a liability you are!" Then she laughs.

I didn't know how much I liked Celestina until now. And I realize I've forgotten Greg's jacket. I left it behind on my bed. Maybe I just don't want to give it back.

"Anyway," says Celestina, "I don't mind losing some shoes and a hat for a good cause." She smiles at me. "Greg's been telling us the Reconciliation Rally's going to be held in the Old City Meeting Hall, on the day before the Agreement is signed, in five months. It's on the anniversary of the massacre." She nods her head. "They're finally acknowledging it. That has to be a step forward."

Jeremiah leans across the table. "Did you like Yoremouth?"

I look up in surprise. Jeremiah never speaks to me. "Well, yes," I say. He's assuming I've never been there before. "Apart from the muggers."

Jeremiah's mouth curls up. "Greg told us," he says. "Nasty." I can tell he only believes me because he heard it from Greg first.

My eyes meet Greg's for a moment, but again his slide quickly away. He isn't the Greg who joked and talked on Limbourne platform. It's impossible to believe that he held me close all last night.

Lunch the next day is the same. I can't stand sitting here while Greg ignores me. And I have a job to do. I just want to get it over with now. I leave quickly and go to the library, because this is the perfect time to get the visitors' book. Then maybe I can sneak it back to Brer Magnus's office this afternoon while he's talking in the auditorium.

"Hello, Verity." The librarian, Mrs. Shelley, looks up as I come in, but then she goes into her office to make coffee, so I have time to get the book down and put it in my bag, tucked inside a file and hidden by a scarf. It would be better if I still had the fastener to hold the bag shut.

Then the loudspeaker cuts through the hush of the library: "All students please make your way to an emergency meeting in the auditorium."

Mrs. Shelley comes over to me. "I think you'll have to go too, Verity," she says. "I know you're working hard." She looks so worried at the thought of my reading being interrupted that I feel a stab of guilt.

On my way down the stairs I start to panic. *Don't take the book into the meeting!* But where can I hide it? The courtyard is filling with pupils waiting to get into the narrow passage that leads into the auditorium. I duck into the bathroom at the bottom of the library stairs and wait for an empty cubicle. If only I had something waterproof, the tank would make a perfect hiding place.

But this is a very old toilet and the tank is one of those high ones, with a chain. If I close the lid and stand on it, I can reach above it. I'm about to tuck the book on the top, toward the back, when something stops me. Fingerprints. Can you leave them on paper? Just in case, I get some paper and wipe the covers. *Hurry up, don't be the last one in!* I wrap the whole book in white toilet paper so that its dark cover is hidden, and place it on top of the tank.

Then I remember to pull the chain, and hurry out to join the stragglers going into the auditorium. I push past a few people so that I can go in as part of the crowd. Jeremiah is hovering near the doorway.

"There you are," he says when he sees me. His eyes flick over to the stage where Brer Magnus is talking to one of the teachers in the doorway.

I bet Brer Magnus has told him to check up on me. "Hello, Jeremiah," I say. "Shall we sit down?"

He turns red. "Yeah, sure," he says. He follows me to a seat.

Brer Magnus takes his place on the stage and sweeps the room with his searching gaze. "A shocking thing has happened," he says. "I don't wish to alarm you, but something has been removed from my office."

A little rustle goes through the room.

That's when I remember: the names! They're still in my art pad, right here in my bag!

Brer Magnus continues. "It was the visitors' book that was taken. It can only be because someone wants the names of those who attend our meetings. I don't have to explain to you what that could mean."

Now an angry murmur goes around the room.

"Your families, your friends. Under the spotlight." He stops and stares around the hall. "I think you all know the kind of attention they could receive."

What kind of attention does he mean? Surely if people aren't terrorists they have nothing to fear?

All the same, doubt takes hold of me. I grip one hand in the other to stop it from flying to my mouth and giving me away. Jeremiah doesn't look shocked at all. Brer Magnus probably told him already. Maybe that's what he was telling Greg when we got back.

"So I've decided to take an unprecedented step."

Stay still, don't move. Keep breathing. I know what he's going to say.

"I very much regret this, but we're going to have to search everyone before you leave this room."

Now there's a buzz of outrage. Could I slip the pages out of my bag and hide them in my clothes? Not now, everyone will be watching. Why didn't I put them with the book or leave them in the library?

"Please make an orderly line past the teachers at the front," says Brer Magnus. "I apologize to you all for this intrusion, but you will appreciate that this could only have been done by someone from within."

Yes, that's me. The enemy within. I want to throw up.

"Before we begin, I must inform you that today a security firm will be installing cameras and other devices in the school, starting with the Reception and Meeting Hall block."

While he speaks, teachers are moving to stand behind the small tables positioned at the front. There's nothing I can do except try to look innocent. I avoid Ms. Cobana's table, though. I don't want her keen eyes looking at me today.

Jeremiah follows close behind me. I think he disapproved of me from the start—he's probably longing for me to be busted. I empty my bag onto the table before I'm asked, and wait there looking casual, my heart pogoing under my blouse.

And it's fine, because there's clearly no visitors' book there. Just a wallet, my pencil case, my file, and my art pad. Containing two hundred and forty names. It's a teacher I don't know. He opens the file and gives it a little shake, just to be sure. *Don't open the pad!* I hold my breath.

"Sorry about that," he says, and hands me both the file and my bag.

Jeremiah's face falls. I still can't breathe.

When I get out of the auditorium I decide that if I can get the book back somewhere where it could have been mislaid, maybe Brer Magnus will stop thinking there's a spy in the school. Maybe now Greg will have to tell Brer Magnus about the hole in the fence. Best not to think about it too much. I hang back so that Jeremiah is ahead of me in the crush of students and I wait until I see him turn the corner toward the canteen.

Then I go back to the toilet and get the book down. I flush away the toilet paper and hide the book in the bottom of my bag. If I can get it back to the Meeting Hall before they set up the cameras, might Brer Magnus think it's been there all along? I'm sure they'll be watching his office. Better go now, before I lose my nerve.

But as I go into Reception, I hear footsteps running up behind me. Jeremiah has followed me. He must have turned back and watched until I came out of the toilet.

"Where are you going?" he asks. His face is happy and excited. He thinks he's caught me.

"Jeremiah!" I say. "I'm glad you're here. I just wanted to go and sit in the Meeting Hall for a little while, after that horrible meeting."

He stops, confused. Everything shows on Jeremiah's face.

"You wouldn't come with me, would you?"

"Er . . ." He takes a backward glance across the courtyard. He looks surprised now. "Well, OK."

"Thanks. It's just nice not to be alone," I say. "It's horrible thinking of someone sneaking around the school." And actually I really mean this. It *is* horrible. A little shudder escapes me.

We walk up the stairs in silence. I watch Jeremiah go over to the bench to take off his shoes, and before he turns, I crouch beside the little table where they kept the visitors' book the night of the Spring Meeting, and slide it out of my bag and under the brocade cloth. Then I move away, still kneeling on the floor, and start to take off my shoes, my breath light and fast, heart racing. I'm banking on Jeremiah not thinking how I could just kick them off while standing.

He's not looking at me. He's undoing his own shoelaces. By the time he stands up, my shoes are neatly deposited in the girls' shoe compartment and I'm waiting by the door. He didn't notice. We go into the hall and sit on our separate sides, divided by so much more than gender.

I look through the windows at the treetops as they sway their gentle dance. I think I've gotten away with it. My heart rate starts to calm. Jeremiah sits quietly across the hall, his head respectfully bowed. Greg would never have fallen for this. A creeping, nauseous guilt takes hold of me. I hate myself.

CHAPTER 23

OSKAR ARRANGED OUR rendezvous in the woods near the big oak, after school. I go back to the Sisters' house and in the bathroom there I transfer the folded sheets of art paper into the top pocket of my jacket. It's sunny and warm, with a breeze that smells of blossoms.

As I walk into Reception, I hear the noise of banging upstairs. They're installing the new cameras and I wonder if they've found the visitors' book yet. Mr. East is happy for me to take Raymond for a walk. He opens the gates for us and we cross the road and walk down toward the clearing where Oskar parks his motorbike. I'm early so I take off running through the woods, Raymond loping beside me, enjoying the sunlight and the washed-out stripes it throws onto the earth. Not far now.

Then I hear voices, just ahead. I stop and listen. Serafina's voice, then Emanuel's.

"What's that?" Celestina's there as well.

I walk forward. "It's only me," I say.

They're all there. Greg and Jeremiah too. All going somewhere without me.

Serafina flushes bright pink. "Verity!" she says. "We couldn't find you, and it's such a nice day."

I look at Greg, but he turns away. "That's OK," I say. "Where are you going anyway?"

"To the Trembling Rock. Celestina's never seen it."

I've never seen it either.

"And where are *you* going?"

Look at that, Greg's talking to me again. I stare hard at him, then down at the dog. "Me? Walking Raymond."

Jeremiah smiles at me. "Now you can come too," he says. "Lead on, Emanuel!"

Greg's eyebrow shoots up. We walk on. The conversation seems to have died now that I'm here. Oskar must be waiting for me not far away on the other side of the clearing. It would be much too risky to try and meet him now. I hope he's not angry.

It's nice in the trees. The sun is warm on my face and our feet crunch pleasantly on the carpet of brown fir needles as we head downhill. Raymond is busy, nose to the ground, following interesting smells.

"It's not far from here." Emanuel jumps down onto a narrow path below us.

Celestina looks back at us. "Come on, then. Let's put him out of his misery. Is it really worth it?" she calls down.

But Emanuel is already pushing his way through the bracken. I'm last, behind Greg. He stops at the bottom of the steep slope and turns back. "Do you want a hand?"

"I'm OK. But you can take Raymond." I pass him the leash. My pumps slip on a tree root as I slide down.

Greg passes me the leash, silently. Our fingers don't touch. I know what's different. He didn't use my name, and he always says my name. I'm surprised by the tears stinging the corners of my eyes.

I blink them away. It's not even my name, is it?

I catch up with him. "Greg," I say. "I still have your jacket."

He looks up. "Oh." His eyes slide away.

"I'll try and remember to bring it to dinner."

"OK."

Why won't you talk to me anymore? But I don't say that. What I say is, "Greg?"

He looks up, but not at me. "What?"

"Don't worry about the Math." I hold on to a silver birch branch to steady myself. "It was nice of you to help me. But that's enough."

Now he does look at me. He opens his mouth and closes it again. Then he shrugs. "It's up to you."

I jump down into the clearing. Jeremiah has observed the whole exchange while trying to look like he's taking a stone out of his shoe.

There's the rock, squatting in the clearing. It doesn't look like it's going anywhere.

"Is this your famous Trembling Rock, Emanuel?" snorts Celestina.

"Yup. Look." Emanuel puts his hands against the rock. Nothing happens. "Come on, guys," he calls. "I don't think one person can move it on their own."

So we all stand with our palms on the rock, which is warm from the sun.

"One, two, three, now!" calls Emanuel.

We push away. Slowly the rock begins to move. Back and forward it trembles, grinding on an invisible axle. Greg starts pushing it harder, rocking it faster and faster.

"Stop, stop!" shouts Serafina. "It'll roll right down the hill!"

"It can't," says Emanuel. "It's been here for hundreds of years."

As the rock trembles, it makes the faintest little rumble. It's rocking on its own momentum now.

When Emanuel starts to climb back up to the path, I turn to look at the rock once more. It's the size of a truck. I go back and touch the rough warm granite again. I can hear the others pushing their way through the bracken behind me, and a blackbird singing in the trees. I can almost hear the rock humming. Then a little crackling noise makes me jump.

Serafina is climbing back down the path. "Verity!" She comes up to me and stands with her back against the rock, hesitates. "I think I know what your secret is."

My heart starts pounding. I have no idea what she's going to say.

"You like Greg, don't you?"

If I tell her she's made a mistake, she'll want to know what my real secret is. So I don't say anything, yet. I stare up at the fir trees.

"It's OK," says Serafina. "Everyone always likes Greg."

I look at her in surprise. I think of Greg—serious, frowning Greg—in his checked shirts, handing things out in the Meeting Hall. Knowing all the answers and getting top grades. Doing whatever Brer Magnus asks. But then I see him drawing in the Art room, charcoal shards flying off the paper. Sitting next to Emanuel in the common room, legs sprawled across the coffee table, laughing. Or wrapping his jacket around my shoulders at Limbourne. Maybe that warm person is the Greg that everyone likes? Even now I'm not sure which one to believe in.

Serafina's still talking. "Don't worry. I won't tell him. Or anyone else."

"Oh. Thanks." Which is as good as admitting it. To change the subject, I ask her, "What about your boyfriend?"

She looks at me in surprise. "I told you. I had to end it."

I watch her profile as she stares ahead. The breeze is lifting her curls. "Was he upset?"

"Yes." She's trying not to cry.

"So why do it?" My voice sounds harsh. "You like him? He likes you? The only problem is he's the 'wrong flavor'?"

She looks at me, shocked. "I thought you understood."

I've been careless. "I'm sorry, Serafina, I do understand," I say. "It's just that you seemed to really like him. But you did the right thing." I nod firmly. What did she say before? "It was like oil and water. There was no future in it."

"Serafina? Verity?" There's a flurry of moving branches as Jeremiah leaps down into the clearing. "Are you coming?"

Good work, K, I tell myself. It's almost impossible to offend Serafina, but you've managed to do it.

—

WHEN WE GET back, I see that Mr. East has dug a new flower bed outside the lodge. His spade and trowel are lying on the dark soil but he's not there. I've never just left Raymond alone before, so I keep the leash on and turn to Serafina. "I need to find Mr. East. I'll see you later."

The others go into the foyer and Raymond and I set off around the front of the building. As we walk under Brer Magnus's open window, I hear Greg's voice. I stop, and that's when I hear him say, "No, sir, I don't want to have anything more to do with Verity Nekton."

The words cut into me. I run noiselessly on the grass, around the corner of the building and down the gentle slope toward the Sisters' house. I don't stop until I reach the rhododendron grove, and then I kneel down beside Raymond and bury my face in his warm fur. He gives my nose a quick lick.

"Raymond," I murmur. "I don't know what I did to make him hate me."

But then I think: it's not what I did; it's what I am. Maybe, somehow, Greg has found out that I'm not really Brotherhood. Maybe he's told Brer Magnus.

When I get back to the lodge Mr. East is kneeling by the freshly turned soil, planting seedlings. He stands up, wiping a sprinkling of earth away from his face, and gestures at the little green plants. "Sunflowers."

I'm not going to hide away anymore, I decide, as I make my way to the Sisters' house. I wanted to help Oskar for good reasons, and in spite of everything I know now about the goodness of the Brotherhood too, those reasons are still true. All I have to do is give him the list, finish my exams, and see out the year.

It isn't me who's stonewalling Greg without even saying why. It isn't me telling Brer Magnus I want nothing more to do with him. But then I think: which one of us has the false name—false everything really—and is here as an impostor? And if Greg does know, or even suspects, that's enough reason to freeze me out.

It's not fully dark yet, and the air is scented with crumpled petals, swirling in the breeze like feathers in a pillow fight. *Not everything was false*, I console myself. I stand under the porch and fish in my bag for my key. Then I hear a scrape of gravel.

Greg is under the arch that leads to the library. "Verity," he says, very quietly.

I step back onto the path.

"I'm sorry," he says.

"Me too," I say.

And then he goes, dissolving into the shadows of the arch. And now it feels much more final than it did before, because our "sorry" isn't really for what has happened between us. It's for things that are too big, things that have gone on for too long, things we can't change.

CHAPTER 24

THE VISITORS' BOOK turns up before the next weekend meeting and although Brer Magnus must know it was taken from his office, there's been no further mention of it. I tape the list of names to the back of my bedside table so that I don't have to keep hiding it and can get it quickly if Ril turns up. But I don't hear from her.

Greg and I are polite to each other but that's all. If he does know who I really am, he's giving nothing away. The only time I can forget is when I go swimming in the pond near the rhododendrons. The rest of the time I am wound up in the tense fear of discovery. The days pass in eating, sleeping, and studying.

Then, on the day before term ends, Brer Magnus gives me a note from Ril.

Dear Verity,

I'll pick you up tomorrow after the garden party. Please have everything ready.

Ril

The summer vacation begins with a bang here. First there's a dance and then a garden party for families too. I know what Ril means by "everything"—the list of names. The cocoon of studying and living here bursts open and all the worries come crawling out again.

It's almost over, this life, and I still don't know whether I'll be coming back after the summer. I still don't know if there's a sleeper cell at the school either—the only reason I came here in the first place. It's the last dance tonight. I lay the deck-chair dress on my bed.

"Verity, you can have this, if you want." Celestina holds up an emerald-green silk dress. It's the one she was wearing the first time I met her. "Try it on."

When I pull it over my head I can see that she's taken up the hem for me. In the mirror, wearing this, my eyes look almost as green as Celestina's. She's watching to see if I like it. If I'm not careful my eyes will fill with tears. They do anyway and I smile at Celestina in the glass.

Serafina looks up. "Oh, Verity," she says. "You look lovely!"

Celestina nods. "Not bad." She picks up her brushes. "I'll do your hair if you like."

"OK," I say. I reckon I'll have to let her, as she's been so nice about the dress. Though in a way, I wouldn't have minded wearing my old friend, the deck-chair. For old times' sake.

Celestina sweeps a comb through my hair, which now hangs past my shoulder blades. It's a serious business to her, so we don't talk. And that's nice. I'd like to tell her I'll miss her, but I don't know how. Somehow I think she knows anyway. Her fingers are quick and light in my hair. I haven't been to a hairdresser for years. No one else has touched my hair since I was a little girl. Then Celestina gets out her makeup bag and does my face as well, humming softly as she brushes and smudges.

Finally she's finished. "Do you want to have a look?" She swivels me around to face the mirror, and just for a moment it's as though I'm looking at Greg's drawing of me. Celestina smiles behind me in the mirror.

—

THE GLASS DOORS of the canteen are open and the party has spilled out to the lawn. It's nearly dark already and the light from the room pools on to the grass outside. Brotherhood parties start late and go on all night: every now and then some random detail like this from Oskar's Manual pops into my head. They must think we citizens are very boring, with our formal civic ceremonies instead.

Inside, dancers swirl around the room, and a band plays wild fiddle music, with flutes and no singers. I don't know these dances, but everyone else knows when to turn and when to stand still. I can see Emanuel dancing, and Greg walking toward us. He's wearing a white shirt. He takes Celestina's hand. They look very comfortable with each other and I wonder again if they're together. Her hair swings around her shoulders as she laughs up at Greg. He whirls her around, and his face breaks into a smile.

I stand in the open doorway. The breeze swishes the silk dress against my legs, so that although my face feels hot, the rest of me is cool. I can see all my friends. I can call them that, on this last night. Celestina is still dancing with Greg. They turn between the two lines of dancers. Celestina laughs, her long black hair spinning out behind her. Greg has had a haircut. I know the shape of his head from drawing him so many times, and I know the feel of it from holding it to wipe the blood from his face. I feel tears welling in my eyes. I never used to cry before I came here. I must stop this.

Serafina sees me and stops clapping to wave. Opposite her, Emanuel dances, his wild curls springing in time to the music.

I turn away and look outside. Colored lanterns hang from all the trees. The sky's blue dark rather than black dark, and there's a half moon hanging above the rhododendron grove. It's so beautiful that I can't stand it. I didn't think this through on the back of Oskar's motorbike all those weeks ago. I'm just about to slip across the lawn into the darkness when someone grabs my elbow from behind.

"Come on, Verity! You have to dance this one!" It's Serafina. She pulls me into the hall, into a circle with Emanuel, Celestina, Jeremiah—and Greg. I'm in be-tween him and Jeremiah. Everyone has their arms around each other's shoulders, but the girls' arms are on top. I have to stretch up to reach Greg's shoul-der, my hand slipping on his cotton shirt. His face is flushed with dancing and his hair is sticking to his forehead in wisps.

He looks down and sees me gazing at him. "What?" he says, laughing. It's as if we've put every-thing to one side for just this dance.

"Hold on tight!" calls Serafina. "Don't let go!"

My right hand is around Greg's neck, and my left around Jeremiah's. The music starts again, and the circle whirls around, faster and faster, till suddenly my legs leave the ground and I'm spinning around like the wing of a fan. All the girls' feet have left the ground. It's a mad and crazy dance, and I'm holding on to Greg and Jeremiah just to stop myself from flying off into the air.

After the dance, we sit on the lawn that leads down to the rhododendron grove. Everyone is here.

Serafina is next to me. Every time she laughs, she touches my arm lightly. It's lovely to feel so wanted, so at home, in spite of everything that's happened with Greg.

Celestina is opposite me. She's very quiet tonight. I keep catching her gazing out into the darkness behind me. She has let a long strand of shiny black hair fall across half her face. I don't know why. If my face looked like hers, I wouldn't hide any of it.

Emanuel is stretched out next to Serafina. He's not talking much either. When he does, it's to Jeremiah, opposite him.

Greg's sitting beside me. He's quiet too, not joking around with Emanuel tonight. He's leaving the Institute for good tomorrow. They've all known each other forever. It must be a sad thing for them, to say good-bye.

"Verity," says Greg, not really looking at me.

"Yes?"

He's speaking so softly that I have to lean closer to hear him.

"Emanuel and I and Celestina are going for a swim tonight," he says. "Come, if you like. We're meeting at the pond after this." He pauses. "It's the last night."

I don't know what to say at first. "Thanks," I say at last. But I know I won't go.

—

ONLY SERAFINA AND I go back to the room. Serafina seems down. She doesn't mention her citizen boyfriend, so neither do I.

"The others are going for a swim," I say.

"I know," she says. "You go, if you want. I don't mind. I can't swim."

"No, it's OK."

I lie in the dark with my arms behind my head. The darkness presses against my eyeballs. It's not too late. I could still go. Greg asked me to. But then I think of Celestina and Greg, and I stay where I am. My last night in the Sisters' house. Eventually I fall asleep.

I wake up as the door creaks open. Celestina is creeping in, just like she did on that first night here. She tiptoes over toward her bed. I can smell the peaty scent of the pond, and now that it's too late, I know I made a mistake. Greg asked me to go. It was the first time he's spoken kindly to me since that night when he stood beneath the arch and said he was sorry. Oh, why didn't I go? He asked me. After tomorrow I may never see Greg again. The thought wedges itself into my throat.

—

I STAND AT the top of the steps that lead to the Brothers' house, in the walled courtyard where strawberries and champagne are being served to students, parents, and visitors. It's the last day, quiet after last night's party on this golden afternoon with its clear light that makes everything look not quite real. Serafina is over by the drinks table, in her favorite pink skirt, standing with her parents and smiling a muted smile. Her parents look as if they're at a wedding. Emanuel is very close to Serafina.

I can't see Greg, or Jeremiah, in the crowd. I put my dish of strawberries on the corner of a trestle table and watch Celestina standing alone with a glass of champagne in her hand. Then I look behind me. Greg is on his own too. His family is still abroad. My friends are lonely; it's not just me.

Brer Magnus's voice goes up and down with the birdsong. "Dark days lie ahead," he intones. "We must all be vigilant."

Reconciliation means dark days for him? I look away quickly, but suddenly he is right in front of me, holding out his hand and smiling. "Congratulations, Verity," says Brer Magnus as I stiffly shake his hand.

But before I ask him what he means, I see Ril coming through the arch toward me. She smiles from beneath her official social worker wig. Instantly I become aware of the folded papers tucked into my pocket. I took them off the bedside table last night, and they've been burning a hole ever since.

—

And now brer Magnus is distracted: Jeremiah's father is patting his shoulder and talking to him.

I start as Celestina touches my arm. "You didn't come swimming last night," she says.

"Did you and Greg have a nice time?"

She leans closer. "You think I like Greg?" she whispers. "Is that what you think?"

"Maybe," I whisper back.

"No." She pauses. "He's a boy." She gives me a quick, sad smile. "He knows my parents don't accept me."

I think back to what she said before: *My parents like me better from a distance.* "I'm sorry, Celestina," I say.

She shakes her head. "It's OK, it's fine. Greg . . . he's the only one I can really talk to." She smiles, brightly this time. "And now you." Then she turns away.

Out of the corner of my eye I see Greg shaking Brer Magnus's hand. He's leaving. Celestina goes and puts her arms tightly around him, and they hug silently. Then slowly Greg makes his way over to me.

"Well, bye then," he says.

"Bye."

I don't move toward him.

There's a long moment when our eyes lock together. I don't breathe. All I can see are Greg's brown eyes. Then he turns away and is gone, down the steps toward the Brothers' house, his feet scuffing up tiny flecks of dirt.

Ril has reached Brer Magnus and is waiting to greet him.

Brer Magnus is speaking to me again, but his voice has blurred into a ringing in my ears. Everything stills in the green and golden air. And there goes the last tiny red sight of Greg, away down through the trees.

All my moments seem balanced on this one moment. What can I offer Greg? Almost everything he knows about me is false. I'm spinning off into thin air.

Far away, I hear Brer Magnus's voice: "So, Verity, what do you think?"

And Ril: "That's tremendous news, Verity!"

I think I must tell Greg who I am.

The deck-chair swishes around my legs as I turn and run down the steps, toward the Brothers' house. I hear shocked voices behind me. Maybe I am too late. Now I'm leaping down the steps two at a time, kicking off my pumps and hitching up my dress, almost turning my ankle. Greg has vanished behind the rhododendrons. He's at the bottom of the steps, where there's an arch with a wooden gate. His hand is on the latch.

"Greg! Greg!"

He stops and looks up, then turns away and pulls the handle down.

"Wait for me!" I call as I reach the bottom of the steps. He's about to open the gate into the Brothers' garden, but he stops.

He waits, his hair flattened to his head by the heat. In the shadow of the wall, his eyes look black. They have already said good-bye to me.

I reach him. I catch hold of his hands. Surprise flickers into his face.

"I couldn't let you go . . ." But I have to stop to catch my breath.

"Without saying good-bye properly?" Greg shrugs.

"No! I couldn't let you go. I can't let you go."

Now he really looks at me. He isn't smiling, but he takes a little step toward me. He's so near that it's easy for me to put my hands on his shoulders and pull him closer. Then I put my arms around his neck to stop him from leaving. His short hair feels as silky as a seal's.

Greg takes my hands, so I have to step back. But

he holds them tightly. "Verity," he says. "I don't want to let you go either."

"There's something I have to tell you first," I say, pulling farther back so that I can look at his face. But it's so good to be able to look right into his eyes without hiding everything that I stop and just smile at him instead. Our eyes fix on each other. You could swear there were no secrets between us. "You don't really know me."

"No, wait. Stop," says Greg. "Don't tell me." He pulls me close to him again. "Don't tell me," he whispers into my hair. "Not yet."

I know I'll have to think about what that means, but not now. Later. At the back of my mind a foreboding lurks, because I know this is one bridge I'll never be able to burn.

"Verity," says Greg, "I have to go now or I'll miss my plane. But give me your address so we can see each other before we come back."

"Before we come back?"

He raises his eyebrows. "Brer Magnus hasn't told you? You got an unconditional offer for junior year." He smiles. "And a Distinction in Art."

Of course Greg knew this before I did. Maybe that's what Brer Magnus was just about to tell me.

"And you?"

He smiles at me. "I'm staying too. I'm not going to go for Medicine now, so I might as well stay here and do Art."

Now I'm smiling.

"It was because of you," he says. "You said, *'It's your life.'*"

I wish I'd said that to myself, when I first met Oskar. But then I never would have met Greg.

"So, your address?"

"I don't have one."

Greg leans back so he can look at me, one of his old looks.

That makes me smile again. "My social worker is here to pick me up, but I don't know where I'm going."

Greg holds me to him. I feel his back through the soft flannel of his red-checked shirt. His hands are warm on my back. I breathe in the smell of him. I feel his heart beating, fast, just the other side of mine.

"We can be together," he says, so softly that I'm not sure if I heard it. It's almost as if he's saying it to himself.

"Even though you don't really know me?"

"I do know you, Verity Nekton." He tilts his head back so that he can look into my face. "I know who you are."

For a long moment we stand there, our eyes meeting.

Greg digs in his pocket for a pen and an old Gatesbrooke bus ticket. "Here," he says. "This is my phone number. My family and I get back in a month. Call me. I'll come and get you. OK?"

I nod. "OK."

He pushes the gate open, but he's holding my hand, so I walk through with him. The Brothers' house is bigger than ours, with a garden and a small cul-de-sac on the side where the road from the main parking lot ends. A taxi waits there, and Greg's bags are on the porch.

I clutch the ticket in my hand as I watch Greg get

into the taxi. It drives slowly away. Then it stops. Greg's door opens. He runs back across the gravel toward me.

He holds my face between his hands, and he stares into my eyes. "Verity . . ." he says. Then we kiss. It's not a kiss-it-better good-night kiss. Not a little bit of nothing. I stop thinking about the future and the past. I feel the ticket crumpling in my fist.

"Promise me you'll call?"

I nod.

"You won't forget?"

"No."

Then he's gone. But I can't feel sad now. Dreams do sometimes come true. Even for me.

CHAPTER 25

RIL IS WAITING at the top of the steps. As usual, she looks tense. But she fixes a bright smile on her face when she sees me.

I speak first. "I'll go and get my bag," I say, walking under the arch that leads to the Sisters' house. I turn back and look through it, at Serafina and her parents, Emanuel with his arm around his mother's shoulders. Children are gathered near the strawberry table, their faces stained pink. I've done it, haven't I? I've convinced Brer Magnus that I'm a Brotherhood girl and I've passed my exams too. But the list is still in my pocket.

I run across the lawn and get out my key. *Do it quickly, before you have time to think.* Inside the house I put the latch down to lock the door, and instead of going upstairs, I go into the kitchenette.

I put the papers in the metal sink and light a match and let it crinkle up the edges with black and then gold until there's nothing but fragments of charred tissue. Then I turn on the tap and leave it running while I fetch Georgette's lemon air freshener from the bathroom. Afterward I shut the kitchen door.

I feel as if a huge weight has been lifted off me. I start humming as I run upstairs for my bag. But then there's a volley of knocks on the outside door. I grab my bags and run back down with them. I'm taking everything with me. It's not much anyway.

Ril is standing there. "I thought I'd give you a hand," she says. "Then I'll take you to your new room."

—

WE DON'T TALK much in the car. She drives into the Old City, past the Meeting Hall, which is caged around with scaffolding. I suddenly see why—it's being cleaned. Ril crosses the canal bridge and turns down toward the shoreline. Old dockyards and warehouses line the waterfront, and the sea disappears into mudflats.

She pulls up outside a boarding house. There are houses on one side of the road only. The other side is taken up by a huge old police station, built from big stones so dirty that they look black. The entrance is directly opposite the front door of the boarding house.

"Up here," says Ril.

My spirits drop as we climb the stairs. The carpet stinks, and on the landing there is the kind of toilet you would pay not to have to use. My room has a bed and a kitchenette.

"Here you go," says Ril. "Now." She sits down on the one chair.

I sit on the high narrow bed.

"A few things to run through. First, there's food in the fridge and the cabinet. Second, there's a curfew for Hoo—for Brotherhood after nine, since the bomb."

"Can't I just wear my own clothes for the summer, then?" I don't like the idea of not being able to go out at night.

Ril looks at me pityingly. "Of course not. You're Verity Nekton now. Continuity, K."

She stands up and takes an envelope out of her bag, "I'll meet you every week to give you your money and check in." She hands the envelope to me.

"Oskar promised me I'd be able to contact him."

"Oh yes, thanks for reminding me." She takes a cell phone out too. "Here you go. I filled it up, and Oskar's and my numbers are in there. There's a load of other fake numbers in the contacts, in case it falls into the wrong hands." She walks over to the door. "One more thing: have you got the list of people who attended the Spring Meeting?"

I walk over to the window and open it. "No."

"What do you mean?" She frowns. "Where is it?"

I turn back to face Ril. Then I shrug. "I couldn't get it," I say. "They've tightened up on security recently, cameras in the Meeting Hall block and everything."

"That's disappointing, K."

I know I should apologize, but I can't bring myself

to do it. I just stand and look back at Ril, waiting for her to go away.

"Well, that's it, then," she says eventually.

—

I DON'T ASK her when I can see Oskar. I can call him myself now. But I don't. There are far too many thoughts churning around in my mind. To keep them at bay, I clean everything and unpack my stuff and make some toast. But as soon as I curl up in the chair by the window, they crowd back in.

It was so easy to tell Greg how I felt. I was so sure, I still am. But I shouldn't have done it, because I can't see how I can tell Greg what I've done and who I really am, and then carry on working for Oskar for another year. And if I tell Oskar I want to stop now, I'll have nothing. I'm nobody.

Down in the street a minibus pulls up outside the police station. Two policemen go around to the back and open the doors. It doesn't take long for them to hustle out the boys inside. And guess what? All of them are Brotherhood.

I look at my watch. Half past nine. Surely they haven't been arrested just for being out after nine? It's horrible to know that I can't go out for a walk along the seafront without risking arrest. And without the Reconciliation Agreement this is only one of the things Brotherhood people have to live with.

At least I have a TV. I turn it on and flick through the channels. Maybe Greg has changed his mind anyway. Why did I pin my hopes on a few words spoken in a hurry?

In the street below, a car shrieks to a halt and four or five Brotherhood boys in masks leap out. No, one of them is a girl. They throw something at the front of the police station, and I hear breaking glass. Then they're back in the car and screaming off again. Moments later they're followed by a police car and a van, sirens shrieking.

I think of the promise I made to Oskar. None of the reasons for doing this, being a spy, have gone away. It's just that now I don't trust him. Does he really know that only a few Brotherhood people are terrorists? These thoughts dance endlessly round and round each other in my mind.

—

A MONTH PASSES. Most days I go out sketching, filling two sketchbooks with studies of the canal towpath or the Old City buildings. Ril checks up on me once a week. I don't know why Oskar hasn't been in touch. Is it because I failed to get the list for him? Ril doesn't mention it again. There's no way around the curfew. Not with the police station opposite and no back door.

I start trying Greg's number from a pay phone. There's no way I'm going to use the phone Oskar gave me to call him. Then one day Greg answers. The weeks fly back and I'm outside the Brothers' house again, having to let him go. But now he says that he wants me to come and stay with his family in their house in the country. I say yes, and I arrange it around Ril's visits so she won't know.

I SIT ON the train, looking out on the rolling hills. *I'm going to see him at the next station.* That's all I can think about, as I stare out at the streams winding through soft green meadows. However strange I might look, I can't stop smiling the whole way there.

Greg is standing alone, looking up and down the platform at the train windows. His hair has grown longer over the summer, not very Brotherhood. He pushes it out of his eyes, squinting against the sunlight. He's wearing long shorts that skim his hip bones because he's gotten thinner.

He doesn't see me until I get off the train. I pull my red suitcase behind me along the platform, feeling so nervous that I'm hanging back, even though I've been longing for this moment, thinking it out so many times that now it's almost as if it's already happened.

Greg sees me. He gives me a beam of a smile: a smile I could never have imagined. We sort of hug each other, not sure whether to kiss. I didn't imagine how much I like him.

Greg laughs. He reaches for my bag. "I've got a car." His arms are brown. "It was for my sixteenth birthday, but we only got it last week."

"I didn't know you could drive." I don't mention that I can drive too, because my driving was kind of unofficial, long ago on the runway of a disused airport, in a tractor with other kids from the children's home.

The car is an old four-door hatchback. As I get in, I see black grease spreading out from under the wheels.

Greg looks down. "It always does that." He drops

his keys on to the seat while he puts my bag in the back. "It's not far."

I pick up his keys. The key fob is a round object. "What's this?"

Greg whistles, and it begins to flash and bleep. "You never know when you might lose your keys." He gives me a sheepish smile.

I shake my head and laugh. He looks sideways at me, a little bit worried. Then he laughs too. He starts the engine and pulls away from the curb.

"Is it nice to be with your family?" I ask. My voice comes out dry.

"It's good," says Greg. "My sisters are driving me crazy, though." He glances at me again. "But don't worry, they'll love you."

Suddenly I feel very nervous. I don't know how to fit into a family.

—

GREG STOPS THE car outside a weathered stone house. The front door is open, and a little girl is skipping up and down the top step.

"That's Angelina," says Greg. "Don't take it personally if she just giggles at you."

A tall girl with long brown hair appears behind Angelina. That must be Meredith. Then I see Greg's parents in the hallway as well. The whole family is framed in the doorway. I can't decide if that makes them look like they're guarding the house or welcoming me. They look close. When I see them I think, *Greg's family*. Not *Brotherhood family*. Oh, but what will they think of me?

Greg puts his arm around my waist and pulls me toward him. "This is Verity."

I glance up at him. He's beaming again. He looks proud of me, and that makes me feel a stab of pain.

Angelina hops down the steps, her straight chestnut hair swinging over her shoulders. She looks up at me. "Are you Greg's girlfriend?"

"Um," I begin, but it doesn't matter, because she breaks into peals of cackling laughter.

"Shut up!" Meredith frowns.

Angelina grabs hold of my hand in her small strong one and drags me into the kitchen, where the pine table is set, ready for dinner.

"Let's show Verity her room first," says Rosanna, Greg's mom.

She takes me up to the top of the house, to an attic room under the sloping roof. Greg follows behind her, with Angelina at his heels.

"This is Greg's room," she says. "He's sleeping downstairs."

Behind her, I see Greg raise his eyebrows. I look around the room. There are books piled under the desk and on top of it too. Outside, trees with feathery leaves whisper against the window.

We go back to the kitchen. On the way down, Greg takes my hand, and I grip it in mine.

"You sit here, Verity," says Angelina, pulling me down on to the seat next to hers. She knocks a fork onto the floor and dives under the table.

Greg sits opposite me. Our eyes meet and he smiles. I've never seen him smile so much. It's almost unnerving. Meredith sets a big dish of chicken in the middle of the table. Greg's dad, Gerontius, opens a bottle of red wine. Rosanna is already at the table, leafing through a medical journal. She pushes her glasses up her nose. "There's an interesting article about ulcerated feet here, Gerry."

"*Mom*," says Meredith.

Greg directs a heavenward glance at me.

Rosanna tosses her journal onto the kitchen cabinet, where it totters for a moment on top of the stack of other magazines, books, and papers. "Help yourself to chicken and rice, Verity." She pushes the dish toward me.

"There's two pieces each," says Angelina quickly.

"Angelina!" Meredith glares across the table. "Don't be rude."

"Well, there are."

I take a piece of chicken.

Gerontius sets a full glass of wine in front of Rosanna. "I got stopped today in town," he says to her.

"Again?" Her voice is sharp.

Gerontius shrugs. "It was a patrol car this time." He pours water into Angelina's glass, spilling some down the side. "They were actually going in the opposite direction. Then they saw me, and that was it. Lights, siren . . ."

A silence falls. Across the table I become aware of Greg's eyes, fixed on me. He and Meredith exchange glances.

Angelina looks from face to face. "Why, Dad?" she begins.

Rosanna shakes her head at Gerontius.

"Who stopped you?" Angelina's voice is insistent.

"The important thing is to remove the necrotic tissue before it spreads to the bone," says Rosanna quickly.

"Oh, yes?" Gerontius helps himself to brown rice.

Rosanna whips around to get her journal and flashes a photo of an ankle oozing pus at them. "See?" she says brightly. "Too late to operate on the foot drop at this stage."

"Ugh!" Angelina covers her eyes.

"Do you have to?" says Meredith. "Please?"

"What?" Rosanna peers around. "Oh. Sorry. Sorry, Verity. I always forget." She reaches back to replace the journal and the whole pile slides off the dresser. "Oops," she says. "Gregory could have been a doctor, Verity." She fixes Greg with a sudden stare, very like the one he's directed at me so many times. "But instead he's throwing away all chance of that and he wants to study cartoons."

—

AFTERWARD, WE ALL wash the dishes together. Greg and I dry, and the girls put away. It's so ordinary, yet so strange to be part of a family routine. When we've finished, Rosanna announces, "Angelina, it's time for bed."

We go into the sitting room. Greg and Meredith and I sit down on the comfortable old sofas, then Angelina comes bouncing in.

"I want you to read my story, Greg."

He gets up, but in the doorway he turns to me and says, "Don't go away!"

I wait there for him, even after Meredith goes upstairs too. I pick up a magazine about Physiotherapy.

After a while Rosanna's footsteps clip down the hall. "Did you get Meredith's passport replacement form?" she says.

I hear Gerontius walking toward her. They're just outside the room. "Yes, I did," he says. "But I wish we could wait until after the Reconciliation Agreement becomes law. Look at the questions." Papers rustle as Rosanna flicks through them.

I don't think I should be listening to this, but I feel too awkward to go out. If only Greg would come back. I try to concentrate on the journal, but it's dense scientific jargon.

But then Rosanna reads out from the form: "If a citizen, go to page thirty-five. If Brotherhood, answer questions eleven-A to twenty-nine."

"Let me see." There's silence for a moment. Gerontius's voice sounds tense with anger even though he's trying to talk quietly. "What sort of questions are these? All your family and friend connections? Detailed information about where you go on weekends? It's outrageous."

"We can't go back abroad knowing Meredith's passport will expire while we're still away. And we must have done it for Greg," says Rosanna.

"Yes, but then we couldn't expect anything better," insists Gerontius. "Now we can. If we could just hold on for a couple of months, there'll only be the one form for everyone. Meredith won't ever need to be on the fingerprint database."

"That's true . . ." Rosanna sounds worried. "She won't need an ID card until she's sixteen anyway . . . But we haven't got any choice." I hear her putting shoes in the shoe rack. "And let's just hope the Reconciliation Agreement isn't derailed," she says darkly.

Greg's family have had years of this to deal with. Thanks, Oskar, for putting *my* fingerprints on *my* ID card when I didn't even need to have one. But I've only lived like this for a few months. I don't think I've ever felt so horrible. Such an impostor.

Suddenly I know I can't ever lie to Greg again. I'm going to tell him the truth, whatever the consequences.

He comes back in. I look up at him. He's smiling the loveliest smile as he sits down beside me. "Hey," he says softly. "What's wrong?"

"Greg," I say, "there's something I have to tell you."

But before he can reply, his mother breezes in. You'd think the conversation about the passport form had never happened.

"OK, you kids," she says with forced cheeriness, "let me help you get your bed ready, Gregory."

It's clear Rosanna wants me to go. Between her and little Angelina, it's going to be almost impossible to be alone with Greg today. And so I have one night to lie in his bed, listening to the swishing of the trees that he listened to when he was a child, remembering his eyes as he said good night. Knowing that we are still friends.

—

WE SPEND THE next morning picking blackberries to make jam. Meredith stirs the bubbling mixture. She's so hot that her hair has frizzed up all around her face. Every now and then she drips a bit onto a plate and tips it to see if it's set. So far it's still running.

I pour hot water into the jam jars on the draining board. It's an old wooden board that slopes down into the porcelain sink, so the jars aren't level. Angelina is sitting at the table writing "Blackberry Jam" and the date on sticky labels.

"You'll never finish that if you do each letter in a different color, Angelina," says Meredith.

"Yes, I will. And I want them in different colors."

Greg hums softly to himself as he rolls out pastry on a marble slab set into the kitchen counter. He has a smudge of flour on his nose and his hair is sticking up wildly at the back. Angelina is humming too, a different tune. Meredith sighs at the jam. She rubs her nose furiously with the back of her hand.

What am I doing here? I feel hot and cold suddenly at the hugeness of my deception. This family has trusted me as a true friend, someone who is the same as them. Not a spy like the passport form, snooping into their lives to find out where they are.

"Are you OK, Verity?" asks Meredith.

I put the kettle down. I must have been standing frozen, holding it. Greg stops humming and half-turns.

"I'm fine," I say. "Just hot."

"It is hot," says Meredith. "Oh! Oh! I think the jam's jammed!"

When all the jars stand full on the draining board, treacly black jam running down the glass, Meredith puts the pan in the sink. She has a big blob of jam on her nose, exactly where Greg has a smear of flour on his.

"You two have matching noses," I say, and they both turn at the same moment to look at me with round brown eyes like owls, and jam and flour on their noses. I burst out laughing.

"I don't think we have to put up with this, do you, Meredith?" says Greg.

"No," says Meredith.

Greg pounces and grabs both my arms from behind. "I don't want Verity to feel left out."

"Me neither," says Meredith, painting cooled jam from the plate on to my nose.

Greg twists around to look at my face. "Maybe just a bit more?" he suggests.

Meredith smears jam on to both my cheeks. I nearly get free, but then Greg starts tickling me.

"What are you doing?" Angelina stands up and stares at us. "What a mess!"

Greg lets go of me and catches Angelina, picking her up and running around the table with her.

"Stop it, Greg!" she shouts. "If you put jam on me I'll tell on you! Stop it! I don't like it!"

Greg puts her down.

She runs over to me. "Tell them, Verity."

"Gregory and Meredith," I say sternly. "You are behaving very badly with the jam."

The happiness of this moment pushes everything else away.

Angelina goes back to her labels. Meredith turns

back to the sink. Greg comes over and stands right in front of me, breathing heavily.

"You've got jam on your face," he says. "Shall I get it off for you?"

He leans close, but at the last minute he grabs the tea towel and wipes my face with it. I grip the drawer handle behind me to stop myself from putting my arms around his neck and kissing his floury face.

"Yours is just as bad," I say. "But maybe it's an improvement."

—

GREG IS IN the garden, taking the sheets off the washing line. I go out to help him. Everyone else stays at the kitchen table, cutting up fruit. I walk down the lawn, my bare feet sinking into the long grass, which is damp with dew. Up until now, I haven't been alone with Greg at all. It's lovely in this home, so different from the quiet, solemn life I lived with Grandma. But I have brought something ugly here with me.

"Greg. We need to talk."

"Oh," says Greg. "'We need to talk,' already?"

"No," I say. "Not *that* 'we need to talk.' But there's something I need to tell you. Something I have to tell you."

Greg passes me two ends of a sheet so that we can fold it together. He takes back the sheet and folds it once more. "Verity." His voice sharpens. "Don't tell me yet. Whatever it is."

I unpeg a pillowcase. "I want to tell you before we get any closer," I whisper. "In case, if you knew, you wouldn't want—"

Greg comes up to me. We're behind a sheet, so nobody in the house can see us. He puts his hand over my mouth. "Shh," he says. "Don't say any more. Or I'll have to tell you . . ." He shakes his head.

"Tell me what?" I push his hand away.

"You see?" says Greg. "If you tell me whatever it is, I'll have to be completely honest with you too. But it's too soon. We haven't had enough of a chance yet."

"I just want you to know who I am."

Greg puts his arms around me. "I told you at the Institute, I know who you are, Verity Nekton."

I open my mouth to tell him that that's who I'm not, but Greg stops me, by kissing me. His face smells of sunshine. He pulls away first.

"Just wait a little longer," he says into my ear. "Then we'll both tell each other everything. We'll find ways to be alone together. Soon, I promise. But not yet. OK?" He looks at me. "OK, Verity? Please?"

He holds my face between his hands so that we are looking right into each other's eyes. His are soft and brown. It's so lovely to be able to look openly into each other's eyes. But then I have to close mine, because everything's not open, is it?

"Greg."

"Please, Verity. Don't tell me," he says. "Just until we get back to school. Please."

"Later, then," I murmur, and we kiss again. I should be relieved because I don't have to say anything now after all. But it hasn't gone away, this thing which is still there between us. Even though, the way we're clinging to each other, you'd think there was nothing wrong.

"YOUR FRUIT SALAD IS READY!" shouts Angelina from the other side of the sheet. She lifts up the bottom and ducks under, standing there for a moment, frowning from Greg to me.

CHAPTER 26

ON THE LAST day of the summer vacation I get the bus back from the Old City to the Institute. Once again, I pull my red case up the drive. Once again, I am entering dishonestly, a citizen spy in Brotherhood clothing. Oskar won't just let me go. Everything I own is in the red case and the wool shoulder bag with its new duffel-coat fastener.

Rosanna sewed the fastener on for me. "It makes a change to sew a thing, not a person, Verity," she said, and it took me a moment to remember she's a surgeon.

I smile at the thought of Greg's leaky car dripping oil along this tidy gravel drive. The gates open for me, and Raymond gives me the kind of welcome only a dog can give. I stroke his lovely silk ears while he bows his head against my leg and fans his tail back and forth. Mr. East's sunflowers stand in front of the lodge, and because it's been a hot summer, they're taller than me. One of them lowers over me like a sad umbrella, too heavy now for its stem. I lift it gently. The seeds are starting to rot here and there, spiraling around, dense black in places. The forked gold petals crackle under my fingers, reminding me that summer is over.

"These are nice," I say to Mr. East, who is standing in the lodge doorway. "Can I still take Raymond for walks?"

"Of course." He looks out at the garden. "They're dying. Need cutting."

"If you're going to cut them, could I have one? To draw."

He shrugs. "I'll cut it now if you like." He shuts the door and comes back a moment later with shears. He snips off the sunflower head so that the stem is about the length of my forearm.

Serafina is in the Sisters' house. It's as if I've never been away. The room closes in around me as she smothers me in a Serafina hug. "Let's go to dinner. Emanuel's here."

I smile, in spite of everything. Even though Greg's not here yet, it won't be long before he is—just another two weeks, then he's back from his last family vacation of the summer. And until he gets here I don't have to keep my promise to myself and tell him the truth about who I really am. I hope he'll still want to know me afterward. But why should he?

We reach the canteen door. Serafina gives me a sudden little grin.

Emanuel's standing there, peering into the courtyard. A smile spreads over his face. "Serafina! Verity!" he says. "Come in."

He looks taller than I remember, but his hair is just the same, a corkscrew halo around his face. There aren't any secrets in his hazel-gold eyes.

—

CLASSES BEGIN BEFORE Greg arrives. Something is different at the Institute—Ms. Cobana has been replaced by Mr. Williams. She didn't say she was leaving and I wish she was still here. Now that we're in junior year we have Life Drawing. Greg should be here too. I close my eyes for a moment and breathe in the smell of linseed oil and dried paint on brushes. It's deeply quiet in the Art room, underneath the rustling of paper and swishing of pencils. Then Mr. Williams turns on his radio. It's the end of the jingle that precedes news, so I start listening. *"Critics urge for an inquiry into the indefinite holding of suspects at Tranquility Sound. A spokesperson from the Department of Security responded that desperate times call for desperate measures."*

What if those people are actually innocent? Imagine being locked up indefinitely then. I used to be pleased that "they" were all locked away. But that was when I was confident that it would be fair. I'm glad when the radio switches back to music.

That afternoon I ask Mr. East if I can take Raymond for a walk outside the grounds. I know I have to stay here, but the more I can get away from the claustrophobia of the Institute the better. Already I miss my walks through the Old City, the hours spent sketching by the canal. And I should check my cell phone. Sure enough, there's a text from Oskar:

Meet me Jubilee Park, 5 pm tomorrow, boating lake

Oskar never asked me about the list. Now that I'm back at school again, it's still supposed to be my mission. But I'm not going to do it. I so wish I hadn't given him Jeremiah's name now.

The light's going blue and there's smoke in the air from the bonfire Mr. East has lit behind the lodge. It'll be dark soon. I want to go and curl up on my bed with a coffee and talk to Serafina about Greg.

But I don't know if he wants to tell anyone about us yet. And will there still be an "us" after I tell Greg who I really am? So I go to the Art room instead—although the rumbling anxiety and guilt are still there, at least I'm studying Art.

I arrange the sunflower on the bench and start to paint. The flower's dead, but it's still so full of life—it's as if it's pulling my drawing out of the paper in sinuous lines. When I've finished, I'll scatter the seeds around; maybe I'll even keep a few and plant them next summer, so that the sunflower can live again.

CHAPTER 27

JUBILEE PARK IS in the New City, near the train station, and I get there the next day just before five. I got permission to leave the Institute because I need to buy some woodcutting chisels. Mr. Williams suggested I make my sunflower painting into a woodcut.

Oskar is leaning against a hut beside the lake.

He walks up to me. "I'll hire us a boat."

I'm good at this, I remind myself. *I can hide my true feelings, just smile like I would have done before.*

Neither of us speaks until the dinghy is in the middle of the lake. Then Oskar rests the oars on the sides of the boat. There's a chilly nip in the air and ours is the only boat out. The water is murky and dark, lapping softly against the sides of the boat as we rock.

"Can I row?" I'll feel less ill at ease if I have something to do.

Once we've changed places, I pull toward the opposite bank, where willow branches hang over the water.

"So, K," says Oskar, "I want to know why you didn't deliver the list."

I look into his eyes. "It's the visitors' book," I say. "Brer Magnus hides it away. I have no idea where he keeps it." This is true . . . now.

Oskar stares back at me. He's just going to let it go? Then he takes a leaflet out of his pocket and hands it to me.

"I want you to go to this."

What now?

"BSF. Brotherhood Student Fellowship," Oskar says. "Don't waste time going to Reconciliation events." He taps the leaflet. "This is where they recruit. For the militant cells." He fixes me with a hard stare. "Your . . . friends . . . from the school. I want to know who goes. Especially those who are close to Brer Magnus."

My heart starts racing, but I stay still and dip my hand into the cold green water. Does Oskar know about Greg?

"The first meeting's tomorrow night. You don't have to say anything, just be there. Don't forget to wear your hat and all the rest of it." He waves his hand over my clothes.

"Where is it?" It's easy to attend a meeting, isn't it? If the others go I just won't tell Oskar. I feel a little surge of relief.

"It's all on the leaflet," he says. "Short notice, I'm

afraid. It's tomorrow at six thirty. I want to know the names of everyone from the Institute who is there. Be careful. Act friendly but don't trust anyone."

"Don't trust anyone." I rest the oars and look at him. "Got it." *Especially you, Oskar.* I give him a lovely, open smile.

He's leaning back, humming a little, stretching his hands open and closed.

I'll go to it this once, Oskar. Because I don't want to rock the boat. Not yet. But I'm not giving you names. A year seems like a very long time now.

Oskar taps the wood with his fingers. "So you'll go?"

"Yes, I said." *Careful, K.* I smile at him again, still on the team. I need him to think nothing's changed, for now.

"Good." Oskar smiles warmly back. "Here, let me row." He clambers across the bench to change seats, and the dinghy pitches from side to side.

Oskar pulls toward the jetty in sweeping strokes. He can't wait to get back now. He's humming snatches of a song.

When we're standing on the bank. Oskar steps toward me, so close that I can smell his aftershave. He looks down at me. "Don't forget to go to the meeting," he says. His voice hardens in spite of the smile in his eyes. "I'll know if you don't. And when they have the Autumn Meeting at the Institute, you *will* bring me the names."

He's not even pretending to be friendly. I nod and turn away. I want to run.

When I'm almost at the gate I collect myself and

turn back to give him a friendly wave. I don't want to go to the BSF, but I think of all the meetings I've been to at the Institute. I'm guessing it'll be more of the same. I can do that, once or twice. That won't do any harm, will it?

—

THE MEETING IS held in the Old City Meeting Hall. Where they've been cleaning the stone, it looks almost as light as the Town Hall across the river. As I walk up the steps, I catch a glimpse of myself in the glass window of the door. Long brown skirt, black jacket, the new brown hat with its red-checked band that Ril just gave me for my sixteenth birthday. For a hat it's quite nice. It's felt, and you can hide your face under its floppy brim if necessary.

I join a straggly line of people. Lots of checked shirts. And hats. And long skirts. But nobody I recognize. An usher shepherds a little group of us down to where there are still some spare seats at the very front of this huge room full of strangers. It's odd how I don't feel ill at ease here. I know I blend in now. I glance around me. Who are they, these Brotherhood students? Are there really people here who want to siphon students off and radicalize them? I'm starting to doubt it. Students like Verity Nekton's parents? But Verity Nekton doesn't exist.

The hall goes quiet. Men walk onto the stage. There are a couple of male students and the guest speaker. He sits down right opposite me, with his gray hair winging up wildly on either side of his head.

His piercing blue eyes meet mine. Of course it's Brer Magnus. Here's where Ril's hat comes into its own. Just by tilting my head a fraction, I can block him out.

Brer Magnus starts speaking. His hair rises with his voice. I make a list in my head of all the things I'd rather be doing than sitting here listening to Brer Magnus. Stuck in an elevator with a rat. Cleaning dog poop off the sole of a shoe. Doing fractions. But that one makes me think of Greg. Where are Emanuel, Serafina, and Celestina? I look around, but to my relief I can't see any of them.

Brer Magnus is building up to the climax. He stares straight at me. Phrases leap out: "FALSE BELIEVERS!" "DECEIVED!" "WALKING IN THE MIRE OF THEIR OWN IGNORANCE!"

Maybe sharing a sleeping bag with a scorpion as well?

Brer Magnus scans the crowd, his arm panning across. "There is somebody here," he thunders. "Somebody who doubts my words, who is checking them in the Book. That person is a FALSE BELIEVER!"

The room goes still, waiting.

"That person should LEAVE!" shouts Brer Magnus in his voice of controlled rage.

Nobody moves, but I feel sure that every last person in this room wants to stand up and shout, "It's me! I'm the False Believer!"

—

IT FINALLY ENDS. I look over at the door, but there is a milling crowd of people between it and me. I still can't see any of my friends. So I edge toward the back of the hall with everyone else. I don't like Brer Magnus's rants, but he isn't recruiting terrorists in the main part of the meeting. If it's happening, it's all under the surface. If I was sure of Oskar, I would keep coming.

When I reach the entrance of the Meeting Hall, I hear footsteps hurrying behind me. I swing around, hoping it isn't Greg.

"Verity!"

It's Jeremiah.

"Verity! Good to see you." He really means it.

"Hi, Jeremiah." I haven't really spoken to him this term. "Did you have a good holiday?"

"Good, good." He walks beside me down the steps to the pavement. "Wonderful to have Brer Magnus here, wasn't it?"

"Does he always lead these meetings?"

Jeremiah looks over my head back up at the Meeting Hall. "Not always."

He walks with me to the bus stop. "Are you getting the bus back?" I ask him.

"No, I'm going to my cousin's tonight. But I'll wait with you." He seems to have something on his mind. "Actually, Verity," he says, "could we go for a coffee?"

I look at him in surprise. He isn't asking me out, is he? Or does he want to tell me something else?

"Great," he continues when I don't answer. "The Pelican's still open?" He points at a coffee shop across the road.

I don't want to go, but I feel guilty about giving Jeremiah's name to Oskar. I no longer believe he would get involved with terrorism—even though he *is* the only other student from Institute that I've seen here tonight. "OK," I say, shaking off my doubts. We cross the road just as a flurry of rain sweeps in from the coast.

CHAPTER 28

THE DOOR DINGS as we go in. It's nice to get out of the cutting wind. Jeremiah shakes the rain from his head. His hair is cut so short that you can hardly tell it's ginger now.

His fingers work at the buttons on his jacket. "Can I get you a coffee?"

"Thanks."

Jeremiah hesitates. Then he goes over to the counter to order our drinks. I perch on one of the high stools in the window, reading the ads for rooms to rent and an old bike to buy. He joins me, carrying a tray. He sits on the stool beside mine, hunched up in his coat. He has done all the buttons up again. He takes a swig of coffee, his eyes flicking from side to side. Every few seconds he peers out of the steamy window at the Meeting Hall.

"Actually, Verity?" He gestures toward the corner table at the back. "D'you mind if we sit down there?"

"Sure." I follow Jeremiah to the back of the cafe, where there's a banquette. He sits with his back to the window. I'm starting to think that maybe Jeremiah doesn't want to be seen with me. That doesn't surprise me. His wanting to meet me in the first place does.

Jeremiah spoons sugar into his coffee. Then he stirs it so thoroughly that foam flies up and lands on the table. He drops the spoon into the saucer and takes a long swig of coffee. Finally he sets his cup down, and looks at me. "So, Verity," he begins, but his eyes slide away to a woman sitting at the other corner table. "How did you like the BSF?"

"OK," I hesitate. I'm sure we've already had this conversation. "How about you?"

"Yes, it's great—great." Jeremiah smiles, but it's a mouth smile. His eyes still dart about, even though the only thing he can really see is the wall. "My cousin goes there too, you know." He lines up the salt and pepper shakers with the vinegar jar. "He's at the university."

"That's nice."

"What about your courses?" he asks suddenly. "Going well?"

"Yes—so far. Yours?"

He nods vigorously, and drains his coffee cup.

"So, what did you do this summer?" I say to fill the silence.

"Oh, I've been busy." Jeremiah picks up his empty cup, and sets it down again. "Some coursework, the BSF, and I've been spending a lot of time with my cousin." He looks at me, and his eyes almost seem to be pleading. "Actually, Verity," he begins. "You . . . with your . . ."

I wait.

But he stares at the table, and then looks back at me with a bleak smile. "It's nice to see you," he says quietly.

This is so unlike him that there must be something wrong. "Jeremiah?" I say. "Did you want to tell me something? Something in particular?"

Jeremiah starts. "No, no!" He tries to laugh, but it's more of a cough.

"You sure?"

"Of course. I'd better go, actually." He stands up, knocking into a chair.

The woman at the other corner table frowns at him. He's in a great hurry to leave now. For a moment I was scared he was going to ask me out, but now I think he's in some kind of trouble. He hurries to the front of the cafe, then stops and waits. I drain my coffee and follow him.

He pulls the door open and holds it for me, trapping us both in the doorway as a woman maneuvers her stroller in. Jeremiah looks at me, opens his mouth to speak, but then closes it again. His eyes stare into mine with a kind of desperation.

"Jeremiah? Are you sure you're OK?"

"Absolutely!" He smiles with his mouth again. His eyes still stare hopelessly into mine.

"You're sure you don't want to tell me anything?" I put my hand on his arm.

He shakes his head. The stroller runs over my foot.

As I step forward, I see Oskar walk past the Pelican. A lurch of fear goes through me as I watch him watching Jeremiah and me, framed in the bright doorway, my hand on Jeremiah's arm. Our eyes meet, but Oskar makes no sign that he has recognized me. He walks briskly toward the bridge.

"Good-bye, then, Verity." Jeremiah flips the collar of his checked jacket up around his neck and hurries off, his plan to go with me to the bus stop forgotten.

I cross the bridge and jog toward the bus depot. Not long ago I would have worried that Jeremiah was spying on me. But now I'm worried about him.

—

THE NEXT DAY I go to the Art room after my other lessons finish and start cutting into the sheet of plywood Mr. Williams gave me. I've gotten used to his radio in the background, and just stepping into the Art room makes me feel calmer. Each blade in my new chisel set comes wrapped in delicate oiled paper. I cut along the line on the block at an angle, the same the other way. Then I can flick the wood out with the tip of the knife. I'm cutting out the yellow bits of my sunflower, just a few crinkled petals. I've already rolled golden ink over the block and printed it before cutting out the gold. Everything is in reverse. Left is right, and right is left. You have to cut away the one thing you want to keep.

After I've cleared away my things, I head toward the common room to fill the time before dinner. But just as I reach the staircase, I see Greg crossing the courtyard from the Reception building. For a moment I just stare at him, delight wiping everything else from my mind. His face is lit by the orange lamp above the glass doors. He pushes them open and comes in.

"You're here." I step toward him.

"Verity." Greg reaches out, puts his hands on my

arms and pulls me into the darkness of the stairwell. "Dad and Mom had to leave early." He bends down and kisses me. His lips are so warm on mine. I can't believe how wonderful it feels to be with him again.

"You're very cold." Greg wraps his arms around me and holds me close.

"Greg?" I say. "What's the matter?"

He sighs. "Something horrible has happened. The others are all in the common room. Talk later?"

"OK. But what's happened, Greg?" The dull sense of foreboding that's forever lurking in the back of my mind flares into life.

CHAPTER 29

THE COMMON ROOM door opens, framing Emanuel in the oblong of yellow light. "Hello, Verity," he says.

Serafina and Celestina are sitting on the couches. One of the new pupils is working in a cubicle, but otherwise it's empty. They both look up with grim faces.

Celestina speaks first. "Have you heard?"

"Heard what?" I sit down on the arm of the couch.

"About Jeremiah," says Emanuel.

"Jeremiah?"

Greg turns to me. "He's been arrested."

"Sent to Tranquility Sound," says Serafina.

"But I just saw him yesterday evening." They must have made a mistake.

"It happened last night," says Greg. "About eight thirty. They took him off the street."

A thrill of fear runs through me. It can't be possible.

But I see Oskar walking past the Pelican. Jeremiah and me framed in the doorway. My hand on Jeremiah's arm. Oskar's words in Yoremouth: *All you have to do is point out anyone you suspect.*

My head starts whirling. How did Oskar even know who Jeremiah was? But he's had plenty of time to look him up since I told him his name, hasn't he? Did he think I was pointing him out last night?

"But, Jeremiah," I say. "Jeremiah can't be, he would never . . ."

"No," says Greg. "We know that. But do they?"

Cold sinks through me when I hear that "they." "They" means Oskar. It means me.

"There's no way he'll be treated fairly." Celestina's voice is bitter. "Not with all the opposition to the Agreement."

"The Agreement?" My brain isn't working.

Celestina looks hard at me. "The Reconciliation Agreement? The one about whether we get to lose the fingerprint database? Live where we like, go to any school we want? Be, you know, citizens of our own country?"

"It's like Brer Magnus said at the end of last term," says Serafina. "Dark days lie ahead."

Greg makes an impatient noise. "It doesn't have to be like that," he says. "We can try and change it. Maybe nothing will happen to stop the Reconciliation Agreement." But he sounds unsure.

I don't speak. I'm replaying the moment when I saw Oskar walk past the Pelican. What did he say all those months ago? Eyes and ears. That's all I am to him. What did I tell him about Jeremiah? Why, *why* did I do it? I can't stay here a moment longer.

I spring to my feet. I can hardly breathe. "I've got to go," I say, and hurry to the door. Just by being here, I'm putting my friends in danger.

Greg is right behind me as I yank my coat and bag off the chair. "What's the matter? Why are you going, Verity?"

"I've got to. I don't feel well." I grab my scarf and hat. "I'll see you tomorrow." I pull open the door. It's a heavy oak door, but I picture it being smashed in.

I don't look back to see if Greg is standing watching me leave. All the way to the Sisters' house, the thought repeats in my head: *It's because of me.* I know Jeremiah wouldn't hurt anyone. Whatever he's worried about, I'm sure it's not that.

I get into bed, still in all my clothes, even my shoes. When the others come in, I'll pretend to be asleep.

Of course I can't sleep. What about Serafina? Emanuel? Celestina? What about Greg? Is Oskar watching them too? What right does he have? How can I go anywhere near Greg now?

Slowly the knowledge of what I have to do grows clearer and louder. It's not a choice. It's something I must do. I have to end it with Greg.

And then I must leave.

It doesn't matter what he or the others think of me. Not anymore. The only thing that matters now is to remove myself from this school before I hurt anyone else. I can't ever come back. Not unless I want Greg to be arrested too.

CHAPTER 30

I DON'T GO to breakfast, hiding instead in the Sisters' house kitchen. After the first lesson ends I wait for Greg at the bottom of the Art department stairs. Normally I'd have to stop myself from smiling with excitement. He'll walk down here when he comes out of the Life Drawing class I missed. I didn't sleep last night, so now I feel sick with tiredness. But I know I have to tell him it's over. Then I'll go. I'll think about where later.

The floor tiles gleam dully, tiny chips of green set into concrete. I mustn't think about Greg. I've zipped up the thought of him in a suitcase. Maybe he isn't there. Everyone else seems to have clattered down the stairs and out the door already.

I walk over to the bulletin board and stare at it, hugging my bag to my chest. It's stuffed full. I put an extra sweater in, along with all my papers and money and the paintbrush Greg gave me. I run my eyes along the gray furrows crossing the pitted surface of the bulletin board.

I jump when I feel hands on my waist. I hear Greg's laugh near my ear before I turn. I close my eyes, feeling his breath on my neck under my hair. He kisses my head.

I turn and look at him. His brown eyes are soft and warm. How can I possibly end this?

I look down at the tiles. "Let's go outside," I say. Nobody will be able to see us by the pond.

WHEN WE GET to the rhododendron grove, Greg twines his fingers in between mine, where they belong.

"You're in a hurry," he says. "Where were you this morning?"

"I didn't have a good night. I overslept."

We walk farther in. I don't mean to, but I can feel my hand gripping Greg's more and more tightly. How will I ever let it go? I think of the tiny snatched moments of privacy in the summer when we held each other close, of all the kisses we never had, of everything we'll never have now. My throat feels as if a fist is gripping it.

"You're very quiet. Guess I should be grateful," he teases, smiling.

"Mmm." I duck to avoid a low branch.

We're in the woods now. I'll have to do it before we go back. Otherwise I know that Greg won't let it go. He'll drag the whole story out of me, and then he'll persuade me that it'll be OK. And I'll want him to, so how will I ever be able to stop him? But now I know it won't be OK. I swallow the sobs banking up behind the fist.

I will plunge into this ice-cold pond, colder than the real one on the other side of the rhododendrons. Now. I pull my hand out of Greg's. He thinks it's because the path narrows here. He stops and waits. My two hands clasp each other, nails digging in.

I open my mouth, and make myself say the words. "Greg." It comes out so clearly. "I can't see you anymore."

Greg's smiling face turns slowly back to me.

"What?"

"It's over." I can't believe how cold and loud my voice sounds. "It was a mistake. I'm sorry."

"What are you talking about?" Greg's not smiling now, but he doesn't look like he believes me.

"I'm sorry," I say again. "It's not going to work. It's not you, it's me. I think we should just be friends."

I can't do this if I don't leave now. "I'm sorry," I say, one more time. Then I turn and walk away as fast as I can.

Greg is shocked into stillness. But then I hear him begin running.

"Verity!" he shouts.

Of course he won't just walk away like that. I duck back into the rhododendrons. I hear Greg behind me, but I hide in the hollow behind two bushes until I hear his footsteps running back toward the school.

Then I jog back the other way toward the lodge. *No tears.* Mr. East is inside.

I catch my breath. "Can you let me out? I left my sketchbook in the Old City Meeting Hall when I was at the BSF meeting last night," I say.

"No walk for you today, Raymond," he says to the dog as he releases the gates for me.

I run down the hill to the bus stop. The bus comes on the half hour—have I missed it? But when I look back up the hill I see it emerge from behind the trees. I see Greg too, running out of the gate.

The bus groans to a halt and I leap on. It doesn't leave straight away. I peer through the rear window to see Greg running down the road. The bus growls and rattles. *Come on!* I won't be able to leave him twice.

The bus cranks into motion. Greg's fist bangs against the window and I start. His face looks up at me, his eyes dark through the glass as the bus draws away. *Don't cry. Not yet, not yet,* I think, in time to the rumble of the bus, and as it crosses the bridge into the New City, *Go back, go back . . .*

—

I RUN ACROSS the square in front of Central Station toward the crematorium, until weariness forces me to stop and walk. A skeleton leaf skitters across the drive. That's my life now. None of it is real. It's all nothing.

I make it into the Garden of Remembrance and find the wall where the *K CHILD* plaque should be. I know it was here because my dead white rose is still crumbling below it. But there's another name there now. I don't even exist in death. I'm all alone. I'm standing by the wall when the howl comes out, climbing and tearing up my throat. I stuff my fist over my mouth to muffle the noise, and I hang on to my scarf as if it's a rope to pull me out. Only it isn't.

Greg. Greg. My lovely Greg.

I fall to my knees and curl up in a ball against the wall. Another cry wells up through the scarf.

When at last I sit up, the day has darkened with rain clouds. Inside the enclosed garden, the grass glows green. Could I have stayed? Explained it all to him? Found a way to make it all right, together? Held him in my arms and never let go?

Of course not. I stand up and pick up my bag. I know I can't stay here in Gatesbrooke. Greg might find me. I know if I see him again I won't be able to hold my resolve. I have to go. I sling the bag across my chest.

Still, when I see the spire of the Old City Meeting Hall across the square, I pause.

Then I remember Jeremiah and me framed in the Pelican doorway. I can't let that happen to Greg. I'll leave first and decide where I'm going later.

I turn my back on the Old City and walk across the square toward the station where I first met Greg and Oskar, where my whole world exploded. Other people are bustling toward it too: office workers, parents and children, police officers, chatty students, all going about their business. I don't look for the difference between us and them anymore.

CHAPTER 31

I'LL GET THE first train out of Gatesbrooke.

That's a plan, isn't it? I walk faster, my shoes slapping through puddles. But when I'm halfway across the square, I stop.

Light glows from the Town Hall windows. That's how dark today is. Its turrets and spires shine in the streetlamps. It's a pale twin of the Old City Meeting Hall. The wind lifts and claws inside my coat.

It's no kind of a plan, is it? But it's all I have. I cross the road, getting out my wallet, and as I do, a card falls out.

I pick it up. It's a plain white card with a phone number on it. I hear Ms. Cobana's voice in the Art room last spring. *"If you ever need help, I'll be there for you. I really mean it."*

So I go to a phone booth and pick up the receiver. Then I slam it back down again, because will I be putting Ms. Cobana in danger too? Surely not, if I'm calling from a payphone? I deposit the coins and key in her number. After four rings I hear her voice. "Hello?"

"Ms. Cobana?"

"Who is this?"

"It's Verity. Verity Nekton."

"Verity!" Her voice lightens. "How are you?"

"I need your help," I say. "Is it, could I, talk to you?"

"Of course." There's a pause. "Where are you?"

"Gatesbrooke station."

"OK." I can hear her thinking. "Can you come to the station where you and Greg got stranded?"

"Yes. All right." I wonder why she doesn't say "Limbourne station." And because she doesn't, I don't either.

"I'll meet you there outside the station. The next train from Central Station. Is that all right?"

"Yes. Thanks."

She did mean it.

—

LIMBOURNE STATION LOOKS different in the daytime. I hurry past the waiting room, so I don't have to think about my night there with Greg, then up the stairs and into the parking lot, where I see Ms. Cobana with her hair flying around her head in a wild black-and-gray tangle.

She pushes her glasses up her nose and smiles at me. "Come on," she says. "This way."

"Thanks . . ." I begin, but Ms. Cobana puts a finger to her lips.

We get in her car and drive out into the countryside. She pulls up suddenly alongside a hedgerow with spiky twigs that rattle against my window. She gets out, and beckons for me to follow. This is weird, because there's nothing here. But I do it. What have I got to lose?

Ms. Cobana takes a piece of paper out of her pocket and holds it up to show me. *Have you got any bugs on you?*

I stare at her in surprise. She puts her finger to her lips again. Then she takes a small handset out of her bag and runs it over every bit of me. When it passes over my hat, it starts to beep. Ms. Cobana takes it off my head and rummages around inside the lining.

Is she mad? But now she holds something up—a small round metal thing like a watch battery. She has a funny sort of smile on her face, half-rueful, half-triumphant. She finishes running her detector over me and then she pops a stick of gum into her mouth, chews it up, spits it into her hand, and fixes the little metal lozenge into it. She places it carefully in the road and jerks her head back toward the car.

We sit and wait. It's not long before a van comes up the lane, and drives off with a flattened blob of chewing gum stuck to a tire.

"Good," says Ms. Cobana, starting the engine.

"Ms. Cobana?" I begin. "I had no idea that was there."

"I know." She turns right onto a mud path, drives a

short distance, and then stops the car in front of a gate. She gives me a brief smile. "We have to walk the last bit."

I look sideways at her as she closes the gate. She never seemed interested in security when she was my Art teacher at the Institute.

At the end of this overgrown lane, a small bungalow is almost hidden among the apple trees, which have sprouted right up to the walls. The grass is knee-high. Apples, mostly brown with rot, lie all over the path and in the grass, filling the air with the sour tang of cider.

Ms. Cobana turns her key in the lock. "I don't get much time for gardening," she says. "Until summer I was living at the Institute, as you know."

I'm expecting a damp smell, but it's fresh inside. I follow her into the kitchen. She fills the kettle and switches it on. She ladles sugar into my mug before I can tell her I take my tea without it. But that's OK, because I haven't had any food today.

"We'll eat in a while," says Ms. Cobana, like a mind reader.

I follow her into the living room, which has colored concrete tiles on the floor and a rag rug in front of the fire. This is the first television I've seen in a Brotherhood building.

Ms. Cobana notices my surprise. "I need to keep in touch with the world," she says.

She puts the tray down on the coffee table. She's made a huge pot of tea with a woolly hat tea cozy on top of it. "One cup's never enough, is it?" She doesn't seem bothered that I'm just nodding or shaking my head.

"You drink your tea. I'll be back in a minute."

I can hear her, going around the house with her bleeper gadget, checking for bugs. I'm starting to wonder again if she's a bit mad. But she found one in my hat, didn't she? The hat that Ril gave me. How did Ms. Cobana know?

Then I realize: because it's not the first time. What else have Ril and Oskar given me? My boots. My bag, with the wooden fastener that disappeared after Greg picked it up on the bus.

Finally Ms. Cobana comes back in and sits down.

"So," she says. "Verity. What's on your mind?"

"Ms. Cobana," I begin. "I'm not—"

"Call me Tina," she cuts in. "Short for Constantina." She makes a face.

"I'm not Verity Nekton," I start again. "My name is K Child."

CHAPTER 32

MS. COBANA LOOKS at me, waiting.

So I tell her everything, and now that I'm finally telling the truth, the words spill out. I stop and watch when she hears that I've never been a real Brotherhood girl. But she doesn't look shocked. She doesn't seem at all like a teacher now.

"Ms. Cobana?"

"Tina."

"Tina . . . Was I bugged at the Institute? From the beginning?" *Eyes and ears.*

She smiles at me. "The Institute has quite sophisticated security," she says. "Even before the visitors' book disappeared. I thought maybe you'd worked it out when Brer Magnus took your boots."

"I just thought he had some kind of boot fetish." The corner of Tina's mouth twitches. "Did Greg know?"

"What do you think?"

Then I tell her about Greg. But it's hard to talk about Greg, and about visiting his family. I dash tears away with the backs of my hands. Tina doesn't say anything.

And now I can't stop talking, but it all comes out in a jumble. I tell her about Verity Nekton's terrorist parents, and about the Brotherhood Student Fellowship, and how only Jeremiah went there, and how now he's been sent to Tranquility Sound, because of me. I tell her about the girl who Oskar and Ril pretended was me, who drowned and whose ashes were scattered in Gatesbrooke crematorium, and how I saw my name on a plaque there. And how since then I haven't told Oskar anything at all, ever, about anyone.

"But it's too late." I can't stop the tears from spilling out. "For Jeremiah," I go on. "I thought he was very militant at first, but still, he's not a terrorist. He wouldn't hurt anyone."

"Hmm," says Ms. Cobana. Tina.

"I don't know whether I should talk to Oskar about him."

"I strongly advise you not to do that," says Tina. She leans forward. "Why did you decide to become Verity Nekton?"

She must think I'm so stupid. Or that I'm lying. So I try hard to give her a true answer. "After the bomb," I say. "I wanted to fight it. I thought I could do something to stop it happening again. And Oskar believed in me." I pause. "I *thought* Oskar believed in me. I wanted to study Art. I didn't think past that . . ." I stop. "I never thought I'd be stuck as Verity. I didn't think it would matter. It didn't feel real until it was too late."

"Well," says Tina. "I think you're going to have to go on being Verity Nekton for the time being."

"I could do that," I say. "But I think Jeremiah was arrested because of me. So I'm scared for the others."

Tina doesn't speak. She picks up the teapot and pours us both more tea.

"I don't know what to do," I say eventually. "I can't go back. Everything's gone."

"Have you said anything about anyone other than Jeremiah to Oskar?"

"No."

"Do you feel you are in actual danger from Oskar?"

I shake my head. "Not me. But Greg." The tears spill again. "I split up with him this morning. Because I don't want Oskar to tell anyone about him, or the others." Greg's face looking at me through the bus window comes back into my mind, and I have to stop.

Tina puts her fingertips against her bottom lip. She pushes a big box of tissues across the coffee table toward me. "I need to think about what you've told me."

I make myself stop crying.

Eventually she says, "I think you've done the right thing in splitting up with Greg."

I nod.

"Did you tell him why?"

I shake my head.

"That's good," she says. "I did try to warn you how close he is to Brer Magnus."

Of course this is what Greg didn't want to have to tell me—that he kept watch on me for Brer Magnus. But I can't think about it. I know I can't trust Oskar anymore but I want to remember Greg as somebody I did trust. So I stop listening to what she's saying.

"Verity?" she says. "I think you should go back to the Institute. Carry on as normal."

I shake my head. "How can I do that?"

"It'll be all right," she says. "But keep away from Greg. And now I think we should eat something." She goes into the kitchen and shouts through, "What do you want—pizza, hamburger, sweet-and-sour chicken, or battered fish?" She appears in the doorway waving a frozen dinner in a cardboard box. "I'm having this," she says. "But you can have whatever you want."

I wonder if perhaps she doesn't believe me. We eat in the living room.

"Can anything be done for Jeremiah?" I say.

She puts down her fork. "I'll certainly look into that."

"And the girl, the girl they identified as me?" I hurry on. "I believed Oskar when he told me she wasn't Verity Nekton, but now I keep wondering."

"I'll need some time," says Tina. "About Jeremiah, especially. Are you absolutely sure that Oskar poses you no threat?"

"He wouldn't arrest me," I say. "I think he does hate Brotherhood people. But he knows I'm not one."

"Good. Of course, you're welcome to stay." She stands up. "But I think it would be much better if you went back tonight. That way hopefully nobody will notice that you were away at all. There's a train in ten minutes."

—

THE LIGHT IS failing as I walk along the drive. The wind has sprayed oak leaves against the wire fence, crumpled brown fairy lights strung against the concrete sky. The air smells of fog.

After Mr. East lets me in I open the door, drawn in by the warmth and the smells of dinner. I hurry as fast as my cold feet will let me, through the courtyard and past the canteen. I could go in. But instead I go up to our room in the Sisters' house. When I open the door a blast of cold air hits me. I left the window wide open this morning, and the fog has drifted in with its sharp smell of sodden leaves. Even the light seems gray when I switch it on. My bed is a tangled mess, with the bottom sheet half off. I close the window and the curtains and write a message on Serafina's pink notepad, then stick it to the door for Serafina and Celestina:

Have gone to bed now, not feeling well. See you tomorrow. V

That should keep them off my back for tonight. I get into bed as I am—I'm too tired to get undressed—but then the door flies open.

"Verity?"

"Serafina?"

Serafina snaps the light on again, twitches back the duvet and looks at my clothes. "In bed, huh?"

I shrug.

She sits on her own bed. "So," she says pleasantly. "What's up? Where have you been? First Jeremiah, then you disappear. Everyone was really worried."

My tired brain cranks into gear, trying to think of a story. Serafina and I stare at each other. She's waiting.

"Serafina," I say. "How . . . how good friends are we?" I'm too tired to talk properly.

"Good?" she says.

"OK," I say. "Good enough for you to trust me, even if I don't tell you anything?"

Serafina picks up my note. "Good enough for tonight, I guess." She stands up. "I'm worried about you, Verity," she says, switching off the light.

"Don't be."

She's gone. I think she must know about Greg. But I'm so tired that I just pull the duvet back up.

A submerged thought bobs up to the surface of my mind and floats there: Greg and Brer Magnus. What did Greg tell him about me? Did he report every little conversation? Did Brer Magnus tell him to help me with my Math? Was I a fool to feel that our friendship was slowly growing, like a blade of grass pushing itself up between paving stones? When did Greg stop reporting to Brer Magnus?

And the thought I can't bear: Did he ever stop?

CHAPTER 33

I SPEND EVERY spare minute of the next day in the Art room, printing olive green over the yellow-gold and orange on my woodcut. When I hear the ink hiss as I pull the paper off the block, it's as if the dead sunflower has come alive. Thankfully I have the room all to myself. Greg has gone to the city for the afternoon with Celestina and Emanuel.

I put the last print into the drying rack and scrub the wood with white spirit. Outside the clay-tiled windowsill there is only swirling gray, with white rain beads spattered onto the glass. Before I leave, I cut away the bits I want to stay green. There's not much standing out on the block now.

—

THE WEEKEND COMES and I know it'll be harder to avoid Greg now that there's just a handful of us here. Dismal light oozes around the curtains. Ten o'clock. I've missed breakfast. I think about the day ahead. Lunch in two hours, then the long, empty afternoon. I throw on some clothes: long skirt, polo-neck sweater, red-checked scarf, leggings, warm socks. I brush my hair, and I've just opened the door a crack when I hear people talking downstairs by the front door.

"I'm going to see Verity." Greg's voice.

"You can't come in the Sisters' house!" That's Serafina. "I'll get her for you."

I grab my bag and put on my coat and shoes. Then I fling the window open.

Just as I'd suspected back in the spring, it's easy to drop down onto the roof of the back porch and then down the drainpipe. I land with a *thud* in the back garden, with its straggling autumn lawn that spreads down to the willow tree and the woods.

"Verity," says Greg.

I jump. He's standing beside the porch. For a moment we both freeze, like cats meeting on uncertain territory.

Then Greg shrugs. "Why use a door when there's a window?" he says. "Or stairs when you've got a drainpipe?"

Is he angry? Is he trying to be funny? I'm not sure what to say. He's so close that I could reach out and touch his face.

But Greg speaks again. "Why talk when you can run away?" He thinks I'm a coward.

Suddenly I just can't do this anymore. "Why not leave me alone?" It's not a pretend shout. It's a real, angry shout, coming up through my feet and out through my face. "Why not get lost? Leave me alone! Leave me alone!"

I see the surprised look on his face, the recognition of genuine feeling. Then I run past him, and I don't stop running until I reach the lodge.

"I'm going for a walk," I say to Mr. East.

"Want to take Raymond?"

"When I get back," I promise.

—

I'M HOT AND tired now, but I keep walking quickly. I don't want to stop. The morning mist is beginning to drip off the trees that line the drive. Some of them have bark that has turned black with damp.

I jump on the first bus into town and get off at the station. I'm going to buy some boots at the New

City shopping center—warm boots with laces that tie snugly around the ankles. But as I look across at the door into the center, I realize that the old building next door is a swimming pool. I go in, up some curving concrete stairs. The reception desk has goggles and swimsuits hanging for sale behind it. I buy a plain black swimsuit and rent a towel.

Beside the pool, the air smells of chlorine, and there's a booming soft echo to all the splashes. It's busy, with lots of children, because it's the weekend.

I ignore the stares as I go into a cubicle. I guess it's not every day that a Brotherhood girl goes swimming in public. After all this time being covered up, it feels strange to come out wearing only a swimsuit. But as soon as I slide into the deep water, I feel I've come home. As my hands cut into the blue water, I can't stop thinking of the things I want: Greg. My name back. Not to have to pretend. Grandma's voice comes sharply into my mind: *"I want, can't have!"*

I plow up and down until I'm tired. When I'm dressed again I decide to skip the shopping center after all and buy some boots in an army shop instead. I put them straight on. The laces and hooks hug my ankles. They're stiff, but they feel good. I cross the bridge and walk down to the canal, along the service road next to the Meeting Hall. They've taken the scaffolding down from the front and now they're working on the side. I stand looking into the canal basin. There's no wall by the water's edge, just a strip of grass. Was I right to tell Tina? Maybe she can't help, but I don't think she would hurt me. I think I can trust her. I watch the rushing water of the dam, so smooth and black for the moment it hangs suspended over the drop, and then so angry and broken into white tumult when it falls. A heron is frozen on the wooden bridge to the houseboats.

—

It's sunset by the time I get off the bus at the Institute. The light is blue, the sky glowing pink and gold behind the firs.

I become aware of eyes fixed on me. Raymond is watching me from behind the gate, tail wagging slowly and hopefully. I promised him a walk, and it'll be good to talk to him and listen to his silent wise dog replies.

As I walk through the gate Raymond trots happily beside me, sniffing from left to right. "He looks with his nose," I say to Mr. East when I reach the lodge.

"Of course he does." He grunts. "He used to be a police sniffer dog."

"Shall I take him for a walk?"

"Just in the grounds now it's dark." He goes inside to fetch the ball.

Raymond trots beside me to the middle of the playing field.

"Raymond," I say. "Do you think I'm some kind of criminal now? For pretending to be someone else? What do you think? You're a police dog. Is that a crime?"

Raymond looks up at me briefly.

When he's finished following scent trails we play fetch. I bring him back before the light goes. A cold flurry of wind skitters leaves along Mr. East's path and Raymond makes a sudden puppy dash for them.

"He's a clever dog," I say as Mr. East opens the lodge door to let Raymond in.

"Working dogs always are. Why do you like walking him anyway?" he asks.

"I just like having someone to talk to." *Someone I can be myself with.* He'll think I'm such a loser.

But Mr. East nods.

"No one better than a dog for that," he says.

CHAPTER 34

WHEN I PUSH open the door into Reception, warmth rushes out.

It's a moment before I notice the figure sitting on the bench. Greg. He glares back at me, his eyes dark. I keep my hands in my pockets. That way, I won't be able to put them around him.

He stands up. "Verity," he says. "You have to talk to me. You can't just break up with me, avoid me, then run off with no explanation."

I feel something in the middle of my chest lurch down toward my new boots. I stand and stare at Greg, unable to speak. He doesn't look like he'll just go away. He stares back at me, a hostile stranger, waiting for me to speak.

I hear words come out of my mouth. "OK," I say. "Let's go in there." I jerk my head toward the waiting room where I first met Ril.

It's empty, and at least in here nobody will hear us. I walk into the room before Greg has time to object. He follows me in, closing the door behind him. I sit down on the couch by the window. After a moment he does too.

Then he reaches out and takes my hand. I hide the tremor it sends through me. I leave my hand, cold and still, in his warm one.

"Why, Verity?" he says. "What's so wrong that we can't fix it?"

I glance at his face. "Everything," I say. "The whole thing. It was a mistake. I'm sorry." Oh, it wasn't a mistake. It was the best thing I ever did.

Greg pulls his hand away angrily. "I don't believe you," he says. "How can you, one minute, be so . . . and then so cold?"

"I'm sorry," I say. Cold. Be cold. "I just don't feel anything for you anymore. I can't help it." I look at the coffee table while I tell this lie. I'm not so good at lying now.

"Verity," says Greg. "Look at me." He tries to lift my face in his hands. But I know I can't trust myself to look at him. Instead I bury my face in my arms. My head is throbbing.

"Is it because of me?" His voice is hesitant, not like Greg at all. "I was going to tell you . . ."

I leap up, and that makes him pause. He wants to tell me how Brer Magnus asked him to watch me. But I don't want to hear it from him. I take a cold, deep breath and look at a place behind Greg's eyebrows. "I don't know how to tell you any other way," I say. "It's over. Finished. So could you please just stop . . . could you please just leave me alone? Please."

There's a crash of the plant pot as Greg thumps the table. His eyes burn into mine. I love him so much. But we've been in here together for too long. What if Oskar is hiding in the woods across the road, watching me here with Greg through the tall windows, the way he saw me with Jeremiah at the cafe? I move toward the door.

Greg springs to his feet too, pushing the couch back so that a picture on the wall above it shudders. "This is what you want?"

I nod.

"I can't believe I got you so wrong." Greg's voice has a hard edge that I've never heard before. "I thought I was a good judge of character."

Like me. I trusted Oskar the moment his hand reached down from the platform for mine.

"Yeah?" I say. "That's why you think Brer Magnus is so great?"

A flash of anger passes over Greg's face. "What would you know?" he says. "You don't have to agree with everything a person says to respect them."

"He's a bigot," I say. "He's an egotistical control freak. He . . ." But I stop, because we're staring at each other angrily, and I know that all it would take would be the flicker of one tiny muscle to turn the anger into laughter.

"*You're* the one who went to the BSF," says Greg, in his hostile voice. "None of the rest of us would go if you paid us. Except Jeremiah."

I remember Verity Nekton's militant parents, and I feel myself flush, because that's where he thinks I come from.

But then he sits back down on his hands. "Verity," he says. "Verity. Are you sure?"

"Yes. Sure."

"OK." He gets up again. "Well. I'll try and stay

out of your way, then." But still he hesitates.

I say, "Thank you." And then I see that he believes me at last.

CHAPTER 35

EVERY MORNING I'M the first person into the canteen. That way, I've left before the others have even come in and I can work in the Art room before school begins.

Today the radio is softly playing the piano music that Mr. Williams likes. I look on the windowsill for the plastic bag I keep my chisels and apron in, but instead there's a cardboard box with *Verity* written in perfect script on the side. Mr. Williams must have done that.

I take the apron out of the box and tie my hair back with a knotted scarf. When I'm printing I can switch off the hum of worry. That's what I think.

"What did you say?" Mr. Williams has come out of the office.

"Sorry? Me?"

He looks around theatrically. "There's nobody else in here."

"I didn't say anything."

"Yes, you did," says Mr. Williams. "I thought you said, 'I don't know what to do.' So I came over to help."

"Oh," I say. "I was wondering how much red to mix into the brown."

But I wasn't. I was worrying aloud. I know I can't just tell Oskar that I want out. *What about Ril and Col?* I wonder uneasily. I need somewhere to live and some money first.

Mr. Williams shrugs. "Carry on," he says. "See

how it goes. That's nearly finished. You should start planning your next print."

It's hard to concentrate when he's around. He whistles or sings along to the radio while he works. He's singing now, in his deep voice, over the drone of the radio news bulletin. Now and again the presenter's voice breaks through: "Reconciliation Agreement . . . civil liberties . . . Brotherhood fingerprint database . . . As mixed Reconciliation Rally draws near, anti-integration activists gain in opinion polls . . ."

I wish he would turn it off and just sing, because now I can't stop thinking about Jeremiah. Is he in a prison cell? Is he alone? What about Verity Nekton's parents, though? Greg will now always believe them to be my parents. I can never tell him that's not who I am. Or that I didn't know about the bugs.

I roll brown ink over my sunflower woodblock, and after I've printed it and washed it with white spirit, I chisel out everything that was brown. Then I get out my sketchbook and draw a row of beach huts with pointed roofs and a ruined castle behind them.

—

THE NEXT DAY I go down to the Old City after school and call about the bike ad I saw on the Pelican bulletin board. It's very cheap. I arrange to meet the owner on the bridge later on. As I pass the Meeting Hall, I see that they've started taking the scaffolding down. Of course, they cleaned it for the Reconciliation Rally.

When I see the bike, I understand why it's so

cheap. But it has new tires and inner tubes, and a rack on the back, and even the lights and brakes work. The Institute is too far from the city to walk, but it shouldn't take more than an hour on a bike. I fix my bag onto the rack and put the lights on. The hill up to the woods is a lot steeper than it seems on the bus. I pound up, my feet warm because of the pedaling, my hands frozen to the handlebars. At last I see the Institute roof, circled by a flock of starlings wheeling and swooping above it.

My cell phone beeps and I can't help jumping guiltily. I stop to read the text. Oskar wants to meet in Jubilee Park at the gate behind the fish market, at four thirty tomorrow. I don't want to reply, but if I don't he might get suspicious. I need to act normally until I'm ready to disappear.

I key in a quick text:

See you there.

The trees trace black veins on to the mauve of the darkening sky, which holds all the colors of my sunflower print around the golden ball of the setting sun.

It's not much, having the bike, but it's the first step to becoming free.

CHAPTER 36

THE WHEELS CRUNCH and flick gravel on the road. As I get nearer to the Institute, I see someone walking toward the gate.

"Verity?" It's Emanuel.

I brake and put one foot down.

"You've got a bike," he says.

"Yes. Just today." I'm still out of breath from the hill. There's a silence.

Then Emanuel says, "Are you all right?"

He speaks hesitantly, in a soft voice, and I have to turn away for a second.

"I'm fine," I say. "Fine." And I smile at him to prove it. And because he's so sweet. "What about you?"

"Good," he says. "Apart from, you know, Jeremiah. Greg's missing you." He hesitates again. "Did you know about Serafina and me?"

"Not really," I say. "That's nice." And I really mean it.

But then I start to wonder whether anyone could be watching me talking to Emanuel. Maybe Oskar has a hidden camera trained on the Institute. I don't want Emanuel to be associated with me. So I put one foot back on the pedal. "Nice to see you," I say. "Bye!"

I cycle off before Emanuel even has time to say goodbye. The wind rears up and shakes the poplars beside the drive, pressing a ball of cold air into my chest.

I put my bike away in the shed behind Mr. East's lodge. When I get to the canteen I see Serafina and Emanuel sitting at the table by the french doors. Emanuel moves closer to her, and they laugh into each other's faces. They don't even notice when Greg puts his tray down in front of them. He looks thin. Maybe because he's wearing a black shirt.

I go and get my meal: pizza and salad. I'm really hungry after the cycle. I sit near the carts. I can hear them talking about the rally, which will be held next weekend in the Old City Meeting Hall the day before the Reconciliation Agreement is signed. I've never heard Celestina so excited. "All sitting together," she says. "No special areas for anyone. And hopefully that's how it will always be."

"I don't know," says Serafina. "Look what's happened to Jeremiah. How can we trust people like that? And how can we stay pure if we get all mixed up? That's what Brer Magnus said anyway." Her voice falters to a halt.

I hear the scrape of a chair and feel someone standing behind me. It's Greg. I don't mean to, but a small sigh escapes from my chest.

"Verity?" Greg half-sits on the chair beside me. He doesn't wait for me to reply. "Meredith sent me some photos," he says. "Of summer. I didn't think you'd want me to keep them." His voice hardens. "So you can have them. Burn them, if you like."

He places an envelope on the table and stands up. I don't know what to say. I look at him, but he's turned away. His face is closed off, not even frowning. He walks back over to the other table.

I know I shouldn't look at the photos now, but I tweezer open the envelope with my finger and thumb to glimpse what's inside. I see Meredith and Greg and me, walking down to the beach, arm in arm. Meredith's brown eyes are just like Greg's. They're both taller than me. I look happy. Greg is laughing. I can almost smell the pine needles in the heat, and see the wood ants scurrying in the brown needle carpet of the path. Angelina took this photo, skipping backward just in front, because it's at a crazy angle and it's slightly blurred. And now it's completely blurred and I have to get out of here fast.

I run upstairs to our room and put the photos under my pillow. I don't look at them until I'm under the duvet, with a flashlight, just in case there's a hidden camera here. I'm turning into Tina.

There's everyone except for Meredith eating the picnic at the beach. There's Greg with his blackberry pie in one hand and his other arm around my shoulders. Rosanna and me sitting at the table, Rosanna frowning up from her medical journal. I'm in all of them. It's OK to cry here, hidden and mercifully alone.

Afterward, I get out of bed and I go down to the kitchen to burn the pictures in the sink. Oskar will never see them now. I go back to bed even though it's so early and I lie awake with my eyes closed, remembering the pictures in the darkness. My hands smell of smoke.

I can't bear another dinner like that.

Now I can't sleep. I get up and pad over to the wardrobe. I open the drawer and feel around in the dark. Right at the back I find something soft and old. As I pull it out, sand dusts across my fingers. I get back into bed and curl up under the covers with Greg's baseball cap under my chin. Nobody will see. It smells of summer.

—

HE GAVE ME his cap on my last day there . . .

He was wearing it, sitting on the bench in the garden. I paused in the open doorway, watching him and listening to the beads on the side of the blind as they ticked lazily against the window.

Greg looked around, his face lighting. "You're up early."

I went over to sit down beside him, but he pulled me onto his knee instead. His arms were cold from the breeze, in spite of the sun. I brushed little kisses all over his face, to remember every detail, and he laughed at me.

"Do you mind going to the beach, all of us together?" he said. "Mom wants us to have a picnic."

"I don't mind." I never expected that we'd have the last day alone.

Greg pushed a piece of hair out of my eyes. "You sure?"

"I haven't been to the beach since Yoremouth," I said. "When I went with . . ." I stopped, unsure what to say. Greg and I didn't go to the beach when we went to the Reconciliation youth meeting together.

Greg waited.

"With Ril. The social worker? When I went away for the weekend."

—

"I FEEL SICK," said Angelina. "You're going too fast, Dad. Are we nearly there yet?"

"It'll be nice when we're there," Greg said.

"Hmmph," said Angelina. But she held on to his hand.

He left his arm resting along the back of the seat, almost as if he had his arm around me.

"Where's your hat, Verity?" said Angelina.

"I forgot it."

"You'll get sunstroke. Won't she, Mom?"

Rosanna glanced around. "Probably not. But it *is* hot today. Maybe we can sit in the shade."

"I've got a spare hat," said Greg. He jammed the old baseball cap on my head, and smiled his half smile.

"That old thing!" snorted Meredith, pulling it off from behind me.

I held the cap in my hand. It was the one he'd worn when he'd followed me to the Old City.

We ate the picnic, and drank plastic cups of sweet tea from Rosanna's striped flask. Meredith lay on a beach mat with her eyes closed. Gerontius went off for a walk along the beach. Rosanna watched Angelina dig a sandcastle.

"Verity? Come for a walk?" Greg was standing beside me.

Rosanna looked up quickly. "That's a good idea," she said. "You too, Meredith?"

But Meredith rolled over onto her stomach. "No, you're all right," she said. "Too sleepy."

"Come on, then," said Greg.

We walked off toward the other end of the beach, crossing the expanse of sand where dogs were allowed to run free. Greg took my hand. I looked at him.

"I don't care who sees," he said crossly. "You're going tomorrow."

So we walked along the beach hand in hand, not speaking. Greg dovetailed his fingers between mine. The beach wasn't long enough.

We reached the rocks. Greg smiled at me. "Let's go behind there."

"OK."

Under the cliff there was a sort of cave, an overhanging rock above and a sandy miniature beach below.

Greg sat on a ledge and pulled me down onto his knees.

"My dad will be hurrying over here to save you," he said. "So we'd better not waste time."

I didn't mean to, but I heard myself sigh. Greg laughed. He said, "Wait until we get back to Gatesbrooke."

"Mmm." But then I remembered that first I had to tell Greg my true story. And that could be the end of us, before we'd really begun.

Then we kissed, while the sea sucked away and shushed smoothly up the beach. I put my arms around Greg's neck, to remember the way his hair felt so downy near the nape, and the shape of his head and his shoulders under my hands. His hands were remembering the shape of me.

We walked back across the sand.

"You're very quiet," said Greg.

"You know why," I said. "Did you like me better the way I was before?"

"I like you any way."

—

BUT WAS THAT true? Would he still have liked me if he knew who I was?

Could he still like me now?

The cap smells of sunshine and summer, but now it's damp with tears.

CHAPTER 37

MY SUNFLOWER WOODCUT is almost finished. I peel back the print with the slicking hiss of ink. This time it's rusty red, the color of old blood.

I cut away the last few bits for the final printing tomorrow. Everything I cut will stay red, everything that's left will be midnight purple. The block is almost all carved away now, in jagged ridges. All that's left is the darkness.

In my sketchbook I rough out views of the sea, from behind the beach huts and then in front. Although I'm imagining it in bright sunlight, the sea looks angry and the huts cast dark shadows on to the pebbles. I can work on it tomorrow, maybe put a figure on the beach.

I clean up by lunchtime and because I have no afternoon classes I cycle into town to go swimming before I have to meet Oskar. As I duck my head into the blue water, so different from the soft green pond, I plan the things I need to do to untangle myself from the life Oskar set up for me. The bike is a good start, but it's not enough.

Then I become aware of the swimmer in the next lane. Celestina is swimming effortlessly along beside me. She speeds up and treads water at the end, waiting for me. I hook one hand over the edge of the pool.

"Hello, Verity," she says. "I didn't know you swam here. It's a bit warmer than the pond, isn't it?"

"Hi." I'm not really surprised to see her. I don't think Celestina minds breaking rules.

"Did you know you can stay upright without treading water? Look." She stops moving and puts both her hands up in the air. There she is, motionless, with her head bobbing on the surface of the water like a buoy.

I can't help smiling.

"You try it," she says.

So I do. And it's true. After the first little panicky moment when I stop moving, I find myself vertical in the deep water while it holds me up.

"There you go," Celestina says. "Not everyone can do it. Greg can't—he tried it that night in the pond, after the dance. Oh, and he wanted me to tell you something."

My heart leaps. My heart sinks. I don't say anything.

"But don't worry," says Celestina. "He wants you to know he's got the message. He doesn't want you to think he's some kind of stalker, so he won't be bothering you again. He just didn't really get it before."

I duck my head underwater.

But Celestina hasn't finished. "Now he does. I don't get it, though, Verity," she says when I resurface. "What's really going on?"

I make my voice cold. "Nothing's going on," I say. "I need some space."

"From all of us?"

I nod.

Celestina pulls a how-about-that sort of face. "OK," she says. She doesn't sound offended. "Fair enough. Although—Verity?" she calls over her shoulder as she strikes out again. "We're all really upset about Jeremiah. Now's the time when we should stick together. And also, I don't believe you."

When I reach the other end, she's waiting for me. "Are you sure you don't want to get a coffee after this?" she says, pushing her dark goggles up on top of her silver swimming cap. "You can meet my new friend, Jo. She's coming to the rally with me. You'd like her, I think. I'll buy you lots of hot tea, no sugar," she goes on. "And then you can tell me what's up, if you like. It might feel better to talk about it."

I look at her. She's thinking of my problem as if it's something she could help with, not something that will make her feel I've cheated and betrayed them all.

So I shake my head. My wet hair slaps the sides of my face. "Sorry, Celestina. I just can't."

"OK," she says lightly. She pulls herself out of the pool in one smooth movement. "Bye, then."

—

I NEED TO set up a whole new life—somewhere Oskar doesn't know about—ready for the moment I can leave the Institute. So I go straight to a job agency near the Pelican, and get an evening job cleaning offices in the Town Hall, starting next week. As I'm here, I cycle down to the canal basin and lean my bike against the little wooden bridge that leads to the towpath and the houseboats.

Normally you can't go right up to the houseboats because of the locked gate. But today it's wedged open with two big cardboard boxes. I slip through and walk along the towpath and I see that the dark green boat with the painted flowers isn't empty today. There's a bang from inside as the doors are pushed open by the heavy box a young guy is carrying. He lets it fall on to the deck with a *thud* and disappears inside again. The box is full of tins of paint, long-handled paintbrushes, and jam jars.

What have I got to lose? I climb onto the deck

and over the bin bags and boxes to the doorway. It's dark inside.

"Hello?" I call.

He appears at the foot of the ladder, peering up at me. He only looks a few years older than me. "Yeah?"

I gesture toward the boat. "Did you paint the flowers?"

He nods sheepishly. "They're not that good . . . I only did them quickly."

"No, I like them," I say. I hesitate. "Are you moving out? I'm looking for somewhere."

He climbs up to the top step and leans back against the hatch. "She's not for rent." He runs his hand through his matted brown hair, pushing it out of his eyes. "To be honest, I've been squatting myself. Moving on now, though." He indicates the heap of stuff on the deck.

"If you're leaving, can I have it?"

He looks at me more closely. "Er, yeah, why not?" he says. "That's how I got her. Friend of a friend. Of a friend." He laughs. "The only thing is, Doug might be coming back in the summer."

"Who's Doug?"

"He's the owner. He's traveling at the moment. But you wouldn't have to worry about Doug, he's very laid-back, so I've heard. Hey . . . want to have a look inside?"

He ducks back down the hatch. I pause. He seems OK, but I haven't always been the best judge of character, have I? I want to see inside the boat though. I won't let him get between me and the door. I follow him down the ladder and into a kitchen. He's at the far end of the cabin, stuffing clothes into a bin bag. Inside it smells of smoke, damp, and fried food and my feet make a sticky noise on the stained planks. I look at the black stove squatting in front of greasy tiles and the bench covered in torn green vinyl.

He looks around too, then shrugs. "Could be cleaner."

I see all these things, yet it feels to me as if people have been happy here. My spirits lift. "So, can I move in?"

Then he laughs. "Why not?" He holds out his hand and we shake. His fingernails are black, mine maroon red from the morning's ink—not even the chlorine in the pool could bleach it away.

I look around the cabin again before I leave. It looks different now that I'm imagining living in it. There is warmth, underneath the cold and the damp. I picture Greg and me at the table, with plates of food. It hurts so much that I grab hold of the door. Instead I imagine Raymond curled up in front of the stove. Or even a new dog, one that I'll find in the street, a thin dog that nobody else wants.

I turn back before climbing the ladder. "Thanks."

"No problem. If anyone asks, you're a friend of Doug's. I'll leave the gate keys under the flowerpot." He points to a small bay tree in a pot beside the gate. "Better get on now. My lift's coming soon."

I check out the flowerpot before I leave. Time to meet Oskar.

As I cycle back into the center of the city, I feel something lift from my shoulders. I've almost finished my sunflower woodcut. I'm going to start my new job next week. I'll leave the Institute one night without telling anyone, hide out here on the barge. It'll give me time to plan what to do and where to go, and I won't be a danger to my friends anymore. Tina said she would try to help Jeremiah.

Soon I'll be able to tell Oskar that I want out. In spite of what happened to my parents, I don't want to live as Us and Them. Oskar won't like it, but at least I'll have somewhere to hide. I'd forgotten what it feels like to believe you could have a future. Even if Oskar gets me thrown out of school, I'll have somewhere to live and a way to earn money.

And then maybe, in the future some time, I can be friends with Greg again.

CHAPTER 38

I CYCLE OVER the bridge to the New City and left along the river. The market square is empty apart from a truck parked in the access road and a van selling snacks. The market stalls are closed up, the bins smelling of fish, and trash blows across the empty tarmac. I freewheel through the iron gate into Jubilee Park. A dense shrubbery hides the boating lake in front and the Aquarium to the right. I wanted to arrive first, but Oskar is leaning against the fence, just inside the gate.

I note his eyes open a little wider as he takes in my appearance. Ril's hat, now free of bugs—does he know? Black wool jacket from the Old City army shop, a skirt that doesn't quite hide my boots. I glance down. I hope I still look like Oskar's idea of a Brotherhood girl. Celestina wouldn't, I think, and she's a real Brotherhood girl.

"Hello," I say.

"K," says Oskar. He's holding two paper cups. "I got

you some tea. Do you want to chain up your bike? Then we can walk."

He watches while I secure it to the fence, his eyes roving behind me to the empty marketplace. Then he hands me one of the cups. He's wearing his leather jacket. His hair looks darker now. The flicky ends rest on his collar. He smiles at me. I smile back to hide the fact that I'm about to break our deal. But I would never have entered into it if he had told me he would remove my own identity forever. Place bugs on my things without my knowledge. If I had wondered then, as I do now, what kind of policeman Oskar is—honest and true or someone who will stop at nothing to get the results he wants?

"Thanks."

"You're welcome." He sets off along the path and I walk beside him holding the tea.

"So, how's it going?" he says. "I see you've stopped going to the BSF meetings." He waits for me to answer, not smiling now.

Of course he knows I'm not going to them. That was a mistake. To buy myself some time I take a swig of tea. It's way too sweet. "Um." I don't know what to say. "I went the other week." I warm my cold hands on the cup.

Oskar turns into a secluded garden, hedged around on every side, a broken fountain in the middle. "We are at war, K." He stares at me. "There's no place for slacking off, or personal feelings." But now his eyes become amused, not angry. He doesn't say anything. He's still waiting for me to speak.

"They're just students," I say. "There might be people there with links to militants, but I don't know who they are. And the ones I do know are just ordinary people. I'm sorry I can't get you the information you want." Jeremiah's face comes into my mind.

"They're Hoods," says Oskar, sitting down on a stone bench. "Most of them would be terrorists, given half a chance." He carries on looking at me thoughtfully. "You don't want to go?"

I think he knows I don't agree with him. I sit down too, putting my cup down. "That's OK with you?" This would be a very bad time to tell him I want to stop. Maybe he could get me arrested. I must hold my nerve.

"Of course." Oskar smiles that warm smile that makes the amber flecks light up in his gray eyes. "So, how're things?"

I need to find something neutral to talk about, so I tell him about my print. I can make my voice sound normal, because it's something I know so well.

I watch Oskar put an interested look on his face. Is that what he's always done? Why couldn't I see it before? "So you got yourself a bike," he says, looking over at the path.

"Yes. That's why I've got a shorter skirt." As soon as I've said this, I wish I hadn't.

But Oskar just nods. "Practical, K." He nods toward my cup. "You're not drinking your tea."

"No," I say. "Actually, it's too sweet for me. I don't take sugar."

"You've given up sugar?"

There's a little pause while we look at each other. Oskar has watched me drink countless cups of tea, and never once has he seen me put sugar in, but he didn't notice because it was of no use to him. What will happen when I'm of no use to him? Why did he even save me?

At last Oskar breaks the silence. "Well, shall we go back?"

I stand, relieved. But why did he ask me to meet him here today? I steeled myself for him to be angry about the BSF meetings and maybe even the list, but he just seems amused. Oskar stands up too and as he leans down to pick up his empty cup, his police ID card swings out on its lanyard.

Ice runs along my arms, tingling into my fingertips. Is he really a policeman at all? My heart starts pounding.

He pushes it back inside and zips up his jacket. And Ril. Who is she? What if she doesn't work for the police either?

He turns toward me. "What are you thinking, K?" he asks quietly.

He certainly seems like a policeman now. I have to say something. "Ril," I blurt out. "How's Ril?"

Oskar looks blank for a second. "Ril? Oh—she's fine."

He walks toward the opening in the hedge. "Would you like to see her?" he asks suddenly.

"Who?"

"Ril."

"OK." *No.*

"Good, then," says Oskar. "I'll call you. Soon. And we can all meet up. Maybe at the weekend. Yes. I'll pick you up, because they'll be diverting the buses on account of the rally." He's already forgotten about my bike.

We walk the short distance to the gate. I'm scared Oskar will guess what I'm thinking. I stoop down to unlock my bike.

Oskar lets me straighten up and then puts one hand on my shoulder. It lies there heavily. "Keep it free." It's an order. "The weekend." He releases me.

"All right." I pull my hat back down over my ears. I mustn't let him see how nervous I am. I have to get a grip on myself.

The corner of Oskar's mouth twitches. "Nice hat."

"Ril gave it to me." I try to keep my voice light. "It's nice and warm." Does he know the bug is gone? Of course he does. But why hasn't he mentioned it?

"Bye, then." Oskar stands back so I can wheel my bike through the gate. "But next time we meet, K," he says, his voice suddenly quiet and cold, "make sure you're wearing proper Brotherhood clothes. I mean it." He points at me. "Make sure you look like a Hood."

I feel very cold when I hear his voice like that. I nod, and go out quickly. But I turn back when I'm outside the park. Oskar is staring intently at something. I glance behind me, but nobody's there. I look back at him, and it's strange, because for a moment I could almost think that Oskar looks sad.

"K," he calls, as I put my foot on the pedal.

My eyes meet his.

He's still in the gateway, his hand grasping the iron frame. "Nothing." He shakes his head. "Good-bye."

The sky has turned to smoky mauve. I pedal through the empty market and along the river, glad to get away from Oskar, aware of his eyes on my back. But when

I'm in the Old City, hidden behind the looming Meeting Hall, instead of heading up the hill toward the Institute, I turn toward the canal. I start to have misgivings. The man from the barge probably forgot to leave the keys. And I don't even know his name.

I feel through the fence, under the flowerpot. The keys are there. I open the gate and go down the towpath to the green boat. My boat. It looks very dark inside. Nobody seems to be around, so I turn the key in the lock and the door opens for me. I don't need to go in now that I know it's here, waiting.

The green barge already looks like home. Nobody will know where I live. Not Greg. Not Oskar.

CHAPTER 39

MEET ME AT *the end of the drive, 6 p.m. Ril will be there. Oskar*

I message back:

OK

But it's not OK; it feels like something I should run from. I should be going down to the rally with the others in the school minibus. I tell Celestina that I lost my wallet yesterday and I'm going to the shopping center to see if it's been handed in.

"I'll meet you at the rally," I say.

I can see she doesn't believe me. "You'll be lucky to find us. It'll be packed," she says. Even so, I'm pretty sure Celestina won't tell anyone what I'm doing.

Oskar has never asked me to meet him at night before. Maybe it's because Ril's coming too. I don't want to see either of them. Now is not the time to run, though. Now is the time to be brave and face Oskar and tell him the truth. That I'm leaving. I'm not sure how he will react. I think I should wait until we're in a public place, just in case. Hopefully in the Old City. I might have to leave the Institute straight away. If the boat doesn't work out, I think I could stay at Tina's for a few days, even though I haven't heard from her since I told her everything. I have it all planned, so there's nothing to worry about.

I don't want Oskar to guess before I'm ready, so I dress more carefully than usual in my Brotherhood clothes, just as he told me to do, even the long red-checked skirt. But I put on the boots. It's too cold not to wear them. I look at myself in the mirror on the back of the door. This long skirt hides my feet anyway.

I'm trying not to look at the thought in the shadows of my mind. That if I can free myself from Oskar, maybe it's not too late to be friends with Greg again. So many things are against this that I can't afford to even hope.

Though I do hope that Oskar will be like the old Oskar, the one with smiling eyes, who made me feel like I mattered. A sudden shower of rain splatters against the bedroom window. I put on Serafina's pink cardigan, which I somehow never remembered to return, then my coat. I grab my wool bag, take one last look at our room, and turn out the light. I'll miss sharing this room.

I tell Mr. East about my wallet and he lets me out. I'm a little late as I crunch down the drive in my boots, hugging my coat around me to keep out the wind that rattles through the brittle poplars by the field. I see the amber streetlight at the end of the drive. But I don't see the car until I reach the second gate. I look back to see if Raymond is in Mr. East's garden, where the headless sunflower stalk sways. But of course he'll be inside, warmly curled up in his basket, paws tucked under his chin.

The car is parked beside the gate. I don't recognize it, but I've never known Oskar to drive the same car twice. The windows are dark, and I peer inside as the gate swings open. I can only just make out Oskar, half-hidden by his baseball cap, in the driver's seat.

He lets down the window with a whir. "It's open, K," he calls softly across the passenger seat. "Jump in."

As I step up to the car, I see Raymond barreling down the drive. He must have come through behind me and he's been sniffing around by the fence all this time.

"Go back, Raymond! Sit! Wait!" I call.

Raymond skids up to the closing gate, but instead of sitting, he rushes through it and storms toward me, barking and snarling, mouth open in a crocodile gape of teeth.

The barking hammers in my head. One moment he's there, Raymond, my old friend, and the next his teeth clamp around my wrist. I jerk my hand away and fumble for the door handle.

"Get in the car! Get in the car, K!"

Somehow I get the door open and fall onto the seat and pull the door shut behind me. The window glass slides smoothly up, shutting out the raging face of fangs and staring eyes. Oskar must have closed the window. I haven't moved since I got in.

In the wing mirror I see Raymond barking and leaping at the back of the car and Mr. East running up the drive.

Oskar starts the engine.

"Don't run him over!" I cry.

"Are you OK?" Oskar pulls into a U-turn with a screech of tires. "Did it hurt you?"

"I'm fine." But my arm throbs sickeningly. I slide my hand up my wrist, under my coat sleeve. "It's not bleeding." It must be the pressure of Raymond's teeth that hurts so much. "It's just a bruise."

I look at Oskar. I'm not the only one who's shaking. His fingers have left damp smears on the steering wheel, and his knuckles are yellow. Maybe he's afraid of dogs.

I look back. Raymond is standing by the gate, his head thrown back. What has happened to my friend, nose tuned to the ground and tail thumping to see me? Maybe he's sick.

Thanks for coming to save me, Oskar, I don't say.

I'll tell him I'm going to stop working for him when I've calmed down. After we get out of the car, while we're walking, before we meet Ril. Somewhere where there are lots of other people.

Of course, I don't know where he's taking me. I glance sideways at the door. It's not locked, so if I had to I could jump out. This is a new car. It smells of leather as it glides sleekly down the hill. We don't talk. I look at Oskar. His forehead is dotted with drops of sweat.

He drives into the Old City and turns into the service road that leads to the canal and the shopping center, even though there's a NO ENTRY sign there today. He pulls over almost immediately. Maybe it doesn't apply to the police. On the right, the side of a multistory parking garage looms over the road, black and featureless. It's very dark and empty here.

Oskar gestures toward it. "Ril's waiting in a bar around the corner." His hand is already on the handle. "I'll go and get her. Can you drive around to the front of the Meeting Hall? There's a place you can park outside it. We'll get a ticket here." He's opening the door. "OK?"

"But Oskar?" I say. "I haven't driven for years. And never a car like this."

He turns back to me. "Don't worry, it'll be fine. It's like riding a bike: you can't forget. Come on." He smiles at me with his usual warm smile, but his voice is firm and cold. A stranger's voice.

Then he's out of the car before I have time to reply. I don't want to make him angry before I've told him, so I shuffle across, taking care not to dislodge the hand brake, and I sit in the driver's seat. The rear mirror fills with the open trunk lid. Oskar's face appears around the side, in the side mirror. He waves his jacket at me. I slide down the window so that I can hear him.

"Got it!" He's barely audible. He almost drops the jacket, sucking in his breath. Then he gently closes the trunk. He's so careful you'd think it was his own car.

I start up the engine, still watching him in the mirror. Now I've lost the chance to tell him I'm leaving before Ril gets here. Oskar stops by the driver's door, pulling on his jacket. It's a khaki one, not his usual leather.

"I won't be long," he says, backing away, only his mouth visible beneath the cap. "Call me if there's a problem. I'll see you in a minute."

"Oskar . . ." Maybe I should tell him now. But he's already out of earshot. He jogs toward the corner behind us and disappears.

I drive slowly down the service road, past the lane that leads to the canal, and make a sharp right toward the back of the shopping center. The Meeting Hall is lit up with glittering lights, the scaffolding all removed now. I feel a pang of sorrow. If I was still friends with them, I'd be there with Celestina, Greg, and Emanuel now. I'm sure even Serafina has gone. There is a parking place outside the Meeting Hall. Oskar has made a mistake, though, because the sign next to it says, *Taxis Only*. I pull in anyway and turn off the engine.

He said he wouldn't be long. I become aware of the security camera trained on the car. It's like the ones in the Institute drive, except that this one doesn't swivel. Its single blank eye is fixed on me. Under my coat sleeve, my wrist throbs and burns where Raymond's teeth closed on it.

Why is Oskar taking so long? Two security guards open the doors of the Meeting Hall and come down one side of the steps. A camera crew follow them, setting up their equipment to the right of the entrance. The guards pull a barrier out of the way and all of a sudden the pavement is full of young people, spilling into the road and up the steps. They must have been lining up along the side of the building. Some are dressed in Brotherhood clothes, many just as citizens. With quite a few, you can't tell. I wish I was there, as myself, with Greg and the others.

Movement catches my eye in the rear mirror. The trunk lid is slowly rising, silently and gently, until it fills the whole space of the glass. Oskar should have closed it more firmly. I reach for the door handle.

Several things blast into my mind:

Oskar running away around the corner. Backing away from the car. Stooped over the trunk, his hands busy inside while I was sliding into the driver's seat. Oskar shaking and sweating. *Not* from fear of the dog.

Raymond flying in a frenzy toward me, catching hold of my arm. Not biting; trying to pull me away. Raymond the police dog. Barking frantically at the back of the car.

Sniffer dog.

Me, driving the car. Under the camera, placed with such care. A Brotherhood girl, the child of bombers, here on the screen, waiting.

Waiting for a spark.

A spark that Oskar will send.

Oh, God.

CHAPTER 40

TIME IS LIKE water now, held in a bowl full to the brim, waiting for the drop that will send it over the edge.

People mill around the car, some giving me grumpy looks for being in their way as they try to cross the road. A detail that shouldn't matter latches on to my brain. There's a girl stepping in front of the car, right in front of it, and she's wearing a sequined silver top, and she's huddling into herself because the top is way too cold for this frosty evening, and now it doesn't even look as pretty as it did before because her arms are going all goose-pimply and gray. She's much younger than me. She looks anxiously around, maybe searching for a friend, but that's all she's worried about, not the real thing she should be worried about, the thing right here beside her in the car that she's almost leaning against.

Or have I got it wrong? When did I become so nervous and paranoid? Ready to imagine that Oskar, the man who saved me in a bomb attack, would be capable of mass murder? And many of these people are citizens. Why was he at the station that day? *Pull yourself together, K.* But I can't stop seeing Raymond as we drove away, barking and barking, no need for words.

Who to listen to? What to do? My hands are on the steering wheel of the still car. The stitching feels like braid under my thumbs. A whorled pattern crosses the leather, like waves churning.

Waves churning below the harbor wall at Yoremouth. Oskar's hand on my back. The water swirling in inky coils below. I think of my own words. *Don't freeze, K. Don't freeze.*

Still I am motionless, while blood pounds around my head. I become aware of the key fob moving gently in a tiny current of air, as if it's waiting. Like me. Waiting to see what Oskar will do. Waiting until it's too late.

A big *NO* roars in my head. *Not this time.*

There are people everywhere, like ants hurrying around the car. They are laughing and jostling. There's no way I could make them move away in time.

My mind soars over the Old City, making a street plan of the whole area. Shopping center. Meeting

Hall. Bridge, main road, service roads. The lane to the canal basin. The towpath and the houseboats are on the other side of the dam. That's it.

I close my eyes and reach for the key. My teeth are chattering. My hand is shaking. Somehow I make myself take hold of it. *It's not the key, K; you know that. You already started the car to get here.* It must be Oskar's cell phone. He said to call him; to trigger the device. Still, I close my eyes as I turn the key.

Foot on clutch. Gear into reverse. Back up slowly until I am around the corner. Then forward, down the lane that leads to the canal. Not too fast, in case there is someone on the grass verge. There isn't.

I drive the car up the shallow curb and onto the grass. Engine off. Hand brake off. Gear into neutral. Get out. Every part of my body is humming with the need to run. But I make myself go around to the back. I place my hands on the body of the car, above which the open trunk lid bumps softly up and down, and start to push. I don't want it to teeter and sway like the Trembling Rock, going nowhere.

At first it doesn't move. I see Emanuel with his hands on the rock. One person can't move it on their own. But then the wheels begin to turn. The car rolls toward the water, and it tips smoothly into the canal basin. I don't wait for the splash.

CHAPTER 41

I DON'T EVEN know I'm running. I'm not out of breath and I'm not thinking.

I'm in the shopping center. I see phone booths next to

the parking garage ticket machines. I duck into one and dial the emergency number with fingers that won't work.

I hold the receiver to my ear. "Bomb," I say. "Bomb . . . in the car . . . canal . . ."

"Can you give me your name?"

I open my mouth to speak, and sounds, but not words, are stumbling over my tongue.

"I'm sorry? Could you repeat that?"

Jeremiah's haunted eyes. Tina's look of disbelief. Of course they won't believe me.

The voice crackles from the receiver as it falls and swings from the cord, shattering the glass wall of the phone booth into a cloudy cobweb.

I crouch down on the floor, where the door is metal, not glass, in case Oskar walks past. I can hear a voice twittering from the receiver as it hangs on its wire. I wait for the explosion. Can a bomb go off under water? If I stay here, someone will find me. And then I can tell them everything: no lies, just truth.

I lift my head. I think how readily people believe lies, and how easily the truth can look like a lie. I see myself in an interview room with two police officers, a woman and a man. *"And how did you know there was a bomb in the car?" "Because of the dog." "The dog?"*

I think of the girl who was cremated as K Child.

Jeremiah, and Tranquility Sound.

Greg, and Celestina, and Emanuel and Serafina.

A fire alarm shrieks through the air.

"LEAVE THE BUILDING. LEAVE THE BUILDING BY THE NEAREST EXIT."

Yes.

I'm not frozen anymore. I slide out of the cracked phone booth and join the surge of people. Police are hurrying down the corridor that leads from the parking garage.

There's no way they will believe me. Why should they? My life is one big lie.

I need to get away before the police get here. I melt into the crowd.

Nobody will believe me.

CHAPTER 42

AND NOW I feel oddly calm. I only have to do one thing. Hide. Get out of here. There are too many people pounding along this corridor. But that's good. I'm lost in the crowd. In my Brotherhood clothes.

My cheek is pressed up against a shop window, flattened against the glass so that all the clothes inside blur into colors. I edge toward the door to avoid the crush, and as the force of the crowd is suddenly gone, I fall into the sale racks by the shop entrance. I'm lucky that these shops stay open late at the weekend. It's easy to crouch under the rail and pull down a pair of pants, and a jacket. They're men's clothes, but they'll do. I put them on inside the tunnel of clothes. I yank off my skirt and stuff it into my wool bag on top of the few things I always carry with me.

When I rejoin the crowd of people, I look like a citizen again.

I'm just one of the crowd now, hurrying toward the exit of the shopping center, my eyes sweeping the faces for Oskar.

I reach the way out and see cash machines on the wall to the left. I take out as much money as I can. It doesn't matter now if I locate myself here because Oskar has already ensured that I'm on the shopping center security camera. Maybe they are checking the cameras already.

Then I walk through the back streets to the bridge and across the square to Central Station. I'm not afraid of the station now. I'm not afraid of the Brotherhood. I know I have to hurry, in case they cordon it off, looking for the bomber. Maybe they already have. I hear sirens all around. The station looks normal as I walk in.

Where can you hide if you have nowhere else to go?

I want to run as far away from Oskar as I can, but I'm not going to. I'm going to face the danger I couldn't see before. I'm tired of hiding. I'm going to make myself go to Yoremouth, where his house is. There must be something there that will help me find out why he did this. I'll just have to be very careful.

I stand in the line for the ticket office. There's a group of young men hanging about, but this evening I'm one of them, not one of Them. It doesn't take long for me to reach the window.

"Single to Yoremouth." How clear and calm my voice sounds.

I drop the cash into the metal dish Then I go down to the platform to wait for my train. I make my body very still while I wait. I breathe on tiptoes, in and out, in and out. When the train pulls in, I get into a car in the middle. It's empty. My breath hisses out in a long sigh.

The train pulls out slowly, leaving Gatesbrooke behind. But I don't follow the thought of all I'm leaving. I stare at the window, while the train takes me away.

There are lights but no heating. I huddle into the jacket I stole from the shopping center and pull the hood over Greg's cap, which I found in my bag. Maybe, if I get out of this, I'll go back and pay for them. My mouth is so dry. I wish I'd remembered to buy—or loot—some water.

I rest my cheek against the cold glass, watching as the train slows down to pass through Limbourne. In the black glass of the opposite window my face appears, thin and pale, like a child waking from a nightmare.

The train rollicks from side to side. *You've taken everything, Oskar.* My barge, my job, my sunflower print, the new life I've been slowly building: all lost. The only thing I have left is my freedom. But for how long? A week? A few days? Hours?

My breath starts to flutter, and to calm myself I turn and stare back at the Limbourne waiting room as it gets smaller and smaller, until it's a tiny yellow cube, then a dot, then nothing. But that's a mistake, because I can't keep the memory of Greg away any longer. The pain thuds inside my ribs, like an actual blow, and I have to push it from me. If I start to cry now, I know I'll never stop.

I face forward again. In the darkness of my closed eyes I see a tiny oval picture, like a little frame with a film inside it. It's as clear as an image on a screen. It's the road outside the Meeting Hall. There's the girl in the sequined silver top. She's glaring at me, shivering in her thin clothes. She has no idea of the danger she's in. But she isn't in any danger, because I'm carefully reversing it away. *I'm doing that, Oskar.*

I did that.

Unless I'm slowly going mad. Perhaps she was in no danger at all; perhaps there was no bomb. What if there's no need to run? How would I know? There's no one to say, "Don't be daft, K, you're letting your imagination run away with you." My only confidant is a dog! I pushed Oskar's car into the canal because of a feeling, but what if that feeling was wrong? I didn't hear an explosion. All the people rushing out of the shopping center seemed unaware of a bomb. Nobody at the station was panicking.

I open my eyes and sit up. I'm not so cold now that the heating's come on. This jacket is all right. It's a padded parka, so I'll be able to zip it right up to my chin and put the fur-lined hood up. I look at my wool bag. There's nothing much in it now, just my wallet, the paintbrush Greg gave me, my cell phone, my father's paintbox, and my mother's folding scissors and the skirt I was wearing. Tina would think it's bugged.

Tina told me to watch myself. Maybe I was right. I'm not just being paranoid.

I take everything out and put the things in the jacket pockets, except for Serafina's dear old pink cardigan and my coat, skirt, and hat. I put them all back in the bag, along with the phone Oskar gave me. Then I go into the space between the cars. I wait until the train slows down alongside a freight train, and I open the window and toss my bag into one of the carts. I watch it disappear. I can almost see Tina nodding approvingly.

Now it's just me and the clothes I'm standing in. I go back into the car and curl up on the seats.

Tomorrow I am going to hunt for Oskar. I will find out why he's done this.

I start to feel warm. I hold tight the thought that I stopped Oskar's bomb, and I say good night in my head to the girl in the silver top, who is still on this planet, and then I let myself fall asleep.

CHAPTER 43

WHEN I WAKE up, the train is still. Outside, I see the Yoremouth platform. Everything surges back and I feel absolutely certain that I made a mistake. Of course there was no bomb. The sky is lightening to gray. I must have slept here all night. My legs shake when I step down from the train.

I see a cafe ahead of me, and even though it's not even seven yet, it's open. I'm so thirsty. I go in and order toast and tea. It's surprisingly busy inside. I find a table at the back in the corner. Just like Jeremiah. I should have made him tell me what was wrong before it was too late. I wolf down the toast and pour myself another cup of tea.

That's when I see the newspaper rack on the back door. I go and get two newspapers and bring them back to my table. I need to look. Just in case.

It's on the front page: *ATTEMPTED BOMB AT GATESBROOKE SHOPPING CENTER.* I skim through the article: *After an anonymous tip-off to police . . . mystery car crash in canal basin . . . triggered remotely but failed to detonate under water . . . police*

want to talk to unknown caller . . . below average height,
slim build, Brotherhood clothing, long black hair . . .

I look at the blaring tabloid headlines next: *HOOD
ATROCITY FOILED! . . . What Price Reconciliation
Agreement Now? . . . WHAT WILL THEY DO NEXT?*

I rake my hands through my hair. My long, Brotherhood hair!

Nobody was hurt.

Oskar tried to blow me up. Now I know it for sure.

They're hunting me already. The police. Oskar. I
have to get out of here. I make myself get up slowly
and walk casually back onto the platform.

—

I NEED TO do something about my hair. I almost sob
with relief when I see the ladies' bathroom. I slip
inside, and a wild-eyed figure stares at me from the
metal mirror. I already look like a fugitive. It won't
be long before they catch me.

I take my mother's scissors out of my pocket. Greg
would be proud of me for being so well-prepared. I
push away the thought of Greg. What will he think of
me when he sees the morning papers?

I unfold the scissors. The sharp metal edges press
into my finger and thumb as I hack my hair off in
spikes. After a while I don't look like a Brotherhood
girl anymore. I don't look like me. My face is as spiky
as my hair, pinched with cold, eyes with huge black
pupils in this dim light.

I scoop up the cuttings into a bundle and shove it
into my pocket. Then I wash the stray strands down

the drain and go outside. At the entrance to the park that runs alongside the railway line there's a compost bin. I drop the ball of hair inside it and stir it into the mulch with a stick.

—

I WANT TO search Oskar's house. Maybe he's destroyed all my old papers, but if there's a chance I can prove who I really am, perhaps I can explain all this. Prove Oskar was using me. I think of Jeremiah and Tranquility Sound, the flimsy "evidence" that sent him there. I walk briskly through the streets like a person going somewhere. I'm pretty sure Oskar won't be there, though if he got wind of my movements he's had more than enough time to drive back. I'm banking on him staying in Gatesbrooke to look for me. But his housemate Col might be in. The thought of Col makes me shudder. I'll have to be careful. But I also have to be quick.

All I have to do is keep walking. I turn left at the seafront and head for the cottage. I need to lean forward against the wind just to keep moving. The sea seethes around the pier supports, white foam endlessly pouring itself on to the land. Although it thrashes so angrily, it can't mean harm. Not like Oskar. I follow the prom under the castle and around to the other bay. The waves unfold to the sky in an expanse of gray. Nothing would last long in there.

Seagulls wheel above the castle. The wind soars around the angles of the rooftops. I see the cottage where I stayed with Oskar in the spring, and my feet falter and stop. But I make myself keep going. *I'm coming after you, Oskar.*

I slow down as I pass the windows. The front room curtains are open, and I can't see anyone inside. The curtains upstairs are open too. That's good. It looks like nobody's in.

I turn down the next street to find the alley behind the houses. It comes out into a small yard, and I can see the shadows beyond the kitchen window. I peer into the empty kitchen. There are dishes in the sink. One bowl, one mug, some cutlery. One person's dishes. I listen, but I can't hear anything. The key is still where it was in the spring, under an upturned pail near the back door. I unlock the door and put the key back. Then I go in and shut the door softly behind me. I stand still for a moment, absorbing the sounds of the house and the silence after the wind.

I go upstairs, stopping on the first landing to listen again. I check the bedroom there first: Oskar's room. My heart starts beating faster, with the hope that I might find something and the fear that somebody will come home before I do.

I look systematically through the desk drawers, under the bed, in the wardrobe, on top of the wardrobe. Then in all the pockets of the clothes. It's clear that Oskar has been living here recently, because in the bin there's a coffee receipt from last week. But there are no papers or letters anywhere.

Why did I think I would find anything? It's hopeless. Of course he would have destroyed everything that linked me with my old life.

The room at the front must be Col's. It's very tidy. I look quickly and carefully through the closet, the shelves, and drawers. But here too there's nothing personal. I don't bother trying to keep my fingerprints off anything, because I'm looking, not hiding. I stare out at the churning sea.

I go back into Oskar's room for one last look. *Come on, K, think. Where would you hide things if this was your room?* Ceiling, walls, floor. Floor.

I kneel down and begin patting the carpet for loose boards. There's one that moves under the window, but to check it I have to lift the bed leg and pull the carpet out from underneath. It's all taking too long. My fingers are fumbling. And then I see that there is a board with no nails.

I prise the board up and edge my hand into the cavity. My fingers find a thick envelope. I pull it out, and tip the contents on to the floor.

Certificates, documents, photos: a life history in paper. Not for K Child, but for Verity Nekton. A real person after all.

I think of the girl who was cremated with my name, and nausea rushes over me. I swallow it, and I push all the papers back into the envelope. I can't read this here.

Now I can't wait to get out of Oskar's house. I'm outside Col's room when I hear a key turning in the front door lock. I don't have time to get downstairs. I dart into Col's room. The only place to hide is under the bed. At least the quilt hangs down to the floor. I crawl underneath. Footsteps thunder up the stairs.

I hold my breath, hugging the envelope to my chest. I forgot to put the carpet back in Oskar's bedroom!

Whoever it is bounds into this room. Col. I stay very still, staring at the piping on the gray quilt.

Music blasts out from Col's radio. I peer under the cover. Feet.

"Hello? Hello?" says Col's voice.

I stay frozen.

"Oskar? You're breaking up . . ." Col goes out onto the landing.

I have to get out. I have to get out now. I roll out and tiptoe behind the bedroom door.

"What?" There's a pause. Col crashes the door into my face as he strides back into the room. The radio clicks off.

There's a little silence. "Here? You're sure?" Col's voice is cold. "This was your last chance." Another pause. Then, "I'm going to say two words: Mona. Talbot." Another silence. "Ril and I will have to leave the country now. You've sabotaged everything."

Col's footsteps thud upstairs toward the attic. "You'd better find her," I hear him say.

I take my chance and run down the stairs, gripping the envelope.

"Hey!" A shout, thundering footsteps on the stairs. "Stop!"

He's behind me, he's seen me.

The front door is making a noise, the noise of a key turning.

Oskar! Oskar is here!

CHAPTER 44

I HEAR THE thump of Col leaping down the last few steps as I bolt through the back door.

I fly down the alley, running out into the street that leads to the seafront. They'll be here in a moment. There's a supermarket, and I duck inside. Blend in. If Col hadn't seen me in the house, I would be getting the first train out of Yoremouth. But now it isn't safe to go anywhere near the station. I grab a cart and force myself to push it slowly through the hardware aisle until my heart stops hammering. I make myself think.

I buy a big bottle of water, some sandwiches, chocolate, and a small backpack to hold them. Then I add a flashlight and a hacksaw, because I might have to break into a beach hut to hide out. *I'm turning into Greg*, I think. Before coming out of the door, I search the street for Col and Oskar and put my hood up. But as I hurry toward the seafront, I see Col on the corner, scanning the promenade. The movie theater is behind me, and now I dart inside and join the line, pulling off my coat to make myself look different. I buy a ticket for the same film as the woman in front of me and follow her in.

I sit in an empty row, in the middle, so that there are two ways to get out. It's good to be in darkness. I zip the envelope safely inside the backpack. Maybe this is a safe place to hide. I can stay in here until it's dark outside. I hug the backpack to me, ready to leap up. Could I read the papers in the bathroom stall? No. People don't spend long in theater bathrooms. I can't do anything that might attract attention.

At first I wait for the footage of the Gatesbrooke Massacre. But of course they don't show it here. The film opens with a train rushing into the night. I stay alert: wide-eyed, forehead creased into a taut frown, staring at the screen but seeing nothing. I jump when a little girl pats my knee, wanting to climb past. When the film ends, I change seats and wait for the next one.

It's 3:15 when I come out of the movie theater. I peer down the street before I step out, but it's almost empty. The sky is dark blue and the streetlights have come on. The wind funnels between the shops. At the end of the street, waves break over the promenade.

I need to hide. I need to eat. I need to sleep. But most of all, I need to read. I clench my precious backpack to my chest. Wind lashes the spikes of my hair. Long hair yesterday, short hair today.

The beach huts. I lean into the wind and push toward the shore, where pebbles rattle and crash against the surf. Verity yesterday, K today. Nobody tomorrow if I don't find shelter soon. Oskar and Col could be watching me now, from a window. It's too exposed on the promenade. I double back and dart down the little road that leads to the castle. Try to breathe calmly.

By the time I come out by the seafront and cross the road, I am as far as possible from Col's house. There's only one car parked at the end of the promenade. It looks empty. I keep my head down, but rain and spray, sweet and salt, lash my face.

The beach huts at this end are the old ones, with rusty metal windows and doors. Maybe I won't even need the hacksaw. I stop outside the last one and check behind me. Nobody. The sea is loud on the shingle, pitching white foam over the breakwaters. I try to smash the rusty padlock on the door with a rock, but in the end I have to saw through it. All the noise is sucked away by the wind. No wonder nobody is out on the beach.

When I've got the door open, I edge inside, trying to pull it shut behind me. For a moment it feels warm and silent, out of the wind. The hut is small and bare, smelling of mildew and damp. There is an iron bench and a table. Behind me, the wind worries at the door. This isn't much of a refuge after all.

I sit on the bench and try to focus on the sound of the waves sweeping over shingle, rather than the thumping of my heart inside my rib cage and the roaring of my blood in my ears. I need to remember who I am. But all I can think about is the girl they called K Child, drowned in the sea. Maybe when I read Verity Nekton's papers I'll find out what really happened to her. I don't think it'll be anything good. I am sure now that they are the same person.

I take the envelope and flashlight out of my backpack. The door begins to bang against the frame. *Bang BANG. Bang BANG.* Wind whips the corner of the hut. Maybe someone will walk their dog past here, the way they do every evening, and wonder why this door is banging today. Or maybe the parked car isn't empty at all. And I can't use the flashlight, because the light will show. Stupid! Stupid! No place to hide.

Then I hear a stealthy crunch on pebbles. I fumble the envelope back into my backpack and tiptoe to the door. I can't see anyone, but I hear footsteps on the promenade behind the huts. I creep out of the hut and hurry down the row, on the seaward side, my breath gasping in my throat.

When I reach the end of the huts I sprint for the promenade, but as I leap my foot slides under a large stone and turns sideways. A sickening splinter of pain shoots up my ankle. I bite back the scream. Footsteps pound on the shingle behind me. I run into the stabbing pain, limping across the road and into an alley.

The alley emerges into a square. Grandma's community center, where Oskar and I once talked, looms over it.

The door is open and people are arriving and going inside. Best way to hide? In plain sight.

Heart thumping, scarcely breathing, but with a vague smile on my lips, I walk as naturally as I can up the steps, wave over the heads of the people in front of me to look as though I have a friend inside, and go into the lobby. But it's all right. I don't look like a Brotherhood girl anymore. I rummage in my bag for a tissue to give me time to look about. On the right there is a staircase and a sign for the ladies' bathroom. On the left there is a men's and a corridor. I go toward the stairs, and when I'm sure nobody is watching, I crawl under them, behind a stack of folding tables.

The moment I sit down, the pain overwhelms me. But it's OK, because this is a good hiding place. It's very cramped behind the tables and I can't take the papers out in case someone hears them rustle. The people in the hall are singing. I put my wrist nearer to the light to look at my watch: 4:20. This is the first time

I've ever been in Grandma's community center, even though she spent half her life here. The last few people don't leave until almost eight. I can hear laughing and chatting by the open door, and an icy draft slices through gaps under the stairs. Finally the door slams.

I wait until I'm sure I'm alone. Then I slowly unravel myself and crawl out from behind the tables, trying not to put weight on my ankle.

I find a place to read the papers in the ladies' bathroom. There's no window, so I can put on the light. A fan comes on too, but it's quieter than the wind. I lock the outer door and sit down on the green linoleum floor, with my back against some warm pipes. I get out the envelope I took from Oskar's house, and everything changes.

—

I EMPTY IT all onto my lap, and I can't believe what I see.

First a letter from my old school saying: *Congratulations! You have been successful in obtaining a place for junior year.* I riffle back to find the date. Just days after I met Oskar. I cast my mind back. I wasn't failing then.

Oskar manipulated everything. He set me up to fail. But why did he choose me?

I put the letter down. The wind is louder now, whining around the side of the building. I must make myself read the papers about Verity Nekton. She was a real person. The first page is her birth certificate.

Mother: Kit Nekton
Father: Ambrose Nekton

With shaking fingers I shuffle through the papers, and I find Verity Nekton's parents' marriage certificate.

Her father's name was Ambrose John Nekton. Her mother was Kit Jane Child.

My mother's name was Jane Child.

Tiny dots crackle around my eyes as I stare at the type. *Kit Jane Child.* Jane Child, my mother. John Child, my father. *Ambrose John Nekton.*

Grandma, what did you do?

I am K Child.

I am Verity Nekton.

CHAPTER 45

I SEARCH THROUGH the papers until I find the photos and peer at them in the dim light. That must be my mother, Kit, holding hands with my father, Ambrose. My mother is pregnant. Kit looked like me. Ambrose was tall, with curly hair. I pore over the photos through my tears, at these people I feel I've never seen. There's another photo, of a newborn baby asleep with arms flung up above her head. Me. And one of the three of us together. I can imagine them choosing a pretty name for their baby girl. Verity. And I'm smiling too, almost laughing with relief, to finally see their faces.

It takes me a moment to notice the Brotherhood clothes my father is wearing. My father was Brotherhood! And my mother too. She wore Brotherhood clothes—she must have joined when she got married. How could Grandma ever have accepted that? Of course: she didn't. Everything suddenly makes sense. My name, K. It's just my mother's initial. That's all my

Grandma could bear to give me. No wonder she never let anyone see me.

Oskar hates the Brotherhood. That's why he hates me. He was never a policeman. But he does work for an organization. One that can provide cars. And bombs.

I scrabble through the rest of the papers. Here's another birth certificate, a copy from when I was two. *K Child*. Grandma must have gotten this one.

Eventually I reach for the bundle of newspaper cuttings, and as I read them, the knowledge seeps into me with a chilly inevitability: something that's always been there, just out of sight.

Grandma's house, where there were no photos. The life I led with her, hidden away, never going to school, never coming here. I read through the articles until I get to the end.

All the clippings are about the bomb that killed my parents. It went off in the concourse at Gatesbrooke Central Station, killing nineteen people. I close my eyes when I read that. Then I make myself read on, even though I'm hardly breathing now. First there's a list of the dead, with names and photos. My parents' faces are there too. Nothing about me.

I turn to the next cutting, and the next. I know what I'm going to find now.

First the calls to find those responsible. Then recriminations. The possibility of a suicide bomber.

And then I finally allow myself to face it. I am Verity Nekton, and Verity Nekton's parents are my parents.

My ears begin to ring. I snatch up the last clipping,

but my vision is blurring. I force myself to hold the paper still and look at the photos.

AMBROSE NEKTON, SUICIDE BOMBER

KIT NEKTON, TERRORIST

How could they have done this?

Grandma must have taken me secretly, changed my name, and hidden me. That's why I never went to school. She was ashamed of me.

I represented everything she hated.

And if I'm the child of terrorists, I represent everything I hate.

CHAPTER 46

I SIT FROZEN for a long time, my head against the knee of my uninjured leg. Gradually I start to hear the ticking sound of the pipes cooling down, and the wind gusting around the building in a shriek. Then I become aware of the crushing exhaustion that pins me down.

I lift my head and the sudden brightness makes my vision explode into dots. Scattered all around me on the floor is the evidence of Oskar's plans for me, the way he took my buried history and twisted it into a new atrocity, so easy to believe. Like parents, like child.

My mother and my father. How could they have thrown their lives away in an act of murder? How could they have left me behind?

It's over. Nothing matters anymore. A great stillness has gripped me, and I can't move at all, not even my eyes, which have locked themselves onto the thin copper pipe at the bottom of the radiator. It's a relief now. That's all I have to do: stare at the pipe while the room grows steadily colder, because none of it matters. It wouldn't matter if I walked outside now and waited for Oskar to find me. I could even go back to Col's house. I could do that. It's just on the other side of the square, minutes away. I know too much. Oskar wanted to kill me, and he'll get me in the end. I could get it over with. It would be a relief.

But first I have to get up.

I turn onto my good leg, trying to kneel. The first movement of my other foot sends pain searing through my body, rocking me so that I lose my balance and fall back against the wall. My good knee crunches onto something thin and round in a burst of sickening pain. Greg's paintbrush rolls toward the newspaper cutting.

AMBROSE NEKTON, SUICIDE BOMBER
KIT NEKTON, TERRORIST

That's not me. I pushed Oskar's bomb into the canal. Everyone who was outside the Old City Meeting Hall last night is still alive.

I pick up Greg's paintbrush and close my eyes, and faces appear on the dark screen of my eyelids.

First Mr. Williams. He's whistling an old tune while he writes *Verity* carefully on the side of a box for the anxious Brotherhood girl who talks to herself while she cuts into her woodblock. For me.

Celestina, floating motionless, upright in the pool, her head tipped back against the water, smiling at her own buoyancy.

Emanuel, so sweet and smiling, looking for me to share his happiness.

Serafina, flung against a tree after her bicycle crash, and the gladness I felt when I heard someone coming to help.

Greg.

And what I see is his uncertain brown eyes, and I hear his voice as he says, *"What's so wrong that we can't fix it?"*

That's when I know I have to see him again. I have to tell them all what really happened.

I open my eyes and let them adjust to the fluorescent light in the quiet bathroom. There is a reason why people should believe me. Because it's the truth.

I won't feel sad. I won't feel angry. I'm going to let myself feel something I've only allowed a little glimpse at until now. Hope. It's a dangerous feeling, I know that.

For the first time in months, everything is here in my own hands. Carefully I put all of it, my whole life, back in the envelope, and I tuck that into my backpack.

I know what I have to do. I must prove who I am and what really happened. I have to stop Oskar from using me for propaganda. But I'm too tired to do anything tonight.

I brace myself, and clamber to my feet, pulling myself up on the radiator. I turn off the light once I'm holding the door handle. Nothing happens. Too late I see that there are two switches. I must have turned on the light in the hall outside. I snap it off, my heart racing. Surely nobody will have seen that momentary flash?

I watch and listen, with the door ajar. There's no sound from the lobby outside. It's dark in the hallway as I edge out, holding on to the wall. I stand and wait in the darkness. When I can make out the staircase in the faint shimmer of moonlight, I creak my way up to the gallery, one step at a time. The pain isn't so bad now. My ankle feels numb.

I only need one more day. Just enough time to call Tina from a pay phone and go to Limbourne. And over the horizon is the thought that if I can clear my name, I can see Greg and explain everything. I have to believe he'll still want to know me. I know it's a big "if." Maybe bigger now than before.

So I pull a long cushion off a bench onto the floor, wrap myself up in my coat with my hood up, and lie down. My ankle throbs against the side of my boot. I don't think I'll be able to get it off now, so I leave it, and shut my eyes.

The second I close them I hear something. It's not the creaks of wood contracting at night. It's not the scurrying of mice.

It's the sound of a person, creeping up, step by step. I can even hear them breathing.

Moonlight shafts through the skylight onto the landing at the top of the stairs. A shadow creeps across the floorboards. I see him.

Oskar.

Just for one moment I think he hasn't seen me. Then I'm blinded, as the beam of his flashlight shines into my eyes.

CHAPTER 47

I SHUT MY eyes. I can't bear to watch him coming closer,

toward my trap between the wall and the bench.

Then he speaks.

"Verity?" he says. "Verity? It's me."

He shines the flashlight on his own face, lighting it up from underneath like a mask.

I leap up, forgetting about my ankle, until the searing pain makes it give way and sends me tumbling toward him. He catches me by my arms.

"Greg! What are you doing here?" I stop, breathless.

Greg lets go of my arms. "I'm sorry." His voice is cold. "I know you don't want to see me. I just came to check you're OK. That's all."

"How did you find me?"

"I followed you from the beach," says Greg. "I knew you were somewhere near the square, so I waited. Then I saw a light go on in here."

He turns off his flashlight. But I can see him in the thin moonlight if I don't look directly at him.

"You look like a citizen," he says. "But that's not surprising, is it, K?"

I feel the blood rush to my head. "What did you call me?"

"K," says Greg. "K."

I'm dizzy. I sit down, suddenly, on the cushions. I try to keep the tears out of my voice. "You know?"

"I know." His voice is cold. He's still standing.

"Why are you here, Greg?"

"Serafina told me you'd disappeared. She said you made up a story about losing your wallet so you could go into the city early and then you didn't come home all night. So she was worried." He half-shrugs.

"Celestina called Ms. Cobana—Tina. Celestina told her you broke up with me, and Tina said she knew—because of Jeremiah."

I nod. He's come a long way to be so cold. "Do you want to sit down?" I say. I wipe my face with the back of my hand.

Greg sits down, at the other end of the cushion. Then he punches it. "Why didn't you tell me sooner?" he says. "About you and Jeremiah?"

"Me and Jeremiah? . . . Greg, what did Tina say about Jeremiah?"

"She just said that's why you broke up with me. You don't have to explain. I don't want to hear about it. It's not as if we were . . ."

I start laughing. I can't help it, and once I've started, I can't stop.

"Shut up, Verity. K. Whatever your name is."

I crawl over to where Greg is sitting. He knows I'm K, and he still came. I put my hand on his arm, but he pulls away.

"Greg. Listen to me. I thought Jeremiah was arrested because of me. He asked me to meet him, after the BSF meeting. He looked upset, so I said I would. And because he was from the Institute and he was your and Emanuel's friend."

"Not really my friend," mutters Greg.

"I was sure he'd been arrested because of me. So I was afraid the same thing would happen to you. That's why I ended it."

He turns to me. "So you and Jeremiah aren't—"

"No! I didn't even like Jeremiah, really."

Neither of us speaks for a moment.

"But it's still dangerous for you to be friends with me," I say. "More dangerous than it was before. Oskar, the guy who set me up, he knows I'm in Yoremouth. Maybe if you go now—"

"Verity," says Greg. "I know who Oskar is, but I'm not going anywhere without you. You were wrong not to tell me the truth."

"I tried to tell you, all the time. It's you who wouldn't let me."

"I mean after Jeremiah was arrested."

"I was so scared I'd hurt you," I whisper.

"You did hurt me." He moves closer. I reach up to feel the shape of his face. His hair has grown longer.

"Greg," I say. "Greg." I kneel up so that I can kiss him.

He puts his arms around me, so tightly that we fall onto the cushions. It's a hard, angry kiss. Neither of us will let it end. Finally I lean away.

"Greg? I want to tell you everything now." I pull myself up to make him listen.

"OK." He sits up too and holds me close.

"How did you know my name? K?"

"Tina told Celestina," says Greg. "I knew about Oskar before, from Brer Magnus." He pauses. "I told you before, I knew who you were. You should have trusted me."

I tell him about Oskar's bomb and the letters I found today.

Greg waits until I stop talking. Then he says, "You didn't know you really were Verity Nekton?"

Now he will despise me. I shake my head.

"You didn't know your father was Brotherhood?"

"No. Did you know? And did you know my mother wasn't?"

"Yes. I told you, I know who you are. I don't care."

There's a silence. I start to move away, but Greg's hand tightens on my arm. "There's something you need to know about me too," he says. "It's the reason why I didn't want you to say who you were. Because I knew that then I'd have to tell you."

"Tell me what?" It must be something quite bad after all.

Greg holds on to me like I might try to move away once I know. "At the Institute," he says. "When you were new? Brer Magnus asked me to watch you. So I was a spy. I spied on you."

"Oh, that," I say. "Yeah, I know."

"You know?"

"I think I always did," I say.

Greg gives a little laugh. "That's why, after Limbourne, I stopped speaking to you." He pulls me closer. "I couldn't do it anymore. I went to tell Brer Magnus."

"I overheard you."

"I couldn't stand it once I got to know you," Greg murmurs. "No, before that. The first time you spoke to me. I was terrified you'd find out I was spying on you."

Now I laugh. "How did you find me tonight?" I ask him.

"I looked through your things in the Art room," says Greg. "I found your sketches of the beach huts. And you seemed to know your way in Yoremouth last spring. Celestina thought you'd come here. So I came in my car. I saw you go into the beach hut. By the way"—his voice sounds much more like it used to, at the Institute—"that was a pretty stupid place to hide, if you don't mind me saying."

"I know that now."

"Not Yoremouth. Oskar wouldn't expect you to come back to his safe house. That was quite a clever choice."

"Now I'm clever?" I pause. "But he does know; Col saw me in the house."

"OK. Not really clever. Slightly less dumb."

I feel better now that Greg's stopped being nice.

—

WE'RE LYING ON the cushion. Greg puts his arm around me so that my head is on his chest. My cheek is next to the soft cotton of his shirt.

"I've never seen you without long hair," says Greg. His fingers brush through my fringe.

I run my fingers down the side of his face, so familiar and so new, from his close-trimmed hair to his earlobe. It feels like silk. I rest my hand in the little hollow where his collarbone starts. I'm warm now. Sleep is taking me down.

"Greg?"

"Mmm?"

"Do you think . . . do you think we're going to make it?"

Greg kisses the top of my head. "We are." He pauses. "I bolted the door on the inside."

We lie there for a few minutes.

"Verity?" Greg finds my hand and laces his fingers

through mine. His palm is warm against mine. "I like this," he says.

"Like this," I murmur.

"Whatever happens," Greg whispers. "We have this."

"I can hear your heartbeat," I say.

"I can feel yours."

I think of all the lonely nights under my duvet, pretending to be asleep so that nobody would speak to me, trying not to think of Greg. And now here he is.

"You're here," I say.

I feel his lips touch my head. "I'm here."

I want to stay awake. I want to feel his arms around me, and listen to his heart beating, and feel his breath on my head. But sleep is pulling me down to an absent place where I won't remember that I'm lying in Greg's arms. I try to fight it off, in case this is our only night together, in case something comes between us again. I try to hold on to wakefulness, the way I'm holding on to Greg's hand and his shoulder, but I can't.

CHAPTER 48

IT ONLY FEELS like a second later when I wake up.

"Verity? Verity!"

Greg's voice hums through his shirt. It's true. He's here. My head is on his chest.

He gives my shoulder a little tug. "Verity? We've got to go. While it's still dark."

He's right. He's in enough danger just being with me.

But when I stand up, the pain in my ankle almost makes me pass out. I collapse onto the bench and pull up my trouser leg before unlacing my boot.

Greg crouches in front of me. "Shall I try and take it off?" He shines his flashlight on my ankle. Above my boot the skin is puffed and shiny.

I shake my head. "I'll just hobble."

I get down the stairs on my bottom, but I know I will be too slow if I try to walk to the car. And too conspicuous.

We reach the doorway at last. The pane next to the door handle is broken. I look at Greg.

"Someone might be outside." He's whispering now. "I had to get in quickly." He nudges the glass into the corner of the door frame with one foot.

"Wow." I smile at him, whispering too. Then I realize something. "I don't think I'll be able to share the driving."

"And that's a bad thing?" Greg eases back the bolts at the top and bottom of the door, and looks around at me with his familiar raised eyebrow. "I don't want my car to end up in the sea."

"Best place for it." I smile. "Except it would cause an oil slick."

"I'll go and get it." Greg opens the door a little and peers out. "It'll only take me five minutes, if I run. Here." He pulls a pair of gloves out of his pocket and gives them to me. "Your hands are always so cold."

"OK." I reach up and touch his face, and he turns back to kiss me, with his hand on the door. I hold it open a little so that I can watch him run across the road and into the castle gardens.

Now that he's gone panic gnaws at me. We should have stayed together. But it's OK; it's just that anxiety has become my default setting. Greg's safer on his own. Oskar won't recognize him without me.

Maybe I should get myself down the steps so that we can leave as soon as Greg comes. I pull on the gloves and steady myself on the door frame, because as soon as I open the door the wind tears around the corner of the building. I can't put weight on my foot, so I bump down to the bottom step, waiting with my eyes fixed on where the road from the promenade emerges into the square.

He should be here by now.

I shouldn't have let him go alone.

I strain my ears into the air, trying to hear past the wind and the sea's roar. Maybe the car won't start.

But now I hear the sound I've been listening for: the whine of an engine revving to get up a hill. I feel myself smile. I stand up, to be ready. It's going to be OK.

There's a gust of slashing rain, but through it I see the car's lights. Rain washes down the windshield because he hasn't got the wipers on. That's not like Greg.

There he is, hunched over the wheel.

He should be slowing down.

There's someone else in the car. Behind Greg, leaning forward. It's Oskar. Oskar is in the car with Greg.

I take a step forward.

Greg winds down his window. "Run, Verity!" he shouts.

Then he speeds up, and the car shoots past me, out of the square.

"No, no, no!" But in the second it takes for me to shout, I see in my mind the one-way system that takes the road past the steps that lead up from the square.

Adrenaline surges through me, and I run across the square and up the steps, ignoring my ankle. I haul myself up with the handrail. *Come on, come on!*

I hear Greg's car growling up the hill, and that gives me hope for one last burst. And now I'm on the road and I can see the lights blinking through the rain.

I stand in the middle of the road, legs apart, arms out. There's no way past me.

I wave my arms. "Greg! Stop!" I yell. But the wind sucks my voice away.

I don't think he's seen me.

But the car screeches to a stop and stalls. I get in before Greg has time to start the engine again.

I'm swamped by sensations as I fall onto the passenger seat.

Gladness, to be with Greg again.

Relief to be sitting down.

The searing pain that rips back, sending waves of nausea over me.

The smell of leather and aftershave.

I turn back, and there is Oskar's face, smiling at me.

"Good girl, K," he says softly.

"Let Greg go," I say. "He's got nothing to do with you."

"Not yet, maybe." Oskar's voice is cold. He jerks something into Greg's neck. It's a gun.

My breath stills.

CHAPTER 49

OSKAR LEANS FORWARD into the gap between the two front seats and jabs the gun into Greg's neck again. "Drive."

But Greg is staring angrily at me, shaking his head.

Oskar twists the gun away from Greg and rams it below my ear. His voice hardens. "Start the engine."

A vein in my neck pulses under the metal.

Greg turns the key in the ignition and the engine splutters into life.

My eyes meet Oskar's in the sun visor mirror. His light up in malicious joy.

I feel my breath seep away.

"My little Hoody." Oskar's eyes smile at me.

Eyes that made me feel safe.

Greg's voice, beside me: "Don't call her that!"

"Greg," I whisper.

"Shut up." Oskar's voice is ice. How could I have missed the hatred before?

My eyes are held by Oskar's. His gloved hand is clenched in a fist on the back of my seat. There are two Oskars. The one with the gun at my neck, who tried to blow me up. And the other one, the one in Fred's Cafe, who laughed and listened. Who saved my life. Why?

"Oskar." I try to speak to the cafe Oskar, even though I can't find him in the mirror. Maybe I can distract him with talk. "Oskar. Why did you do this to me? When you didn't even know me?"

Oskar barks a brief laugh. "You gave me the idea," he says. "You made it so clear that nobody would miss you. And when I got Ril to look up your lovely family, I couldn't believe what a gift you were."

I try to hold his gaze in the mirror, but his eyes slide away.

He punches the seat, close to my head.

Out of the corner of my eye, I see Greg start.

"But then I had to identify Mona as you." Now Oskar does meet my eyes.

"Who is Mona?" I speak softly.

"Mona Talbot. *K Child*. You should be the one who drowned, not her."

This time I have to look away.

He continues. "But it's not too late." He laughs. "I can still put one thing right." He jerks the gun into Greg's neck.

As we follow the road downhill, spray spatters over the roofs of the fishing cottages by the quay. I'm frozen, frozen with the weight of Oskar's gun between Greg and me. The wind buffets the car. Clouds scud over the low morning moon, and the road rises white against the hillside. Pastels, on black paper: that would be the best way to capture it. We'll be out of Yoremouth soon.

"Turn right," Oskar says to Greg as we reach the end of the bridge over the river Yore.

Greg brakes and the car stalls. Oskar slams the gun into the side of Greg's head. My breath sobs in my throat.

"Hurry up! Hurry up!" Sweat beads glisten on Oskar's forehead. In the mirror, his other hand is clenched in a fist.

I swallow the sobs. *Don't freeze, K. Don't freeze.* But there's nothing else to do right now, with the gun lined up beneath Greg's ear. I look sideways, without moving my head. I remember the silk feel of Greg's earlobe, which is now pressed flat by cold metal. Greg shouldn't be here. I shouldn't have led him into this trap.

Greg starts the car and turns the wheel. For a moment I think he's going to turn all the way around, back toward Yoremouth. But Oskar flings the gun back against the side of my chin, forcing my jaw almost out of line, and Greg swerves into the narrow lane. On the left a cliff face rises above us. On the right a low wall separates us from the sea, which churns in the harbor, darker than the road. The white foam dashes against the windshield.

We've reached the end of the road, even though Greg is driving so slowly. All that's before us now is raging black sea. I see his fingers trembling on the steering wheel and anger surges through my body. Everything sharpens.

"Stop the car," Oskar commands.

Greg brakes. The car stalls.

"Don't move." Oskar's voice is deadly cold.

I hear a sigh as Greg breathes out. A word slips from his mouth. "Verity."

Then there's a flurry from behind. I can't see the gun. Oskar's two gloved hands grasp Greg's hair and his collar. Greg's head flies forward. His forehead cracks against the steering wheel.

I scream.

"Shut up," says Oskar's quiet voice. "Don't move." He waves the gun through the gap between the seats, swinging it from me to Greg, from Greg to me. Oskar's hand is shaking so badly that he has to grip his wrist with his other hand to steady it. He's watching Greg to see if he will sit up.

But Greg is still.

Greg might not be dead. I don't know for sure. Hold

on to that. I manage at last to take a gasping breath.

Maybe it isn't too late. A wave smacks over the wall and splatters against the windshield. It's been cold for weeks. Nobody could survive long in there.

Oskar opens his door and climbs out. Everything stops working in a submerged car: doors, windows. I slip off the gloves, undo our seat belts. I'm not getting out. Not without Greg.

The back door slams, and Greg's door opens. My heart plummets as Oskar jerks the key out of the ignition. He throws it onto the floor near the driver's door, in the dark where it would take precious seconds to find. I force my brain to think. Why did he do that? Why didn't he just shoot Greg, and me?

His face turns to mine. I feel my back weld itself to the seat.

"Bye-bye, K." Oskar smiles. "It's good that your Hoody boyfriend is here too. You can be remembered together, for your bomb in Gatesbrooke, when they round up all the other Hood scum."

"Oskar." My voice is a whisper. "Don't do this. You don't have to do this."

Oskar steps with one foot into the car, onto the pedal. Then he reaches across and moves the gearstick into neutral. He points the gun at me. His hand isn't shaking anymore. "Oh, I do," he says. "I was trying to save citizens that day. I should have left you under the train at Central Station." He smiles at me. "I would have, if I'd known what you really were. But then you gave me the perfect way to put things right with Col. A Hood who nobody would miss, another suicide bomber to kick-start the Strife again, to put the Hoods back where they belong."

That's why he wants it to look like an accident, a lovers' suicide pact. He still thinks he can get away with it, and somehow redeem himself with Col and Ril.

How could his smile ever have made me feel safe? How did he veil the hate before?

Oskar's voice changes. It takes on a friendly, conversational tone that sends terror trickling through me. "I quite liked you at first," he says. "I even thought about pulling you out, that time in the woods? Maybe I would have, if you hadn't gone native so quickly. But it's not too late." He bares his teeth in a grin. And even now, his eyes are smiling too. "You can still help me out." He glances at the gun. "I don't want to use it. But I will if I have to. By the way," he adds. "Thanks for the idea." Then he slams the door and disappears behind the car.

"I stopped you before, Oskar," I whisper.

He begins to push. Nothing happens at first. I know that—it took me moments to get the wheels turning before I pushed Oskar's car into the canal. In front of the hood I see the lip of a curb, a few feet away. It'll slow him down a little. I wait. Slowly the car starts to move. Once it begins, it rolls under its own momentum.

CHAPTER 50

TIMING. IT WILL all rest on timing. I force myself to remain still.

My fingers long to jerk up the hand brake. But I need to wait for the right moment.

Now. I lick my lips and purse them and try to whistle. It's not working. My mouth is not working. Concentrate. The car is moving now. I close my eyes and think of Raymond, calling him back to me in the woods, and a whistle bursts from my lips.

From the floor Greg's key ring beeps and flickers. I lean toward Greg, under his face, until I feel the key in my hand. *Don't drop it. Don't drop it.* Carefully, slowly, not breathing, I put it in the ignition.

As I pull myself back under the steering wheel, something drips onto my face. *Don't, don't think about that.*

The car rolls toward the sea, faster now. The front wheels bump against the curb. *Now. Now. Now.*

I sit up and take the envelope out of my backpack. I open the door and hold it outside, clinging to it with both hands as the wind tugs.

"Oskar!" I yell. "You forgot this! Everyone will know it was you!"

Oskar's face shifts from effort to surprise, and then to a snarl. He lets go of the car and runs toward me, reaching into his jacket. I slam the door and press down the central lock.

I push Greg's head up and back and climb over the gearstick and hand brake onto his lap. It takes an agonizingly long time. My limbs feel like they're not moving. I'm wedged under the steering wheel, but I reach my feet down until they find the pedals. Pain sears through me, but then a wave of adrenaline sweeps it away and I slam my foot down on the clutch as I turn the key in the ignition. Gear into reverse, lift up on the gas, slowly, carefully, point of balance.

There's a crash next to my ear. The window shatters. Oskar, right there, by the broken window, pointing the gun. I stare into the side mirror. *Come on, K. Greg's not dead. He isn't dead, but you must get him away. You've almost done it.* The car vibrates. Then I slam it backward, down the narrow road.

I duck to look in the rear mirror, and I see the rock wall. I'm going too fast. I lift my foot off the gas a little. *Keep going. It's going to be OK.* Oskar is in front of the car now. He's raising his arm. I twist the steering wheel away, toward the sea. The windshield shatters in a shower of silver flakes. I feel the bullet whip past.

He won't miss next time.

The car stalls. *Get it started again. Now.*

I lean forward. Turn the key. Start the engine. Moving now. Oskar's face, lunging at my window. Turn the steering wheel, look into the rear mirror. Rock wall. Too fast.

Oskar's hand is on the door handle. *Don't worry, it's locked.* But it's opening. It's opening!

The door flies open and Oskar seizes my arm. I scream into his face. My foot tries to find the gas, but Oskar is pulling me up and out, crushing Greg. He's trying to yank me out of the car. I wedge my legs under the steering wheel, but he's too strong. My body is being dragged out of the moving car. My legs twist under the wheel as Oskar pulls me out. I fall on to the ground. Oskar hauls me up with one hand, and his other arm jerks back to hurl the gun into the car.

The car crashes into the rock wall. Greg flies forward and back, and forward again.

From the road comes the whine of sirens. Too late, too late. Oskar drags me toward the steps down to the sea, where spray plumes up and over the wall.

I'm not afraid of deep, dark water.

And I don't know why, but in this last long moment, between the car and the sea, I notice how the headlights shine into the water on the road, and how a rainbow glows where oil has leaked from Greg's car.

I stretch up and seize Oskar's arm.

Then my feet slip in the oil, sliding and lurching away, and Oskar and I are falling and then there's a little *crack*.

Then nothing.

CHAPTER 51

I'M AWAKE.

I lie still, eyes closed.

I can't hear Greg's heart beating, or feel his breath on my hair. There's something I don't want to remember. But I remember it anyway.

A howl tears out of my mouth, and once it starts it just can't stop.

Hands are on my bare arms, a voice is hushing me. I open my eyes. A woman in green hospital clothes leans over me.

"You're awake!" she says. "Lie quietly."

"Where's Greg?" I shout. "Where is he?"

"I'm so sorry," she says. "So sorry for your loss."

I try to sit up. "I want to see him. Where is he?"

"Shh," she says. "Your friend . . ." She stops. "I'd better get the doctor."

She hurries out of the cubicle. I sit up, even though

my head throbs. I'm dressed in a hospital gown.

I hear the nurse talking softly to someone just on the other side of the curtain. "She's come around."

A man's voice replies, too low for me to hear.

"No," says the nurse. "She's in no state to identify bodies."

I strain my ears, but I can only hear that their hushed voices are arguing.

"Your investigations will have to wait," the nurse says. Her feet clip away.

I swing my legs over the edge of the gurney until my feet touch the cold linoleum, and my bandaged ankle splits into shards of pain. I make myself stand up, holding on to the cabinet. I reach for the curtain and pull it open.

The nurse turns from the console and rushes toward me. I try to push her away, but she propels me back to the bed and I fall onto it. She sits beside me, holding me there.

A man in white clothes comes in. "I'm very sorry," he says.

"No," I say. "Greg didn't die." The gunshot missed him. The car was moving slowly. He's young, he's strong.

The doctor looks into my eyes. "Your friend is dead. His head injury was too severe. We tried to save him."

I manage to push the nurse away and sit up. "Where is he? I want to see him."

They look at each other and then the doctor nods slowly. "All right. But you'll have to wait until a police officer is available." He looks at the nurse. "You see, the assailant is also on this ward."

Noise roars into my head. "Oskar is here?"

They both stand up. "You're lucky he ran out of bullets," says the doctor. "Wait a minute. Someone will be along shortly."

They pull the curtain closed. But I can't wait any longer. I get to my feet and look out. I guess immediately where Greg is lying, because there's a policeman guarding a cubicle on the left: Oskar. All the other curtains are open except for one, only several feet away. I bunch up the curtain between my space and the next one and climb through, holding on to the fabric to support myself. The next bed is empty.

But the one beyond it is where they have put Greg. He's lying on the hospital gurney. The white sheet is over his face.

The roaring is too loud. I step forward and put my hand on the side of the gurney. "Greg," I say. "Greg."

I collapse onto the chair beside him. I want to see his face. I want to tell him I love him. But I can't move.

Until I lift the sheet I can put away the realization that waits for me, in the corner of the room, like a dark sack ready to spill open. For precious seconds I can pretend he's only sleeping.

From beyond the curtain I hear voices and footsteps moving toward us. And the rattling of a gurney.

I lean forward, and take the corner of the sheet, because now I know I am running out of time. And I never told Greg how much I love him.

A man's voice speaks. "Take this one first. Then you can come back for the Hoody murderer."

CHAPTER 52

THE WORDS SEEP slowly into my brain. *Hoody murderer.* Hoody murderer? I look at the shrouded figure on the bed. I pull back the sheet.

It's Oskar.

I'm frozen, gazing at his face.

It is calm and still, his eyes closed. There's no injury or wound, but beneath him the bed is damp and the damp is pink.

Where is Greg?

She said "bodies."

He said the assailant is still on this ward.

I stumble to the end of the bed and tweak the curtain apart. Someone is pushing a metal gurney toward me. There's a policeman outside this cubicle, with his back to me, and at the end of the room I see another policeman sitting on a chair outside a closed curtain.

Greg.

I let the curtain fall, but underneath it I see the policeman's feet.

I hear another male voice talking quietly. I can't hear what he says. Then a new voice says, "Yes, sir. Until they take him away."

The rattling noise stops outside. I hear the word "mortuary." They're going to take Oskar away.

They want to take Greg away too. Now I have one thought in my mind: to reach him first.

I wait for the roaring in my ears to calm. Then I crawl under the curtain, past my bed, and into the next space. There's someone on the gurney, but they're asleep. The next cubicle is empty. I slip under the curtain into the last one.

There's no sheet over Greg. He's lying on his back. His eyes are closed. His face is the same waxy color as Oskar's and his eyelids are sealed shut, as if they've never opened. You couldn't guess now, if you didn't know, that underneath were liquid brown eyes, flashing light and fire.

He looks so like Greg. But so still. His silky brown hair is hidden under a bandage. He looks so much as if he's sleeping. He looks slim and young, like a boy.

I bend my face down close to Greg's. "I love you," I say. "I always loved you. I love you, I love you."

I hear the rattle of the gurney outside. They're coming to take him away.

I lean down and kiss Greg's lips. And they're soft and dry.

CHAPTER 53

SOMEONE SIGHS GENTLY.

I look up.

Greg's eyelid flutters.

I lean closer.

At first I don't believe it. Then it twitches again. I've never seen anything so beautiful. I stare at his eyelid, waiting.

His eyes open.

Greg's eyes are dazed and fuzzy as they focus on mine. He tries to speak, but his voice is too quiet. I want to listen, but instead gulping sobs storm out of me.

"Hey," says Greg, into my ear. "I knew it was you.

No one else is so noisy."

I hold his face in my hands and kiss it again and again; his lips, his eyebrows.

Greg lies still.

"Greg?" I stand up. My head spins. "Can you not move?"

"My hands."

I look down. I can't believe I didn't notice before. Greg's wrists are handcuffed to the bed. I stare at him in horror. He shrugs.

I climb onto the bed and lie down carefully beside him.

We're both thinking of the handcuffs and what they mean.

There are voices outside. They are going to take Greg away, after all this, like Jeremiah. I hold on to his shoulders as tightly as I can. The curtain is yanked aside and now the room fills with people: the green nurse, the young policeman, another much older policeman, and the doctor in his white coat. They all freeze when they see us lying together on the bed.

The policeman at the back has a gun, pointing at us. I cover Greg with my body.

"Let her go!" shouts the policeman.

"Verity, do what he says," says Greg.

I hold on to him more tightly. "Leave him alone!" I shout. "Go away!"

The green nurse plows into the middle of the room. She stands in front of Greg and me with her arms stretched wide. "Get. Out. Of. My. Ward!" she shouts. "With that *thing*." She's quivering with anger.

There's a frozen moment, but then the policeman with the gun steps forward anyway.

Someone is pushing her way into the room. Tina. She flips open an ID badge as she passes the policemen in the doorway.

"I think we can clear this up, gentlemen. Verity. Greg." She nods in our direction. Her eyes fall on Greg's hand. She turns back to the policemen. "You need to get rid of those," she says, pointing.

I wait for them to slap some cuffs on her too. But the young policeman comes over to Greg and unlocks his wrists. Greg doesn't move. Neither do I. I'm not letting go of him now, no way, in case it's a trap.

"There's no further use here for armed response," says Tina. And they leave, just like that.

"Not before time," snorts the green nurse. She points sternly at me. "You should be in cubicle three. But you can stay here for now."

That's good, because I'm not going anywhere.

"Verity?" says Greg's muffled voice. "I can't breathe."

I sit up. Greg does too. He puts his arm around me heavily, because he hasn't been able to move for some time.

"Tina?" he says.

She slips the ID badge into the top pocket of her jacket. "What can I say?" She smiles and gives a little shrug. "I have two jobs."

"Does Brer Magnus know?" Greg's voice sounds slightly outraged.

"Well," says Tina. "I think he will now, don't you?" She sits down on the chair beside the bed.

"I thought they were going to take Greg to Tranquility Sound," I say. "Like Jeremiah."

"I came as soon as Celestina phoned me," says Tina. She turns to Greg. "Unfortunately you'd already left."

"Why did they want to arrest Greg? They called him the assailant."

"The gun was in the car with Greg," says Tina.

"Oskar threw it into the car," I say.

"He fell onto the steps and drowned," she adds. "So he seemed to be the victim. You fell and hit your head on the sea wall."

"Typical," says Greg.

"It was your fault," I say. "Your stupid oily car. And your door locks are broken too."

Tina looks at me. "Now. Jeremiah," she says. "He wasn't arrested because of you, Verity. It was because of his cousin."

Jeremiah was with his cousin, that very first night at the Institute, after the Spring Meeting. The conversation I overheard between them and Brer Magnus was the reason I suspected him in the first place.

"His cousin really is in a militant cell," says Tina. "Jeremiah didn't know. But he helped his cousin put some bags of fertilizer in a lock-up. Jeremiah believed they were for his cousin's gardening business."

Greg gives a little snort.

Tina half-smiles at him. "It was an easy mistake," she said. "Most people don't use it as an explosive. Jeremiah's been released now."

She looks at me. "I feel I let you down, Verity," she says. "I didn't understand that you didn't know who you were. When Brer Magnus told me about the bugs, I suspected that Oskar was involved with an extremist group. I just didn't know which one until after you came to see me. And both Brer Magnus and I underestimated Oskar's group. Neither of us realized that Oskar was in the CPP."

"The CPP?" I manage.

"The Citizens' Protectorate Party." She takes off her glasses and balances them in her curls. "Unbelievable as it seems, they're a political party. They want to fight the next election, but you know their real agenda, K. Nothing Oskar told you was true. He wasn't a policeman. He was recruited by the CPP when he was a student and he's been with them ever since. So he knew how to manipulate you."

She hesitates. "You asked me about the girl who drowned, K. I'm sorry, but she was someone who got involved with the CPP and then tried to leave. You don't get out of the CPP alive. She was Oskar's girlfriend, Mona Talbot. That's why he was so desperate to get back in their good graces."

"Are you a citizen?" I ask her, because she looks like one today.

Tina looks at me. "Maybe it doesn't matter who's a citizen and who's Brotherhood," she says. "Maybe I'm like you, Verity," she adds. "K."

"I don't think so," I say. "Your parents weren't . . ." I tail off, because I don't want to say it.

But Greg pulls me closer. "That's not who you are, Verity," he says.

Tina puts her glasses back on. "Actually, K," she says. "Verity?"

"Just call me Verity."

Tina takes her glasses off again so that she can rub her eyes. "It's by no means certain who planted the bomb that killed your parents. It could have been either side. It could have been them. Or it could have been someone who targeted them for being in an illegal mixed marriage."

"But the newspaper cuttings . . ."

"Yes." Tina smiles a tired smile. "You haven't seen some of today's papers, have you?" she says, "with your picture all over them? As a failed bomber?"

I don't know why I'm shocked.

"So that's why I have to ask you," she says. "Today the Reconciliation Agreement was signed. But things would have been very different if that bomb had gone off, with you as another Brotherhood bomber." She hesitates again. Her face is clouded with doubt, making her suddenly look much younger. "Would you give an interview? Tell your story to a newspaper reporter?"

I feel sick at the thought.

"You don't have to do that," says Greg quickly.

Tina leans closer to me. "If people know what the CPP really stands for, K," she says, "they'll know what they would be voting for. And their political party status will be revoked if they can be proved to have committed terrorist offenses." She waits for my answer.

But I made my decision when I saw the girl in the silver sequined top, who didn't deserve to die, outside the Old City Meeting Hall.

"I'll do it," I say.

CHAPTER 54

I CLOSE THE door of the wood burner. I've got the hang of it now, and the cabin is warming up. Greg is in the galley, cooking chicken and rice. He has his back to me, frying onions. I put my arms around him and he half-turns. He has a smudge of tomato puree on his nose. He turns back to the sizzling chicken and starts humming again. Greg always hums when he's cooking.

I have another look around the cabin. The table has six plates in a pile next to the glasses and the mats. Greg brought four of them from the Institute. Everything's ready, everyone's coming. It's late, but there's no curfew now. The rice is on the table already, in a pot, with oven gloves on top to keep it warm.

Greg comes into the cabin. "That's done," he says. He sits on the green bench and pulls me down beside him. "I've got something for you." He slides his backpack toward him and takes out a flat package. "Open it."

I rip off the paper to reveal the back of a picture frame. When I turn it over, my sunflower print leaps up at me, gold flashes of light shining against the green and brown of the faded petals and the midnight blue of the sky.

"Mr. Williams gave me one," says Greg. "Is the frame all right?" He looks at me, a little unsure. "You like it?"

I put my arms around him and kiss him. And then there's a clatter of shoes on the deck outside and a loud knocking on the door. But it doesn't matter, because we have all the time in the world now.

"They're here." I stand up. "I'll let them in."

Celestina comes in first, shrugging the cold off her shoulders. She gives me a quick hug and then calls behind her, "This is Verity's palace, Jo."

Her friend Jo steps down into the galley. "Nice," she says. "It's very cozy." She puts a box of chocolates on the draining board.

The cabin looks much smaller once Emanuel and Serafina have come in too.

Celestina opens the door into my bedroom. "I see you're keeping it shipshape, Verity," she says. "It looks a lot better now it's clean, thanks to me."

"You can all sit down now," calls Greg. "Food's nearly ready."

I take the coats over to the pegs by the door and hang up Serafina's purple jacket, still cold and smelling of the freezing fog that drifts over the canal basin.

But when I turn back to face the cabin, everything is suffused with the yellow light from the lamps, warmer because of the black squares of the curtainless windowpanes. If I was going to paint it, I would use watercolors, so that I could bathe the paper first in the same amber shade as the withered sunflower petals.

Emanuel is stooping to climb onto the bench without hitting his head on the glass lampshade, and Serafina is arranging the pink flowers she brought in a jam jar on the table. Celestina is still showing Jo around, and they're laughing at how small the bathroom is. Celestina looks over at me suddenly and smiles as if she knows what I'm thinking. She gives an enigmatic little Celestina nod.

I look at Greg in his red-checked shirt, and I remember the first time I saw him, in the station before the bomb. I don't think the Strife will return now, because the tide has turned. Greg is unaware of me gazing at him because he's stirring cream into the pan, but then he glances up and our eyes meet before he gives me his raised-eyebrow look.

This moment is perfect. I don't have to pretend anything. We know the best and the worst of each other, and here we are.

ACKNOWLEDGMENTS

I would like to thank:

Lisa Cheng, my editor at Running Press.

Allison Hellegers of Rights People.

Barry Cunningham, my editors Imogen Cooper and Rachel Leyshon, Rachel Hickman, and all at Chicken House.

My critique groups: Katherine Barnby, Mike Thexton and Catherine Randall, and online group YACritique: Nicky Schmidt, Kathryn Evans, Jackie Marchant, Pat Walsh, Carmel Waldron, Ellen Renner, and Vanessa Harbour.

Amanda Swift, for her mentoring support before I sent the book out and Olivia Phelan, for her generous feedback.

SCBWI, and the interesting writers and illustrators I meet through it. Everyone who kindly read the manuscript.

My family for all their love and support: Pete, Rory, Kirsten, and Cara. My parents, Alan and Rena, who filled our childhood with stories, and my sisters, Mairi and Alison.

Dougal, for the walks that helped me plan the story.